accidentally *hers*

ALSO BY JAMIE BECK

In the Cards

Worth the Wait

accidentally hers

A Sterling Canyon Novel

Jamie Beck

Montlake
Romance

Published by Montlake Romance, Seattle

www.apub.com

Amazon, the Amazon logo, and Montlake Romance are trademarks of Amazon.com, Inc., or its affiliates.

ISBN-13: 9781503947023
ISBN-10: 1503947025

Cover design by Laura Klynstra

Printed in the United States of America

To my brother, who remains one of my all-time favorite skiing partners, and who, like the hero in this story, always wears his heart on his sleeve.

Chapter One

Grey instructed his group of clients to double check their ski bindings and avalanche transceivers before approaching the edge of the snowy cornice.

"Only thing that beats a deep-powder day," Trip began with a grin, "is a little après-ski action at On The Rocks. You in?"

Unlike his friend and employee, Grey'd had no time for women since he'd moved to Sterling Canyon in December to buy the back-country ski-expedition business, Backtrax, from its founder. Detaching the skins from his skis and stuffing them into his backpack, he replied, "The only action I'll be seeing tonight involves a shitload of paperwork."

Trip smacked the side of Grey's leg with his ski pole, his six-foot-three-inch frame casting a long shadow across the snow. "Hey, buzzkill, loosen up or this will be my one and only season working in this town."

"Promises, promises," Grey joked in a deadpan voice. "Seriously, I can't chase women when I've got less than eight weeks to plan post-season climbing programs."

"Oh man, you're looking at this all wrong. The way I figure, we've got only that long to enjoy this little ski town while it's still packed with women. Good-looking, fit women on vacation. Women who aren't expecting a commitment. How 'bout you have some fun before you prematurely age."

"I have fun." Grey locked his bindings and zipped his jacket. "But I've sunk everything into buying this business."

"Suit yourself, but don't wait up for me." Trip's self-assured grin curled the corners of his mouth. "I'll be snuggled up with a soft, warm body, preferably in one of the swanky hotels with quality bedding."

"I won't send out a search party." Grey couldn't help but chuckle, knowing Trip's infamous charm and swagger would ensure his success. "Set your alarm, though. If the predicted storm doesn't screw up our scheduled tours tomorrow, I need you ready to go by six thirty."

"Hey, I welcome any excuse for an early-morning escape." Trip glanced around the group and then over the cliff's edge, into the Rock Creek coulee. "Looks like everyone's set. You gonna lead?"

"You know it." Grey's entire body hummed in anticipation of the drop into the gulch.

The rush of adrenaline from cliff hucking always made up for the ninety-minute hike up the ridge to the twelve thousand five hundred-foot-high peak. Some might call it a sick addiction, but he'd been hooked since adolescence.

Only sex delivered a bigger bang.

"Yahoo!" he hollered as he shot into the canyon.

Champagne powder sprayed around him as he ripped down the steep slope under a fantastic bluebird sky. After several cuts to confirm stable conditions, he turned, stuck two fingers in his mouth and blew hard. Blankets of snow muffled his sharp whistle. He raised one pole over his head, giving his tour group an all-clear signal.

He'd witnessed nature's finest while working as a ski instructor and backcountry guide at resorts from Utah to Alaska throughout the past thirteen years. But the out-of-bounds regions of Colorado's San Juan Mountains ranked among the most starkly gorgeous—if not exactly death-defying—peaks he'd skied.

Few enjoyed his brand of freedom—flying downhill with the warm sun on his face and cool snow at his heels. Fewer got to live their dream. He traversed the remainder of the chute feeling like a lucky SOB despite the financial headaches awaiting him at the end of the day.

Three hours later, Grey collected the transceivers from the team, pocketed his three hundred bucks in tips, and headed into his office.

A perfect day.

Or it had been until now.

Grey dumped the transceivers in a plastic bin, stripped off his hunter-orange-and-black Gore-Tex outerwear, and collapsed into the desk chair. He flicked on the computer and stared at the nemesis threatening his aspirations—a spreadsheet. A seriously challenging nightmare for someone with dyslexia.

Numbers and text scrambled in the gray-white glare of the computer screen despite the intentionally enlarged font. His hand balled into a fist, but he stopped short of punching the keyboard, mostly because he couldn't afford to waste seventy-five bucks on a new one.

Unfortunately, spreadsheets and insurance forms had become a permanent part of his life. Sighing, he stuffed another grape Tootsie Pop in his mouth and, after making a final entry, he then stowed his tips in the petty cash box.

Grey raked his hand through the heavy bangs hanging over his eyes. The vinyl office chair squeaked as he leaned back and stretched his legs. Smiling to himself, he scanned the small, windowless back office. Some might balk at the stark, dingy room, decorated with ugly metal file cabinets and a worn wooden desk with sticking drawers, but not Grey.

It may be ugly, but it was all his, thanks to an inheritance from his grandfather and the fortunate timing of meeting Bill Batton just when the man wanted to sell his business.

Now Grey owned a small commercial property, a bunch of equipment, and an exclusive U.S. Forest Service special use permit to lead guided tours on certain acreage in the San Juan National Forest. Failure was *not* an option, and not just because he refused to prove his dad right by losing everything.

His stomach growled, reminding him he hadn't eaten any real food since the two bananas he'd wolfed down hours earlier. He called in a take-out sushi order, grabbed his coat, and jumped on his mountain bike.

Overhead, the gray clouds swelled, obstructing the moonlight and stars. As he biked the several blocks to Plum Tree restaurant, he smelled the pungent mineral zing of the impending late-February blizzard.

Along the way, he surveyed the late-nineteenth-century, brick-and-clapboard Victorian buildings while navigating spotty patches of ice. The old silver-mining town, declared a historic district in its entirety, had grown into a premier winter-resort community since the early seventies. Despite its similarities to his hometown near Lake Tahoe, this resort didn't suffocate him with sad memories.

Grey leaned his bike against an obliging tree and entered Plum Tree. While waiting for his order, he wandered over to the sushi bar to watch the *itamae* prepare *futomaki*. The chef's precision with the knife held Grey's focus until a bright, feminine laugh—almost a giggle— snagged his attention.

He glanced over his shoulder in the direction of the enticing voice, to where a cute brunette was relaying a story to her friends. In a town filled with faded denim and muted, earth-tone pullovers, she stood out like a bowl of rainbow sherbet.

A neon-pink coat draped the back of her chair, and a snug canary-yellow sweater hugged her sweet curves. Her pin-straight hair, the color of milk chocolate, hung down to her shoulders. Dimples became more pronounced when she laughed. Her hands gestured wildly then covered her eyes as she shook her head in the middle of her story.

Her vitality stood out in the middle of the crowded restaurant, entrancing him. The energy she exuded reached across the room and tugged at his gut and his groin. He noticed little details like the absence of makeup and jewelry, though from a distance he couldn't make out whether her eyes were blue or green. They were sparkling and round and faintly curled upward at their outer edges and—*oh shit*—she just met his unflinching gaze.

Apparently stunned by his boldness, her doe-shaped eyes blinked three times in rapid succession.

Bambi.

Usually it took him a while to choose someone's nickname, but this one leapt to mind before he'd even had a chance to introduce himself. In any case, she didn't look away. Bambi might've been startled at first, but clearly she had confidence.

As if he weren't turned on enough.

She'd already busted him gaping at her, so he might as well make the most of the opportunity. He held her stare and winked, feeling pretty good about the fact she hadn't averted her eyes. Then her two friends turned toward him and he recognized Kelsey Calllhan. *Hell.* Grounded before takeoff.

Kelsey had seemed like a normal girl when he'd met her last month. 'Course, he'd been drinking with Trip that night. He must've been temporarily blinded by her sex appeal when he kissed her in the back of the pub before heading home alone.

Since then, she'd sent him several texts and somehow managed to regularly bump into him in town. Granted, in a town of barely twenty-two hundred full-time residents, bumping into folks wasn't uncommon. Still, Kelsey screamed *needy*.

Grey didn't do needy.

Maybe the fact she appeared to be friends with Bambi was a sign. Getting Backtrax to thrive remained his priority. He couldn't afford romantic complications, and despite her appeal, Bambi had *complication* written all over her.

"Your order's finished," called the cashier.

Grey nodded at the table of attractive women with a half smile then quickly paid his tab and strode out the door. As he unlocked his bike, he stole a final peek through the window, but only caught a glimpse of Bambi's back. The three girls were leaning into the center of the table, probably listening to Kelsey's tales about him.

Yeah, no doubt she was cock-blocking him.

Grey shook off the sexual buzz still gripping his body and hopped on his bike. Yet Bambi's vibrant laugh and animated face kept looping through his thoughts, tying him up in a way he hadn't felt in more than a decade.

A lifetime ago.

Bittersweet memories doused his libido and diverted his thoughts. He hand-signaled a left at the intersection of South Coyote, vaguely registering the shouts coming from a group of pedestrians. When he saw the car careening toward him, he wrenched his handlebars toward the sidewalk.

The driver swerved, but the car's rear fender struck the back wheel of Grey's bike, flinging him into the air. A God-awful crashing sound from across the street punched the air before Grey hit the pavement. He landed in a twisted heap on the road, popping his knee.

Shock seized his muscles and thoughts. *Am I dead? Paralyzed?* He wiggled his toes and fingers. Sweet relief gushed through him despite feeling like his knee had snapped out of place. He winced before looking down at his leg, expecting to see blood and bone poking through his jeans. Even just that slight movement sent fifty knives slicing through his side. *Motherfucker.* Had he broken some ribs, too?

Distant shouts and icy snow slowly assaulted his senses. Between shallow breaths, he twisted his neck to search for the car, which was now wrapped around a metal lamppost on the opposite side of the street, steam rising from its engine. The crumpled vehicle didn't bode well for the driver.

Several pedestrians began running toward him and the car. Some were calling 9-1-1. Others were snapping photos. *Assholes.*

Pain, hunger, and chaos mingled together. A wave of nausea roiled in his stomach as he removed his cracked bike helmet. He closed his eyes to clear his light-headedness. Goddammit to hell, a knee injury meant big trouble for him and Backtrax. Grey stole a second look at the car, but still didn't see the driver emerge.

Unbe-fucking-lievably bad luck—for both of them.

◆ ◆ ◆

The prickly imprint of attraction lingered on Avery's skin after the gorgeous man left the restaurant. No, not gorgeous. Sexy. An incredibly sexy man whose two-day stubble covered his jaw, surrounding sensual, full lips. Whose disheveled, walnut-colored hair called out to be touched. Whose gaze—intense, steely-gray eyes fringed with long lashes and hooded under straight brows—had burrowed inside her body, making her hot and restless.

He'd stared at her with open desire, but then ducked out after he'd won her full attention.

Was he a tourist? Would she ever see him again?

Hopefully.

"That's him, guys," Kelsey chirped. "That's Grey!"

Emma choked on her sake. "*He's* the guy you've been crushing on lately?"

"Yes." A wistful expression swept across Kelsey's face. "Greyson Lowell. Yummy."

Crud. Avery couldn't even consider him if Kelsey called dibs. Kelsey, whom she loved dearly, but who also fell in and out of "love" with all the drama and duration of a winter snow squall.

"Remind me, because I forget. What's his story?" Avery had stopped listening to Kelsey's mooning over this guy weeks ago, unwilling to indulge her friend's habit of pining after someone who didn't appear to return her affection.

"He moved to town in December after he bought Backtrax. His friend Trip works for him and they have plans to expand into summer mountaineering so it becomes a year-round business." Kelsey waved her hand. "I met them at On The Rocks one night after work last month. Grey kissed me in the back corner just before closing."

"Ew, barroom PDA?" Avery scrunched up her nose. "Hmm, I could've sworn we'd all graduated from high school twelve years ago."

"Kelsey, you ho!" Emma teased.

"Sadly, he didn't give me the chance to be a ho. He left with Trip when the bar closed. But even drunk, he was a great kisser." Kelsey's eyelids fluttered. "Really *hawt*, and sweet, too. Unfortunately, he's hard to nail down." Kelsey frowned. "Trust me, I've tried every trick in the book."

"Good gravy, Kels, promise us you're not stalking this guy." Avery dipped her spicy tuna roll into the wasabi soy sauce, tuning out Kelsey's "really hawt" bragging, which had been stuck on auto-replay in her head. She slid a sideways glance at her friend and paused, her chopsticks midair. "You *are* stalking him, aren't you." Avery plastered her palm to her forehead.

"No! Maybe I've texted and called him a few times, but he's really focused on building his business." Kelsey straightened her napkin and cleared her throat. "If I'm patient and friendly without smothering him, maybe he'll come around once ski season ends."

"Well, he's hot," Emma said. "I say go for it. Nothing to lose. It's not like this town is bustling with great-looking, available, self-employed men."

Kelsey looked at Avery, whose raised brows and soft sigh must've spoken volumes. "You disagree?"

"You know my feelings about ski guides and instructors." Avery squeezed Kelsey's hand.

"Come on, they aren't all cheaters like Matt," Emma interrupted. "Don't judge every man in the ski industry based on the one who burned you."

Matt's duplicity had surprised Avery, but she'd ultimately considered their split his loss, not hers. She'd hardly shed a tear—at least not in public—when he finally left town with the wealthy client who'd stolen his heart.

"It's not just Matt. I've spent my life watching those ego-driven adrenaline junkies—including my brother—preying on the tourists and the rest of us locals." Avery shook her head, somewhat grateful Grey's career would lessen any regret she felt about not getting to know him better. "Anyway, it's not just skiers. The older I get, the less convinced I am that I'll ever meet a nice guy with a normal job who won't end up either taking me for granted or trying to change me.

"I get sick when I think of all the little things I started giving up—the compromises I made—just to keep Matt happy. Look where that got me! Dumped and publicly humiliated." She waved her hand to sweep away the unpleasant memory. "Besides, the absolute last thing I *ever* want is to turn into my mom. No, thank you." She sipped her drink and then set it down, sighing. "Flirting is fun. But I like my independence, too. If I'm going to accomplish my goals, I can't get sidetracked again."

"With that attitude, I'm surprised you stick around this town," Kelsey said. "Wouldn't you have a better shot at opening your own physical therapy clinic in a big city like Denver?"

"Maybe. But for better or worse, this is home." Avery glanced at the dark silhouette of the San Juans, which was visible through the window. A warm smile spread across her face. "Besides, I could never leave you guys."

Emma and Kelsey had been her closest friends since middle school, and the bond forged by their differing yet complementary personalities had carried them through fad diets, Emma parents' messy divorce, the births of Kelsey's adorable niece and nephew, and more campfire escapades than she could count.

No, she couldn't imagine life without them. Nor would she want to leave her childhood home, which she and her twin brother, Andy, had bought from their parents a few years earlier. Thinking of him brought a smile to her face. Her playmate, confidant, best friend. The only man who loved her *because* of her grit, not in spite of it.

"Well, I'm not ready to give up on Grey." Kelsey nodded in confirmation of her own statement. "I can tell he's a good guy. Once he settles into a groove, he'll be more available."

"You know what my brother always says about reading a guy's 'just not that into you' signs." Andy had fostered Avery's no-BS attitude toward the opposite sex thanks to several frank discussions during her high school and college years. Since then, she'd always walked away with her head held high the minute any guy's interest waned. "Maybe you should consider his advice and back off."

"But then Grey'll think I'm not interested." Kelsey twirled her blond curls around her fingers, pouting. "My sister never played games, and she's married with kids."

"Games?" Avery shook her head and looked at Emma for support. "Tell her the truth, Em. Tell her maybe the guy would respect her more if she weren't so obvious."

Emma meekly shrugged without confirming or refuting Avery's claim.

Avery shooed her hand at Em and clucked. "Stop acting like such a politician."

"Stop being such a pragmatist," Em shot back.

"Avery, you just don't get it." Kelsey looked at Avery, her amber eyes brimming with pity. "You've never been a romantic."

Avery burst into laughter. *Oh, Kels, you sweet, starry-eyed thing.* "Well, I can't argue with that, friend."

Romantic or not, Avery might've enjoyed a little flirtation with Grey—Greyson.

Sadly, he'd remain off-limits unless Kelsey fell for some other guy before things progressed. Probably a fifty-fifty shot of that happening within a month. Not bad odds. Maybe she could overlook the ski-bum thing if she were willing to explore a more superficial relationship.

"So, if I can hang on for several more weeks, I've got a chance. Come on, help me figure out how to entice him." Kelsey beamed, apparently convinced her friends could dispense some kind of miracle.

Avery shook her head with a little snort, then sighed. It amazed her that Kelsey could be so driven and savvy with her real estate business, yet so flighty in her personal life.

In any case, clearly Grey wasn't an option for Avery even though he made her insides tumble and tingle at first sight. In fact, all the better for her not to fall so quickly under some skier's spell. Last time hadn't worked out so well.

And, unlike Kelsey, she had never wanted to fall hopelessly in love. *Hopeless* perfectly described what she'd seen too often: a woman sacrificing more of herself and her ambitions to accommodate a growing family's needs than any man.

Perhaps some couples balanced those competing goals better than others, but on the whole, traditional gender roles still persisted in Sterling Canyon. Maybe Avery would feel differently if she were more maternal or romantic. Maybe she'd even welcome the idea. But, "for better or worse," she knew her limitations.

She saw no reason to give so much up for a man when a man couldn't always be trusted to hold up his end of that bargain, especially a ski pro like Matt and probably Grey Lowell, too.

Gulping down the rest of her Sapporo, she forced herself to muster enthusiasm for Kelsey's chatter about how she planned to woo Grey.

It would be a long night.

Her phone rang while they were waiting for the check. The display read "Sterling Canyon Medical Center." As an orthopedic physical therapist, Avery often dealt with the hospital, but rarely this late on a Saturday night.

"Why the scowl?" Emma asked.

She held up her pointer finger as she answered her phone. "Hello?"

"Avery, this is Nurse Harding over at the med center. I'm calling about your brother Andy. He's been involved in a car accident. Are you able to come to the hospital now?"

An accident?

A mystifying sense of calmness descended despite her unsteady hands. "Wait, what?" Avery uttered, her mind wiped clear of all thought. The hum of background conversations seemed to grow louder, but that couldn't be right. "How bad is it?"

"He's in critical condition. How far away are you?"

Throughout the many years Avery had interacted with Janet Harding, she'd never before encountered this dire tone. "I'll be there in ten minutes."

Her hands trembled as she shoved her phone in her purse. "Andy's been in a car accident." She stood to go, then remembered she hadn't paid the bill. Her body overheated as she dug around for her wallet and keys. Absently, she threw forty dollars on the table. "I've got to get to the emergency room. Let me know if this doesn't cover my share of the tab."

"Wait a second." Emma grasped Avery's forearm. "We'll come with you."

"No, please." She patted Emma's hand. "Don't come. I'll call if I need you, I promise."

"Aren't you going to call your parents first?" Emma looked anxious.

"Not until I have all the facts. Sorry, gotta go!" Avery exited the restaurant and sprinted to her car.

Ten minutes later, Avery darted through the emergency room doors. Fortunately her frequent interaction with the hospital staff afforded her quick service. Janet whisked her out of the reception area and into the bowels of the facility.

"How's my brother?" Avery fixed her gaze on Janet.

"He's sustained a concussion, some broken ribs, and a traumatic pneumothorax. The puncture was significant, requiring surgery to insert a chest tube. The doctor couldn't wait for consent before getting started. Andy'll have to stay here to be monitored for several days while the lung re-expands and stabilizes."

Flattening her hand against her breastbone, Avery gasped. "Can I speak with him?"

"He's still in surgery, then he'll be in the recovery room beyond the end of visiting hours. You probably won't be able to see him until tomorrow morning, but if you want to leave him a note, I'll make sure he gets it." Janet handed Avery a notepad and pen.

In her peripheral vision, Avery noticed two policemen hovering nearby. Frowning, she whispered from the side of her mouth, "Why are the cops here?"

Janet's gaze darted from the officers to Avery. "They must've just finished taking the victim's statement."

"Victim? What happened—a robbery gone bad?"

"No." Janet grimaced. "Andy's victim."

"What?" White noise rushed through Avery's ears as her heart rate sped up. "Why?"

"Andy was drunk when he hit the cyclist."

Chapter Two

Avery exited the hospital the next afternoon, her body aching as if she'd been the one who'd undergone surgery and was facing criminal charges. Her parents had just called her to say they were only minutes away, having made the nine-hour drive from Phoenix in record time.

Squinting, she shielded her eyes with one hand. The incandescent sunlight reflecting off the fresh snow clashed with the occasion. She needed sleep. She needed a shower. She needed the police to back off and let her brother rest.

Clasping her cashmere scarf to fend off a sudden breeze, she navigated the ice patches covering the sidewalk—ice patches similar to those that had contributed to her brother's accident.

She collapsed onto a bench and raised her face to the sun. Minutes later, her parents walked toward her from the parking lot. Her mother's shuffling gait suggested she'd taken too much Xanax. Now she leaned heavily against her husband's arm for support. A common scenario—literally and figuratively.

Seeing her mom so weak made it difficult to envision that same woman as a premed student with an academic scholarship—all of which she'd given up after marrying Avery's dad. She'd traded Bunsen burners and a chem lab for a bottle warmer and pie pans.

From Avery's perspective, it seemed those choices had slowly drained her mom's spirit and strength. If love had so transformed her once-ambitious mother, then surely Avery could fall victim, too. In fact, hadn't she allowed Matt's demands for her time and attention to take priority over completing a business plan for her own clinic? Proof of her own vulnerability.

Avery stood and approached her parents with open arms. Her mother hugged her, sniffling, but her father simply rubbed his big hand over his eyes.

"Oh, Dad, you look exhausted." Avery stroked his arm. "You should've flown in rather than driven."

"Avery, please. No lectures." He turned from her and strode toward the hospital entry. "I need to see my son."

And I don't need another car accident in this family! Normally she was quick to challenge her dad's dominance, determined he not dictate to her the way he did to everyone else. Today, however, she bit back the remark and followed him. "He's awake but still confused because of the concussion. The cops were questioning him again, but the doctor asked them to come back later."

As they entered the elevator, her mother's knees buckled, forcing Avery and her dad to catch her before she hit the floor. "Mom? Are you okay?"

"My baby could've died," she whimpered. "And all the police care about is sending him to jail?"

"Gina, come on now. It'll be all right. I've called a lawyer. We'll meet him tomorrow." Her dad's no-nonsense tone held little compassion, no hint of softness. Funny her softhearted mother had fallen for someone lacking empathy.

Granted, the current circumstances were rather dire, but just once

Avery wanted her mom to reclaim her backbone rather than fumble and falter and lean on her husband for support.

"Andy's resilient, Mom. It'll take a couple of months for his injuries to heal, but if he's careful, there's no reason to think his lung will collapse again." She reached over to massage her mother's shoulder. It had taken most of Avery's strength not to break down when she'd first seen the violent purple bruising and scrapes covering Andy's head, neck, and torso, so she worried about her mother's reaction. "Prepare yourself, though. He looks bad."

Avery's mom squeezed her hand while her father stared up at the lighted numbers until the elevator came to a stop.

When they reached Andy's room, Avery gave her parents a few minutes alone with him. Her raw nerves couldn't tolerate additional tension. She'd barely had a moment to take in everything that had transpired during the past twelve hours.

The disgrace associated with the cause of Andy's injuries made everything more difficult, at least for Avery. How many people in their tight community would now judge her brother by this single mistake rather than by his history of living with a ready smile and helping hand?

Her father strode into the hallway, his face drained of color. "Tell me exactly what the cops said."

"Although this is Andy's first DUI, the fact he injured someone elevates it to a class-four felony. If convicted, that typically carries a two-to-six-year prison sentence." As she spoke those words, that reality tightened around her throat. "Arraignment should occur within three to sixteen weeks, depending on Andy's health and the court schedule. The DMV will also pursue suspending his license."

"My son, the felon," her dad muttered, with a harsh curse.

Avery noticed her father's hands grip his waist as he shook his head. "Dad, please don't harp on the criminal charges right now. A positive attitude is critical to Andy's recovery. Let's focus on his health first."

"You think I don't want him to get better?"

"No, of course I don't think that. But sometimes you can be so . . . judgmental. Please try to temper your opinions, at least until he's out of the hospital."

Her father's hands flexed at his side as he stared into the distance. When he glanced back at Avery, he rubbed his surprisingly glassy eyes with the heels of his palms. "When will we get to talk to the doctor?"

Accustomed to her father's cool demeanor, Avery was taken by surprise by his unexpected display of emotion. Perhaps stoicism was merely a shield he used to hide his fear. Or maybe he'd simply been preserving his strength. Either way, seeing his vulnerability tipped her off-balance.

"I'm told the doctor will stop in before early visiting hours end. Afterward, we can all go home to rest and shower . . . maybe grab a quick dinner before coming back this evening."

"You go on home for a while. We'll stay with Andy until they kick us out, and then we'll come meet you." Unexpectedly, he pulled her to his chest.

Despite everything, being held inside the cage of her father's arms and hearing his steady heartbeat settled her for the first time since she'd received Janet's call. He might be gruff and unyielding, but he did know how to reassure her, regardless of whether he could resolve Andy's problems. At this moment, Avery would take the false sense of security and run with it for however long it would last.

Tears pooled in her eyes for the umpteenth time. She blinked them away before withdrawing from the embrace. "Okay. Let me go say good-bye to Andy and Mom first."

◆ ◆ ◆

Thirty minutes later, she turned in to the wooded enclave of homes three miles outside of town known as Artistry Row. Each of the seven homes in the cul-de-sac where she'd grown up boasted uniqueness, whether in design or color or both. Her own, stained the cheerful green shade of Early Spring and nestled amid a copse of aspen trees, resembled a tree house.

When her folks had decided to retire and move to Arizona a few years ago, Avery had practically begged them to sell her the family house at a below-market price. She couldn't stomach the idea of another family living in the home that held most of her happiest memories. Just because she wasn't a romantic like Kelsey didn't mean she lacked sentimentality.

Her parents relented and agreed to informally finance the arrangement. They'd sacrificed the possibility of a higher, lump-sum payment in exchange for her happiness, which made Avery all the more grateful. But even at the market's lowest point, going in on the house with her brother had been the only way to afford it.

Secretly, she hoped to live out her days there, and eventually leave her current job to start a private practice, like Richard Donner had done years ago. She assumed Andy would sell her his half of their home once she could afford to buy him out. Funny how those daydreams had sometimes made her eager to get him out of the house, when now she'd give anything to have him there rather than at the hospital.

She entered the ominously silent home and flung her purse on the kitchen counter. While pouring a glass of water, she noticed one of Andy's red hoodies carelessly tossed over the back of the sofa, a pair of his sneakers by the side of a chair.

Drained, Avery simply passed the discarded clothing on her way to her bedroom, unable to deal with cleaning up before her parents arrived.

She fell across her bed, limbs heavy and numb. So tired. She closed her dry, scratchy eyelids and inhaled slow, deep breaths. Her body melded into the mattress as her mind skirted the edge of consciousness.

Ten or forty minutes later—hard to tell—her phone rang, jerking her from sleep. Groggily, she fumbled around in her purse, praying it wasn't bad news from the hospital.

"Avery? Where are you?" Emma asked.

Avery lay back on the bed and flung one arm across her eyes. "Home."

"I heard Andy's lung collapsed. Is he okay?" Emma's voice cracked, which didn't surprise Avery. Her friends thought of Andy as a brother, too. "Why didn't you call us last night?"

"I didn't leave the hospital until after midnight. I planned to call you once I got my parents settled. Andy will be there for a few days, but his prognosis is good. I guess you heard about the cops, too?"

"Yes. Listen, I know you've been dealing with a lot." Emma paused. "What can I do to help?"

"Nothing, thanks. I've just got to brace myself for dealing with my parents for the next few weeks. You know I hate watching my dad take over and my mom act like June Cleaver." Avery rubbed her eyes. "No doubt my dad and I will go several rounds throughout the coming weeks."

"Maybe it's time to quit being the family peacekeeper. You can't keep defending Andy or your mom against your dad's expectations. Putting yourself in the middle of this situation will be exhausting, Ave. Come stay with me while your parents are in town."

"Thanks, Em, but I can't leave Andy to face my dad on his own. It'd be a bloodbath."

"It's Andy's first offense, right?"

"Yes, but he's facing felony charges because he hurt someone." The lump tightened in her throat. Fighting the tingling sensation in her nose, she closed her eyes and prayed for strength. "I know drunk driving is wrong. I know someone innocent got hurt. But I can't bear to think of Andy in jail."

"Me either," Emma croaked.

"Town must be buzzing with this gossip." Avery swiped at her nose.

"Mostly from the old busybodies," Kelsey, who must've been listening on speakerphone, broke into the conversation. "It'll die down soon, especially since Grey will be okay."

"Greyson Lowell?" Avery rolled to her side and propped herself up on one elbow. "*That's* who Andy hit?"

"It must've happened right after he left the restaurant."

The fact Avery's brother hit Grey on the very night she'd first laid eyes on him struck her as a ghoulish coincidence. Of course, in a town as small as Sterling Canyon, improbable coincidences happened with freakish regularity.

Suddenly curious about Grey's condition, Avery asked, "Tell me, how bad was he hurt?"

"He tore his ACL. His doctor is waiting two weeks for the trauma to die down before he'll operate." Kelsey paused.

"Kind of ironic, isn't it?" Emma chimed in. "What if you end up being his physical therapist? How awkward."

"I'm sure he'll prefer to use someone else." When she considered what Grey's penetrating eyes might look like when angry, she shivered.

"Um, I wouldn't be so sure about that, Avery. There are four PTs in town. Only two of you have ortho specialties. With Richard Donner still in Florida helping his mother recover from her hip replacement surgery, you're the *only* ortho PT in town for the foreseeable future."

Awkward didn't begin to describe how Avery would feel if forced to work with Grey. Plus, there were bound to be ethical conflicts, under the circumstances.

"I can't think about Grey right now. I just need to get through today." Avery rubbed her forehead. "Tomorrow I'll face other people and their judgments."

"You do realize you have nothing to feel guilty about," Kelsey decreed. "*You* didn't do anything wrong. Andy did. He made a huge mistake, and he'll pay the piper. But he deserves compassion, too. He didn't intentionally set out to hurt anyone. It was a terrible, terrible *accident* caused by a moment of bad judgment. Who out there hasn't had a moment of bad judgment? No one, that's who! Most of us are just lucky none of ours ended in tragedy."

"I'm sure he'd appreciate your empathy and support, but the fact Andy's not the first to get behind the wheel after one too many doesn't excuse him or fix the fallout." Avery sighed. "I'm sorry, guys, I can't talk right now. I'm dead on my feet. I'll call you later."

Avery set the phone aside and rolled onto her side, hugging a pillow. She forced Andy's troubles from her mind, including the recurring images of him lying bruised and beaten in his hospital room. How must Grey look? Her last coherent thought, as she drifted into the soothing peace sleep promised, was of Grey's seductive eyes.

◆ ◆ ◆

Grey lumbered out of the doctor's office on crutches, carrying his pre-surgical instructions. Thankfully, Trip had pulled the Backtrax van up to the curb for him. After several clumsy steps, Grey handed his crutches to Trip and gently slid into the front seat.

"How're you feeling?" Trip tossed the crutches in the back of the van and slammed the door.

"Shitty. Wish I didn't have to wait another ten days for the surgery." Grey shifted uncomfortably in the front seat and winced. Thankfully the painkillers helped numb the sharp twinges of bending and straightening the joint. But stuffing his leg into the car kinda sucked. "How were today's treks?"

"Let's get home and settled before we talk about business, okay?" Trip turned south out of the hospital driveway. "You need surgery. Maybe your first concern should be your health."

"Don't remind me." Grey rubbed his thigh just above the knee with care. "I know it could be worse, but this damned injury screwed me during the final weeks of ski season."

"Well, the driver got hurt, too." Trip glanced at Grey from beneath the brim of one of his dozen cowboy hats. "I hear he's looking at felony charges."

"Should I feel bad about that? Seems he got what's coming to him as far as I can tell."

Trip shrugged. "Can't blame you for those feelings."

"Right? Not only am I out for the rest of ski season . . . this leg means I won't be able to climb this summer. Puts a real crimp in my plans and bottom line." Grey tapped his fingers against his thigh. "Maybe I can assist with some basic training by June."

"You know, some of our friends feared the accident would do you in, but really, it's gonna be stress that kills you." Trip shook his head. "You need to get some perspective."

Grey folded his arms across his chest, eyes on the windshield. He hated talking about the accident, but he really hated being lectured to by Trip. "Well, hello, Oprah. When did you arrive?"

"At least you haven't lost your sense of humor." Trip grinned then turned up the radio and whistled along with a Kenny Chesney song.

"Trip, I know I'm asking a lot, but what I need from you is help—with the business, not with me, personally."

"Believe it or not, I understand what's at stake for you. You'll have to trust I've got your back." Trip shot him a look of pure challenge.

"You're right. Sorry." Grey's shoulders eased a bit. He stared at the yellow center line of the winding country road for a minute, trying to drown out the twangy music. "Hey, can we at least agree on some other station? Anything but this sappy, sad country stuff."

Grey had been surrounded by music his entire life. His mother, a music teacher, had gifted him with both an appreciation of music and a natural talent for playing the piano. His talent had propped him up when he'd felt defeated by his dyslexia. He'd habitually turned to his piano in times of trouble or stress, which meant his keyboard would be getting a good workout in the upcoming months. Despite his broad tastes, however, country music had never quite captured his interest.

"Driver controls the radio, pal. Suck it up." Ten minutes later, Trip parked the van in the paved lot adjacent to the office building and retrieved the crutches. "Do you need help?"

"I think I've got it." Grey took the crutches and hobbled toward the entrance to the upstairs apartment. The skyrocketing costs of real estate—a downside to the town's popularity—forced him and Trip to bunk up in the small apartment above the office. Not ideal, but the one-flight commute made up for the lack of privacy, at least for now.

"Damned ice everywhere is a menace."

"Can't live in a ski town without running into snow and ice."

"I know." Grey lumbered up the narrow steps, and his golden lab, Shaman, bounded toward him as he entered the apartment.

"Whoa, whoa, boy." Grey struggled to balance himself on the crutches while preventing Shaman from hurting his knee further or knocking him over. He scratched under his dog's jaw and accepted a sloppy kiss, ignoring the shock of pain piercing his knee. "Good boy. I missed you, too."

Shaman's tail wagged, but he quickly became distracted when Trip tossed a dog biscuit in the opposite corner.

Once Shaman settled with his treat, Grey went directly to the sofa. "Hey, Trip, can you grab me a bag of ice?"

While Trip filled the blue rubber ice bag and got a dishrag, Grey twisted his neck to alleviate the remaining strain in his shoulders.

Home.

Better than some places he'd lived, but not particularly warm and cozy. Just a small beige living area, sparsely decorated with used brown leather furnishings and a square oak table with four chairs.

No drapes. No pictures or paintings. No personality or style.

Nothing but Shaman's dog bowls and the Yamaha piano keyboard in the corner to suggest Grey Lowell lived there. He'd lived a nomadic life for so long—always running, as if distance could make him forget *her*—he'd never accumulated the possessions or normal friendships most other men his age had in their lives.

At thirty-three, he craved something more, but had neither the time nor money now. *Hell.* He shoved aside his maudlin thoughts.

"How's Jon working out?" Grey laid the towel across his leg and placed the ice bag on top. "He did his first solo gig yesterday, right?"

"He's okay. Clients seem to like him." Trip grimaced, tugging at the brim of his cowboy hat. "Poached him from ski patrol. He likes the tips."

"I hate not being able to get out there to check out his skills." Grey pulled a bag of Dum-Dums out of his jacket pocket and stuck a grape sucker in his mouth.

"He's certified, Grey. PSIA, AIARE, yada yada." Trip sank into the chair across from Grey, removed his cowboy hat and placed it, upside down, on the table.

"Certifications don't mean shit if the guy doesn't have the right combo of personality and restraint on the mountain."

"He's seasoned and mature. Available on short notice. Definitely good enough to get us through the rest of ski season."

"Every time I think about the extra salary expense, let alone my personal loss in tips, I could strangle Andy Randall." Grey locked his hands behind his head. "But I appreciate the way you've been picking up the slack these past couple of days."

"No problem. But don't micromanage the money for the next few months. It's a setback, but you gotta focus on the big picture. Take a long-range view." Trip stared at Grey's sucker and then motioned for one with his hand. Unlike Grey, he immediately began crunching on the candy after shedding the wrapper. "Just get through surgery and start with therapy right away. I've heard it takes seven to twelve months before you can ski."

"Don't worry." Grey pushed up his sleeves and started sifting through the mail on the coffee table. "I'll recover quickly." He stopped at the hand-addressed yellow envelope.

A card?

Curiosity spiked, although he suspected it might be from Kelsey. She'd texted him a couple of times since the accident, offering to help out. He wished she'd take the hint and stop trying so hard. She was nice enough, just not really his type. Still, he didn't know how to shake her off without hurting her feelings.

He pulled the get-well card from its sleeve—a girly card with a picture of a branch with pink flower buds. At least the text was in a large, clear font. "Wishing you a quick and complete recovery." However, the handwritten note gave him some trouble.

Using his index finger to track the words, he concentrated his best on the feminine, loopy scrawl. Two minutes later, he tossed it on his desk, surprised and frustrated.

"What's that?" Trip asked.

"Best I can make out, it's an apology note from Randall's sister. You know how hard it is for me to read cursive. I can't read her name."

Trip picked up the note. "Avery Randall." Apprehension edged Trip's voice, which made no sense.

"Avery," Grey repeated.

"This is either a real nice sentiment," Trip began, setting the card back on the table, "or the cunning work of a woman trying to get on your good side so you won't sue the shit out of her brother."

Grey toyed with the TV remote and frowned. He'd never been a big proponent of litigation. Seemed like the only sure winners in any lawsuit were the lawyers.

But now everything he owned hung in the balance. He couldn't work. He was bleeding money. He had a lot more medical bills to look forward to in the future. And God forbid this injury truly sidelined him from the demands of safely skiing the backcountry in the future.

His new lawyer, Warren Adler, advised him to hold off on accepting a payout from Andy's auto-insurance carrier because Andy had only carried the minimum policy limits. Adler needed time to investigate Andy's assets, and to determine Grey's "maximum medical improvement" in order to accurately assess damages. He'd said it could take up to six months to determine the MMI. *Six months!* Grey just wanted the whole thing to be settled quickly so he didn't lose everything in the process.

"You're right about one thing," Grey said, tossing the remote aside. "I need a good therapist."

Trip wrinkled his nose. "Well, I asked around about the local PTs, but I doubt you'll like what I have to say."

"Why not?" Grey sat forward, grimacing when his knee accidentally bumped the edge of the table. "I thought there were good orthopedic therapists in this town."

"There are two. One's an old dude who's temporarily living out of state with a sick parent."

"So what's wrong with the other one?" Grey crunched on the remaining bit of lollipop then tossed the tattered stick on top of last month's *Powder* magazine. "Is he some kind of freak show?"

"*She* is not a freak show and has an excellent reputation." Trip sat back with a smirk on his face.

"You think I can't work with a woman?"

"Maybe not *this* woman." Trip leaned forward, resting his elbows on his knees. "It's Randall's sister, Avery."

"Get the fuck out." When Trip nodded, Grey picked up the get-well card again, studying her handwriting as if that would make the situation more tolerable. "Why didn't you tell me sooner?"

"'Cause after the accident, I dreaded giving you more bad news."

"Well, isn't that just peachy?" Grey scrubbed one hand over his face, using the other to tap the edge of the card against his thigh.

"It's thorny. But honestly, Grey, she's not to blame for her brother's screw-up."

"You think I don't know that? Still sucks. That drunk asshole screwed with my future, and now I'm going to have to work with his sister each week?" He shook his head in disgust. "God, this is an unholy mess. Watch her blame me for her brother's injuries. I bet she thinks he wouldn't have swerved and hit the lamppost if I hadn't been on the road." Grey frowned, shaking off his own niggling feelings of guilt.

"You know it's not your fault." Trip sank deeper into the chair and crossed his legs at the ankles. "He'd been drinking."

Grey pitched the card across the table. "I know. But if I hadn't been out there on my bike, he might've made it home without hurting himself or anyone else."

How many times had he replayed the events of that evening? Five minutes either way would've avoided the whole thing. Fate chose to test him instead. At least a physical test was one he had a chance of passing.

"We could look into PTs elsewhere. It'll probably involve a thirty-mile drive or farther each way. Could be a problem until we get through the snow season."

"No. This could work in my favor. Maybe I'll learn something about Randall that could help move my case along faster. Besides, I want the best so I can get back on the mountain as early as possible." Grey drummed his fingers on his thigh. Shaman trotted over and rested his head on the sofa cushion, waiting for affection from Grey, which he promptly received. Grey petted Shaman's head, gazing at nothing in particular. "If she's the best, then that's the end of the discussion. I've dealt with tougher situations."

"Of course, she might not want to work with you." Trip cocked one brow.

Grey's voice hardened as he glanced at the card on the table. "She'll work with me. It'll be her way of making up for her brother's mistake."

"That's harsh—and unlike you."

"I'm feeling pretty harsh right now." Grey rubbed at his thigh again. "I've got very little in savings and a three-hundred-thousand-dollar loan hanging over my head. I could lose everything in a New York minute if

I'm not looking out for myself. I can't take any chances. And if I have to apply a little pressure to get what I need, then so be it." Grey sighed at Trip's shocked expression. "Don't pull a face. You know I'll be nothing but polite—compassionate, even—but Avery Randall *will* agree to work with me."

Chapter Three

Grey exited the cab on crutches and lumbered toward the rehabilitation center, bracing for a confrontation with Randall's sister. During the past twenty-four hours, he'd felt like two wildcats were wrestling inside his chest.

Working with Randall's sister was either brilliant or plain stupid. Guilt over her brother's actions could spur her to work harder, or make it uncomfortable and awkward. Gripped by indecision, he knew only one thing was certain: aggressive therapy.

He drew the crisp mountain air into his lungs before opening the door of the bustling clinic.

Inside, sunlight flooded through the large windows, bouncing off the wall of mirrors lining the spotless exercise area. State-of-the-art gym equipment filled the airy space. That and the citrusy-clean scent improved his mood considerably, although his muscles still twitched in anticipation of their introduction.

He trudged to the receptionist area, pleased to discover a candy dish filled with Jolly Ranchers set upon the station's counter. After fishing around the bowl for a grape piece, he tossed it into his mouth. Lollipops were preferable to Jolly Ranchers, which always stuck to his teeth, but honestly, he'd never met a grape candy he didn't like.

"Good morning." A chipper young lady smiled at him. "Are you here to see Dr. Randall, Mr. White, or Ms. Hastings?"

"I've got a four-thirty appointment with Dr. Randall," he replied. "Grey Lowell."

"Super," she said. "Did you print out and complete the paperwork?"

"I'm not a patient yet. I'm just here to meet with her." He dug into his jacket pocket and pulled out folded-up papers. "I did fill out these forms in case we end up working together."

"Okay. I'll hold on to these for now." She took them and then pushed out of her chair. "Let me show you to the conference room."

Grey followed her into a small room. He leaned his crutches against the small table and sat in one of the plastic chairs with his back to the door. "Thanks."

"She'll be here in a minute." The receptionist smiled and left him alone.

While waiting, he scrolled through his email, then texted Trip with a reminder to pick him up at five.

"Mr. Lowell."

He looked up at the source of the soft voice.

"Bambi?" His ears burned as soon as the word flew from his mouth. Bambi was Randall's sister? Good God, another stroke of bad luck—or maybe not. Damn, she was just as pretty as he'd remembered.

Despite his discomfort, her confused expression made him smile.

"Excuse me?" Her stunned voice yanked him from his lusty daze. He noticed her eyebrows had risen to her hairline. "Did you just call me *Bambi*?"

Sky blue, not green. Sky blue eyes dappled with warm flecks of gold. Mesmerizing, but not as bright as the first time he'd seen them. Now faint dark circles beneath them underscored the strain she'd been under.

"Uh, yeah." He rubbed his jaw, trying to look nonchalant despite the rush of embarrassed heat racing up his neck.

She paused, clearly flabbergasted by his ridiculous remarks. *Way to be impressive, Grey.* He tucked his phone into his pocket. Unlike the other night, today she wore simple black sweats and a white, Alpine PT-embossed pullover. The boxy clothes did little to conceal the womanly frame underneath. She'd been seated when he first saw her, so he hadn't known if her figure would be as cute as her face. Apparently this girl had it all.

"I'm sure I'll regret this question, but where did that come from?" She held his gaze, just like the first time he'd seen her.

Backbone.

He liked it. A lot.

Maybe too much.

"From the way you reacted to me at Plum Tree." He shrugged, grinning. Something about her provoked the hell out of him, which prompted him to push her buttons and watch her respond. He decided to roll with the pleasant buzz traveling through his limbs . . . and elsewhere.

"Reacted?" She closed one eye and scratched at her temple, pretending to think back. "Gee, and here I recall you ducking out before we even spoke."

A ripple of satisfaction skimmed through him upon confirming she remembered their near encounter. He leaned close enough to smell her light perfume.

"When you looked up at me, your eyes got real wide and you blinked a few times." He paused, smiling at the memory. "Well, like a deer in the headlights."

"I did not!" She tugged at her ponytail, but she didn't back away. A good sign. "Anyway, that name's demeaning."

"Is not. Everyone loves Bambi." He squared his shoulders. She might claim not to like the name, but the subtle quirk at the corners of her mouth gave her away. He affected her, which revved him up further. "Regardless, it's how I always think of you."

Oh Jesus, he might as well have simply used the word *fantasize*. *Real smooth, Grey.* When he finally found the balls to meet her eyes, he noticed a hint of temptation in her expression.

"That's . . . interesting. But we should probably stick with my real name." She held out her hand, smiling. "I'm Avery."

His pulse kicked up a notch when he clasped her hand, more than it had from kissing her friend Kelsey. *Not good.* He didn't want to let go. "Avery."

"No. Avery," she repeated.

"Isn't that what I just said?" His mind struggled to focus on their conversation, which seemed impossible with every nerve ending in his body on high alert.

"Uh-uh. You said *A-vree*. But it's three syllables. *A-ver-ee*." Up close he could tell she enjoyed poking at him. Playful—he liked that, too.

He bit his lower lip and leaned forward, speaking in a low voice. "Guess I'll stick with Bambi then."

"But I don't like it."

Sure you don't. He chuckled. "Since when does a person get to pick their own nickname?"

She narrowed her eyes as if about to lay something good on him, but then her expression fell serious. "I suspect my name, real or otherwise, is the least of the awkward things between us."

Dammit. He'd been flirting as if they were at a bar instead of in a clinic dealing with a sticky situation.

"Yeah." He tried to catch her eye again. "But I'm hoping we can put aside any personal matters and work together."

"I'm not sure that's possible." She shuffled her foot.

"My issues aren't with you. You're not responsible for your brother's screw-up. *You* didn't put my whole future at risk."

Avery winced. "Gee, thanks. But your ill will toward him may be a problem for me. Despite his mistakes, I love him. And I've got professional ethics to abide by. Taking you on as a patient is a conflict of interest."

Grey scrubbed his hand over his face. "You didn't cause the accident. What's the conflict?"

"The conflict is that your recovery will affect your claim. Working with you would put me smack in the middle of a messy situation with my brother, especially if you don't achieve the results you desire."

Not achieve the results he desired? The mere idea pissed him off, but he wouldn't alienate her by letting his anger bubble to the surface.

"Well then, I've got a problem since the only other ortho PT in this little town isn't even in Colorado right now." He could see her struggling with the decision, so he applied more pressure. "From what I've been told, the sooner I start therapy, the better my chances of recovery. On top of that, I've been told you're the best. If that's true, then you should want me to work with you instead of some lesser PT. Aren't *you* my best chance at getting back on the mountain ASAP? Won't a speedy recovery mean less trouble for your brother? So the way I see it, it's in both our interests to work together. No conflict there."

One of her brows shot up. "Subtle."

"I can't really afford to play nice, so I'm respecting you enough to play it straight. I don't think that's unfair unless, somehow, you blame *me* for this mess." He watched her withdraw, which was not the result he wanted. His ham-handed approach was proving her fears right. Time to change tactics. "By the way, thanks for the get-well card."

The fight in her eyes dimmed, but her arms remained crossed.

"I wasn't sure about the etiquette, but it seemed like the right thing to do. I'm sorry about your injuries." Her voice had dropped to just above a whisper. Misery and disgrace washed over her features. "And I don't blame you."

When despair shone through the cracks in her tough shell, he yearned to offer the comfort of his arms.

Hell. Maybe she was right. Maybe they couldn't work together without creating bigger problems. But he wanted to work with her, and deep down he knew it wasn't only because she was the best PT around.

His body came alive around her. Every little thing she did or said stirred him. Therapy would put her in his orbit a few times each week, a positive outcome of an otherwise dire situation.

"Avery, despite my current mood, I am sorry your brother got hurt. I'm sure his troubles are at least as big as mine right now, and I'm sorry about how it all affects you." He meant it, too.

"Thank you." She glanced up, misty-eyed, petal-pink lips parted, eyes lit with appreciation. "I would've assumed you'd be glad to see the book thrown at him."

God, his heart was already pumping hard and they hadn't even begun therapy. Her obvious gratitude temporarily robbed him of speech.

Avery's particular blend of bluntness and reluctant vulnerability made him want to jump off the table and kiss her. Of course, he did think her brother should be convicted, but watching Bambi—another innocent victim—struggle with the consequences of the accident made his desire for vengeance seem petty.

Suddenly, in spite of his tough talk with Trip, his need to pressure *her* to be his therapist took a backseat. Maybe he could find another option that wasn't too inconvenient. "Look, I'm not trying to cause you more trouble. If you can't legally treat me, or even if you're too uncomfortable with the idea, I'll figure something out."

"You're full of surprises." She tilted her head and studied him for several seconds. He held his breath, wondering what she would decide, and whether he inspired any of the same animal attraction in her. "Despite the impression I've given so far, I can be professional. I'm assuming even if this butts against the ethics line, the hardship factor of Richard Donner's absence can probably clear the way as long as you sign whatever waivers or such that need to be signed."

Thank you, God! "Well okay, A-ver-ee, 'cause I need to get my knee in top shape ASAP. It's critical I be back on the slopes by November."

Her expression turned doubtful. "Nine months isn't ideal. As you well know, skiing is especially demanding on the knees because of constant impact and side-to-side motion. Best practice would be to wait a full year. I'm sure it sounds like forever, but your long-term results will be greatly improved if you're patient."

"It's not negotiable. I've got to be ski-ready by next season." His rough tone appeared to startle her. "My business depends on it. I've got no Plan B if this venture fails. I need to know you're committed to doing everything you can to get me back on the mountain as soon as possible."

"I'll do my best, but you need to listen to my advice and your body's signals. Can you follow my orders?" Her perceptive eyes locked with his for a second before she stepped back. Once he nodded, she continued, "Let's take one step at a time. First, I'll complete an evaluation and get some baseline statistics. I'll give you a home program to do leading up to your surgery. After your procedure, I'll go over your surgeon's plans and we'll work from there."

"Deal." Grey followed her to the exam room next door.

She examined the swelling. Her fingers lightly feathered around his knee. "In addition to ice and elevation, you need to begin working on restoring range of motion by doing some simple exercises like heel slides, and quad sets, and such. Flex your quad for me and hold it a few seconds." When he did, she squeezed the muscle as if testing his strength. "This feels pretty good."

Pretty good is right. He nodded while focusing on the slender hands massaging his knee. Holy hell. Watching her touch his body sent his thoughts straight to the gutter.

Totally inappropriate on so many levels. Not that he could control his visceral reaction to her—or even wanted to at this point.

Before he'd arrived, he'd thought having Avery Randall as his therapist would be problematic because of her brother. Now he realized another kind of trouble arose from having Bambi touching his thighs. She'd be a major distraction at a time he couldn't afford any, yet nothing would persuade him to walk away now.

"So, one thing we can check is quad lag. Do a straight-leg raise for me so I can watch your knee and see if you can hold it without bending."

Grey repressed a grunt and tried to keep his leg as straight as possible, without success.

She droned on about studies and neuromuscular electrical stimulators for a few minutes, but Grey had stopped listening, opting instead to openly stare at her like some kind of lovesick puppy. He'd seen and dated beautiful women throughout his adult life. He barely knew this girl, yet something about her awakened a part of his heart he'd long ago buried with Juliette.

Perhaps the fact the potential lawsuit, her brother's criminal charges, and her loyalty to her friend Kelsey killed any chance his fantasies could ever become reality spurred his competitive nature. But really, he suspected it had more to do with her ability to go toe-to-toe without shrinking or playing coy.

She caught him gawking again. His body flushed, hot and needy, when he noticed the artery at the base of her neck throbbing. Maybe he had a chance after all.

Avery replaced his brace, then handed him a set of instructions. "Follow these at home. No more, no less. Don't overdo it."

"Got it, Sarge."

She handed him his crutches, chuckling. "Well, at least that's better than Bambi."

"You think?" He winked as he slid off the table and onto the crutches.

"I don't know. I'm partial to Bambi."

"No one ever taught you to quit while you're ahead?"

"That's no fun, A-vree." He encroached on her personal space.

Her cheeks pinked up, making him wish they were someplace other than her office. Some place dark and private.

Of course, he couldn't push. Hell, she was concerned about whether or not her brother would end up in jail. Meanwhile, he was preparing to sue the guy. Heck, there were a million reasons why he needed to forget all about her.

But he couldn't escape his lust-driven urges.

She walked with him to the door. Grey saw Trip parked out front. "See you after my surgery."

"Yes," she said, resuming a professional demeanor. "Remember to continue with the ice and elevation." She opened the door for him and waved good-bye before disappearing.

Trip jumped out of the van and helped Grey. "Please tell me that pretty lady is Avery Randall."

Grey shot him a warning glance, but Trip merely laughed in his face. "Looks like something good might come out of this mess after all, my friend."

Doubtful. But for the first time in years, Grey hoped he was wrong.

◆ ◆ ◆

Avery returned to her office, closed the door, and dropped her head into her hands. Could she have been *less* professional? She'd been preoccupied all day preparing to face Grey's anger and judgments. Yet he'd ground her preconceptions into dust with a single word: *Bambi*.

The silly nickname elicited a flicker of pleasure. He'd used his flirty, easy manner to segregate his connection to Andy and convince her to go along with him.

But most surprisingly, he'd thrown her with his compassion. Now not only was she skirting an ethical violation for the potential conflict of interest, but she was setting herself up for another violation due to her intense physical attraction.

He'd wrecked her nerves for forty-five minutes. Yes, clearly her will-power with men *was* nearly as weak as her mother's. Could she endure such bittersweet torment a few times each week? Had she made a monumental mistake? No. She was safe. As long as he remained her patient, she absolutely could not flirt or engage in any kind of romantic relationship.

God, she was exhausted. And her parents were still camped out at her house. The last thing she wanted was to go home and spend the evening in her depressing, tense household, listening to yet another discussion about her brother's predicament. Not to mention, her father was probably going to have an opinion about her treating Grey, too.

As if she owed her dad an explanation.

Maybe marriage required blind obedience, but Avery wasn't his wife.

Today she'd agreed to treat Grey despite the obvious pitfalls. The threat of her dad's worst bullying wouldn't make her go back on her word. Nor would Grey Lowell's banter. Avery would prove to herself she was capable of handling both men without crossing lines or crumbling.

Her text alert rang, drawing her from her thoughts. Kelsey and Em were meeting for barbeque at The Mineshaft. She accepted the invitation with a quick reply and grabbed her coat.

"Let's get straight to it, Avery." Kelsey rested her chin in her palms as she leaned across the lengthy, family-style picnic table in the underground restaurant, designed to resemble a silver mine. "What did you think of Grey?"

"How did he treat you?" Emma's concerned expression contrasted greatly with Kelsey's dreamy one. "Was it uncomfortable?"

Avery couldn't help but laugh. *Heck, yeah, it was uncomfortable. Uncomfortable in a flummoxing "I wish my best friend didn't have a major crush on you and my brother didn't injure you and we weren't here in public" kind of way.*

Heat scorched her cheeks. Hopefully her friends would write off her odd reaction as an inability to cope with difficult circumstances instead of the rush of lust coursing through her veins.

Avery took a deep breath and answered Emma first. "It was tense at first, but Grey treated me fairly. In fact, he offered to go elsewhere if I wouldn't work with him."

"You didn't take him up on it, did you?" Kelsey's panic-stricken face caused Avery to shake her head and grin.

"No, Kelsey, I didn't. Despite my ethical constraints, Richard is indefinitely unavailable and there aren't other options nearby, so I agreed to work with Grey." Avery cleared her throat, remembering the well-defined contours of his thigh muscles: vastus lateralis, vastus medialis, semitendinosus. *Stop!* "You know I can't really tell you about his therapy. But he's very determined and strong, so I'm optimistic."

Avery conveniently omitted any mention of "Bambi" or Grey's flirting. The whole situation presented quite a pickle. Kelsey, her brother, ethics. If only she didn't like Grey's attention, it would be so much easier. She had to control her feelings.

"That's not what I mean, and you know it." Kelsey scowled. "What did you learn about him personally? Give me something I can use next time I see him. Something to show how compatible we would be."

"Honestly, Kelsey, do you think he met me and started spilling his secrets?" Actually, he did in fact do that a little, but not in any way that would please her love-struck friend.

Kelsey wrinkled her nose and shrugged one shoulder. "I guess not. But promise you'll try to help me if the opportunity arises."

The best way to help Kelsey would be to redirect her overblown infatuation elsewhere, because Grey apparently had no interest in what Kelsey was offering. Of course, that wasn't what Kelsey meant. Still, Avery's response wasn't exactly a lie. "I promise to help you."

"You look exhausted," Emma interrupted.

"Gee, thanks!" Avery teased. "But honestly, I need this cold beer."

"Drink up, 'cause I've got gossip." Kelsey picked a warm corn muffin from the basket in the center of the table and slathered it with honey butter.

"Ooh, sounds good." Avery could use a juicy distraction from overthinking everything with Andy, her parents, and Grey. "I hope it's fun." She edged closer to the table.

"Well, I don't know how you'll feel about this, actually." Kelsey paused. "I hear Matt may be coming back to town."

Avery straightened her spine and glanced at Emma for confirmation. "For a visit, or for good?"

Emma shrugged. "I don't know. He called Grizzly's to see if they still needed an off-season bartender."

Kelsey cut in. "Apparently things aren't so hot with little Miss Silver Spoon anymore."

"Phht," Avery said, waving one hand dismissively. "Didn't take too long, did it?"

"So, does that weird face you're making mean you wouldn't take him back if he returned?" Kelsey asked.

"Why would you think I'd take him back?" Avery bugged her eyes. "Do I have *chump* written across my forehead or something?"

"Because you loved him and you guys had talked about the future, even if you weren't officially engaged." Kelsey's sincere consternation galled Avery.

"I *thought* I loved him, until he dumped me and took off!" Avery's mouth twitched. She picked up the sweaty, cold bottle of Blue Moon Harvest and took a swig, wishing the beer would wash away the shame of being duped by Matt. "Honestly, as if his betrayal wasn't enough, do you think I'd want to go back to the mousier version of myself I was becoming in that relationship? No, thanks. He pulled me under once, but I'm free now. I've never made the same mistake twice, and I'm not about to start with Matt."

"But—" Kelsey began, but then Emma interrupted.

"Kels, Matt isn't any of our business."

"Sorry. I didn't mean to upset anyone." Kelsey slumped back into her seat. "I just want to see *one* of us in love and happy."

Avery adored Kelsey's mushy heart, even if she never did understand it.

"Since when has *love* ever guaranteed happiness?" Avery fixed her gaze on the bottle in front of her. She picked at the edges of its wet label, then raised the rim to her lips and chugged a good portion of its contents. "Besides, none of our hearts have done a good job of picking a partner. Just as well, from what I've seen of marriage, anyway."

Silently, Avery vowed to be smart. To see the heady swirl of lust and infatuation for what it was instead of pretending it was something more. To remember that flirtatious nicknames, sultry eyes, and full, kissable lips were merely tools of seduction, not love.

Chapter Four

Avery's blissful moment of relaxation—nestled into the corner of the sofa, sipping her chai while flipping through *Shape* magazine—ended when her father stormed into the living room from the garage, the vein in his temple straining beneath his skin.

"Avery, what's this I hear about you working with Grey Lowell?" He came within a few feet of her and then folded his arms. "I had to learn about it from Joe at the hardware store. Said Andy must be grateful that you're trying to butter up Lowell. Made me feel like an ass."

"Joe's an idiot, Dad. And I didn't mention it because there's already enough tension in this house." Her dad's continual disappointment hung over the roof like a dense fog, each swipe he took at Andy exploding like a grenade in the living room. Snide remarks like Joe's only made her dad more irate.

She'd been grateful for her parents' help caring for her brother during his recovery this past month, but now she wished they'd return to Arizona until his trial.

Avery continued reading the magazine, determined not to let her dad destroy another Saturday morning. "Anyway, I'm just doing my job."

"Don't give me that malarkey, young lady. Nobody's forcing you to work with that man. In fact, I can't believe you're allowed to treat him, under the circumstances."

"*That man* is not the enemy." She rested the magazine on her lap, her hands tightly gripping its edges. "He's a patient who recently had knee surgery. There aren't any other ortho PTs within thirty miles of town, so I'm working with him. It won't be a problem."

Even as the words fell from her mouth, she knew them to be untrue.

"Surely you can't be so naïve. You know he's going to sue your brother. You'd be wise to remember Andy's chief asset is half of this house." He gestured up to the ceiling and around the open space. "You know your mom and I count on the monthly loan payments as part of our retirement income. We can't afford for Grey Lowell to pocket your brother's half of its value in a forced sale."

An uneasy pit opened up in Avery's stomach. She'd been so focused on her brother's more immediate health and criminal concerns, she hadn't really thought about the house. And if Grey came after it, she and her parents would inadvertently be entangled in the legal mess between her brother and him.

The weight of responsibility for her dad's current stress bore down hard.

"You're always jumping to the worst-case scenario. What makes you think he'll start some major legal battle rather than settle up with the insurance company?" Her pulse began to speed up, but she didn't want her dad to notice he'd succeeded in making her doubt herself.

"He hasn't accepted Andy's insurance company's offer, so apparently he considers it insufficient." Her father huffed in that superior way he'd perfected by the time she'd turned ten.

Still, the news surprised her. Grey hadn't struck her as greedy.

"So what are you suggesting? I should drop him as a patient?" She tipped up her chin to hide the shiver sliding down her spine. "Would that make him more or less cooperative, do you think?"

"You always have an answer for everything, don't you. But mark my words: this won't end well. Not for your brother, not for you, and not for your mom and me." He turned on his heel and marched toward his bedroom to continue the argument with her mother, she presumed.

Avery tossed the magazine aside, her dad's warning ringing in her ears, echoing her own secret fears. Suddenly, she was no longer interested in the healthy peanut butter bar recipe she'd been perusing before her dad had ruined her mood. She glanced around her living room.

Large picture windows offered a distant mountain-range view. The décor resembled something along the lines of mountain-treehouse-meets-Mexico. Earth tones and exposed beams grounded the space, but festive drapes, pillows, and carpets splashed vibrant color and patterns all around.

Her parents had nearly dropped over in shock the first time they'd come back to visit and seen all the changes she'd made. She'd done it to please herself. To make it hers instead of theirs.

Cosmetic changes did not, however, erase her memories of growing up there: building pillow forts with Andy, sleepovers and secrets, the first kiss on the back deck, report cards on the refrigerator, and her favorite tradition—eggnog French toast every Christmas morning.

Treasured memories in her beloved home—now a home at risk.

If Grey filed a lawsuit against Andy, she'd have to drop him as a patient. And what if he won? Of course he'd win, but how much? Enough to force Andy to sell the house to pay him? Enough to wipe out her entire family's finances?

At least she had a stable career and a respectable paycheck. Andy and her parents would really suffer if they lost the house.

She scrubbed her face.

Helpless.

Helpless didn't suit her. She hated being vulnerable to someone's whim or will. Watching her mom live under her dad's thumb had been a huge turnoff for most of her life. And yet, she'd ultimately let herself fall under Matt's spell.

He'd influenced everything from her appearance to her opinions, and even had her questioning the wisdom of living out her life in Sterling Canyon. That mistake in judgment resulted in public humiliation when he cheated, and, worse, utter self-disgust. *Never* again could she allow herself to be so weak for a man.

But men weren't at issue now. Legal battles were on the horizon.

And as much as she'd like to blame Grey for her current predicament, she couldn't.

Normally, her brother's tendency toward irresponsibility was harmless: paying a bill late, losing his car keys, shrinking her favorite shirt when trying to "help" with the laundry.

However, Grey sustained serious and potentially life-changing injuries thanks to Andy's carelessness. Andy had broken the law and put all of their financial situations in jeopardy. *He* was to blame, not Grey.

A streak of resentment stabbed her heart. She inhaled deeply to relieve the mounting tension. But the walls around her pressed against her from every angle. She needed to go do something productive. To be anywhere else.

She heaved herself off the sofa and grabbed a large garbage bag from under the sink before going into her room to purge her closet.

◆ ◆ ◆

"This is a good bundle of gently used clothes, honey." Mrs. Johnston, the proprietor of Finders Keepers Thrift Store, refolded the last sweater in the pile and pushed it aside. While Avery stuck the receipt in her wallet, Mrs. Johnston tucked her chin and peered over her glasses. "I haven't seen your poor mom in town. Is she in hiding because of all this business with Andy?"

Prickly heat swept through Avery's body. "No one's in hiding. My mom's simply taking care of Andy while he recovers from his lung surgery, but I'll be sure to give them both your regards." Avery hoped her hint of snark nipped at Mrs. Johnston's conscience. She turned on her heel and exited the shop as quickly as her feet could move.

Her patience for prying "friends" like Joe at the hardware store and Mrs. Johnston had worn thin. Having her family constantly scrutinized by everyone stank. The fact their opinions bothered her really stank.

Avery shuttled along the sidewalk, looking around at the storefronts lining the street: a Technicolor version of the Old West towns in black-and-white movies.

Sidewalks were wet with snowmelt from the banks of dirty snow at the edges of the road. Fewer pedestrians clogged the sidewalks nowadays. The busiest time of the year was winding down, with only the die-hard skiers still visiting.

The refreshing cool air tempted her to remain outdoors despite the lack of sunshine. Cupping her hands over her mouth, she breathed into them to warm her fingers and nose. She zipped up her jacket, stuffed her hands in its pockets, and turned left toward the small town square where she often went to think.

When she arrived, it didn't surprise her to find it empty. Only a fool avoiding reality would sit in a park surrounded by a handful of random graying mounds of old snow. She slid onto an ice-free bench and stretched her legs while admiring the cathedral spires of the San Juans, which surrounded town like a fortress wall.

But even Mother Nature's spectacular beauty failed to occupy her mind for long.

Then a loud bark drew her attention. She looked up at the beautiful golden labrador racing toward her. After a sharp whistle split the air, she heard a familiar voice yell, "Shaman!"

Grey trailed behind the dog. Oh God—the absolute *last* person she needed to see right now. She'd been seeking a quiet place to think and ended up coming face-to-face with the very source of her dilemma.

Shaman slowed his pace but still approached her, nuzzling her legs, seeking attention.

"Aren't you sweet?" Avery scratched the dog behind his ears, avoiding eye contact with Grey until she could slow her heart rate. "Yes, you are."

When Grey finally reached the bench, his enormous smile somehow brightened her otherwise dreary day. "Hey, Bambi, no wonder he saw you from a mile away."

Avery continued petting the dog, pretending not to be stirred by Grey's presence. "And what does that mean?"

"You're a kaleidoscope in a sea of gray."

She looked down at her sky-blue corduroys, lilac sweater, and lemon-yellow jacket. When she grimaced, he quickly added, "I mean it in the very best way."

Grey leaned his crutches alongside the bench before sitting beside her. He found a short, thick, broken branch on the ground and tossed it to his left. Shaman barked and took off after his prize.

Despite her mood, a smile formed. Grey had that effect on her, darn him. "If you slip on patchy ice so soon after surgery, you're risking another ACL tear and jeopardizing whatever progress we've made these past few weeks."

"Shaman needs to run." The dog returned and dropped the stick at Grey's feet. He picked it up and tossed it again. "Besides, I'm going crazy sitting around. You said motion is important. I brought the crutches so I could ease up if needed. Trust me, no one wants to get stronger more than I do."

Avery sighed, wishing she could read Grey's mind and determine whether he was willing to take her house, or planning to testify against Andy in the criminal proceedings. If she stopped lying to herself, she'd also admit to wanting to learn more about Grey Lowell the man.

"He's a beautiful dog." Avery watched the dog tearing up the ground to retrieve the branch. "How'd you come up with that name?"

Grey stretched his legs out and rubbed his thigh. "It's an Indian word for medicine man."

"Very cool." She glanced at Shaman, who was already returning.

"He's a healer, like you." Grey grinned.

That grin melted her insides a little.

"I'd prefer Shaman to Bambi." She playfully cocked one brow, even as she resented succumbing to his charm.

"Just accept the fact you don't get a vote." He winked at her. The words *heart aflutter* had always sounded corny to her until that moment. His silken waves of hair called to be touched. His intense gray eyes sparkled with mischief. His lips . . .

Don't be stupid, Avery. Too much at stake.

She crossed her arms and refocused. "Where exactly do you live? Because you really shouldn't be pushing it."

"Above the office, just a few blocks away." Grey withdrew a small bag of lollipops from his pocket and offered her one. When she declined, he grabbed one for himself and shoved the rest back in his coat.

She straightened her spine. "Backtrax is more than a few blocks. Pretty far for this stage of your recovery, especially with the pits in the sidewalks and roads."

"Are you worried about me?" His good knee brushed against her thigh when he twisted toward her to toss the branch in the opposite direction. She kept her leg still, maintaining contact. Apparently her body didn't care about her brain's warnings.

"More like I'm worried all my hard work will end up down the drain."

"Nah. I'm tough."

She believed that about him. Saw, had seen, the evidence. Well-developed calf and thigh muscles. A strong core and sinewy arms and shoulders. A sculpted body earned through years of healthy, active living and sports, not from protein powders and calculated weight training.

"You'd have to be in your profession." She'd skied the backcountry with her brother from time to time, but they'd never pushed too hard. Would it be fun or frightening to ski with Grey? "Do you like Sterling Canyon?"

"So far, so good. The skiing's pretty sweet, and the town is beautiful." Grey gestured around with his arm. Then he looked right into her eyes. "Just like one of its residents."

Avery caught herself blinking again, like flippin' Bambi. Meanwhile, he remained completely comfortable and confident, as if it were no big deal at all to tell her he thought she was pretty. His grin widened at her silence.

Flustered, Avery deflected. "Is that so different from your hometown?"

"Not much. I grew up in Truckee, outside of Lake Tahoe, but I left a couple of years after high school and traveled around, working at different resorts. Colorado, Utah, Alaska." Grey tilted his head. "Guess that makes me a vagabond, huh?"

"Or just very well traveled, unlike me." Funny how the notion Sterling Canyon might be just another pit stop for Grey came as a letdown instead of a relief. "So then, will your time here be short-lived, too?"

"Depends." He flashed a smile, the one that should come with a "hazardous to your health" sign.

"On what?" Curiously, she'd stopped breathing for a second.

He grinned again, like he'd noticed her anticipation, but then his expression grew serious and he glanced away. "On what happens with Backtrax."

More accurately, with his case against Andy—a topic they couldn't discuss.

Grey's livelihood and Andy's freedom both hung in the balance, with her family's finances caught in between. The heaviness of heart that had driven her to the park returned.

"But I hope I'll be around a long time," he finally said, breaking the gloomy silence.

"Do you ever miss your home?"

Before Grey looked away, she saw the light in his eyes dim a bit. "Home is where the heart is, right?"

"In other words, butt out?" She grinned despite feeling a little deflated.

He closed one eye and tapped his index finger against the side of his nose. She dropped the line of inquiry, although curiosity about his past tickled her psyche.

"Why aren't you skiing on your day off?" Grey's casual tone couldn't conceal his obvious desire to change the subject. "The mountain closes soon."

Now it was her turn to obfuscate. She turned her face away for a second and then looked straight ahead. "I usually ski with my brother. But even if he were healed, having fun isn't a priority right now." Her jaw clenched at another reminder of her brother's dismal future. "Funny how life moves on, when all I want is to turn back time."

She gripped the edges of the bench and glanced at her shoes. Like every other time she imagined Andy going to jail, she got teary. His looming fate made her feel selfish for worrying about her house. She hid her tears behind the wall of hair shielding her face. Heat raced to her cheeks as she considered what Grey must think of her odd behavior.

But then his warm hand covered hers in comfort, and her heart skidded to a halt.

"You're thinking about the criminal charges?" he asked.

She nodded, lungs tightening. "We're all so afraid about what might happen to him while he's behind bars."

"If only I would've stopped by your table and talked to you that night, everything would've been better for all of us." Although she heard sincere regret in his voice, she couldn't look up at him.

Shaman barked in the distance, having found something of interest near a bush. Without uttering another word, Grey threaded his fingers through hers and squeezed her hand.

A perfect, simple gesture of friendship.

She welcomed his silence while her gaze remained glued on their interwoven fingers. The heat from his hand spread up her arm and through her core, coiling low in her abdomen.

Desire. Forbidden, risky, uncontrollable desire.

For a few seconds, she closed her eyes and pretended they were different people sitting on a different bench in some different town with no connection to anything or anyone but each other. Pretended Grey might be that one-in-a-million guy who wouldn't try to change her or make her helpless.

The fantasy didn't last long. Guilt crashed over her when she thought of her dad's angry face, her career, and Kelsey's hopes, so she slipped her hand free and cleared her throat.

She stared at the worn leather-and-silver bracelet she'd noticed him wearing during therapy. The one obscuring the tattoo encircling his wrist. A tattoo she'd grown quite interested in recently.

"You always wear that bracelet." She dabbed at her eye before flipping her hair behind her shoulder. "Are you purposely covering your tattoo?"

He extended his arm and twisted the bracelet around once or twice. "Sort of."

"Why?"

His brows pinched together, easy smile fading. "Don't like looking at it."

"Why not get it removed?"

His gaze grew distant, shifting toward the skyline. "'Cause I don't want to forget, either."

"That doesn't make sense." She tilted her head and crossed her arms to keep herself from touching the bracelet.

"Does to me." Grey shuttered his eyes once more. He shifted his body, as if preparing to stand, just as a fat raindrop splattered on Avery's nose. Followed by another and another.

"Dang it!" Avery wiped the spatter from her cheek.

Grey's head whipped toward her, revealing an adorably surprised expression.

"Did you just say 'dang it'?" Grey chuckled.

"I don't like swearing." Avery shrugged, resisting the urge to squirm. He stared at her like she was some sort of quaint alien species he'd newly discovered. She braced for a judgmental comment about her being old-fashioned—prim, prudish, snooty—like Matt used to tease.

"Good to know." Grey whistled for Shaman, apparently unbothered by her straitlaced standards or the raindrops pelting his head. He stuck another lollipop in his mouth and said, "Well, dang it, A-vree. Guess I'm gonna get soaked."

She couldn't repress her smile at his devilishly cute grin. Once again, he'd set off a series of somersaults in her stomach. *I'm in trouble.*

"My car is just two blocks away. I'll run for it and pick you up on the sidewalk right over there." She pointed then stood and yanked her jacket hood over her head. "Be right back."

Three minutes later, she pulled up to the curb to ferry the now-drenched man and his dog home. Shaman whimpered and sniffed at her car, quickly filling the space with doggy odor.

Grey climbed in carefully, wincing in pain.

"You pushed too hard, didn't you?" She shook her head.

Grey waved away her concern with his hand, quickly changing the subject. "Why am I not surprised by the color of your car?"

"What's wrong with it?" She shifted into drive.

"Nothing." He stared out the windshield, humming.

Avery loved her Hydro Blue Jeep Wrangler. "First my clothes, now my car. What have you got against color?"

"Nothing." He swiveled in his seat. "I like color, especially on you."

Wiggling his brows made him appear childlike, especially considering the lollipop stick dangling from his lips. His flirtatious manner kept her emotions knocking around like a pinball.

She shouldn't be spending time alone with him, and it certainly shouldn't be so enjoyable. But as long as she didn't cross any lines and remained objective when it came to his care, she could treat him.

When she pulled up to his building, she shifted the car into park. "Let me help you deal with the dog and the crutches."

"Sure." He let Shaman out of the backseat. "Be warned, this place isn't much to look at."

Wet clothes stuck to Grey's body. His hair hung in wavy ringlets. Her breath caught in her throat at the sight. *Don't worry; I won't be looking at your place when there are more tempting options.*

Avery hid her red cheeks by retrieving his crutches from her car. She followed Grey and Shaman up the stairs. When they entered the apartment, Shaman darted for his food bowl.

"The bathroom's back there if you need a towel." Grey pointed toward the back of the apartment.

"That's okay. I should get going." She shouldn't be here cozying up to the man with the power to devastate her family. They'd keel over if they knew she'd spent part of her Saturday hanging out and holding hands with Grey Lowell.

She scanned the living room. Grey hadn't been falsely modest about his apartment.

Barren. Brown. Boring.

"No wonder you tease me about color."

"Told you." He grinned.

Nervous tension pulsed in the air, holding her captive.

Her own soggy clothes clung to her body, making her cold and uncomfortable. She should go.

Really.

It was well past time for her to go.

Yet her stupid feet refused to budge. Being near Grey felt a little bit like being gently pulled under water by a whirlpool, one too strong to fight. She glanced around again and noticed the keyboard. "You play?"

"Yeah." His cheeks actually turned pink for a change. "My mom's a music teacher."

Another interesting layer to explore. "Will you play something for me?"
He tilted his head and shrugged. "Any requests?"

"One of your favorites," she suggested, hoping to learn something about him from his selection.

He sat on the cushioned bench, twisting the bracelet around his wrist a time or two, deep in thought. Finally, he began.

The first quick notes were played with one hand until suddenly the song burst into an unfamiliar, turbulent melody.

Affecting.

Complex.

It captured the tone of her day, making her fascinated and uncomfortable.

She watched him play the melancholy tune, the faraway look in his eyes revealing a pensive side.

"What is this?" She stepped closer, transfixed. The energy rolling off his shoulders brushed across her body, awakening some forgotten hope.

"George Winston's 'Sea,'" he replied without looking at her.

"I love it." She wanted to touch him. Might have, too, if the apartment door hadn't suddenly swung open.

"Well, hello there, drenched ones." A giant, dark-haired god of a man in ski clothes waltzed into the living room. "Tell me, Enchantress, what magic spell did you cast to get Grey to play for you? It's usually 'hell no' whenever I ask."

The music stopped as Grey swung himself around on the bench.

"Trip, this is A-ver-ee, my PT." He paused. "And she doesn't like swearing."

"Apologies, sweet therapist." Trip held out his hand. "Pleasure's all mine. In fact, right now I'm plotting a tumble down The Cirque so I can get in on this action."

Oh, Trip was a player. Too bad Kelsey hadn't fallen for his sweet talk over Grey's less practiced flirtations. Grey's special blue-jeans-brand of sex appeal had its allure, but Trip was Armani-model handsome.

Together they were a lethal combo.

"All you pro skiers are smooth operators." How utterly frustrating! In addition to all the other reasons she shouldn't indulge illusions about Grey, she'd forgotten he belonged to that particular fraternity of womanizers. A single, thirty-something man whose idea of a "good relationship" probably involved a weekend-long fling. Just like that, she found the life jacket needed to keep the whirlpool from taking her under. "I always warn Em and Kelsey about guys like you, but they never listen." *And apparently neither do I.*

"Kelsey?" Trip glanced toward Grey, chuckling, and clapped. "She's friends with Boomerang?"

"Boomerang?" Avery scowled as she pivoted toward Grey. "What? Do you have some kind of little black book of nicknames? *Boomerang* is awful!"

Before he could respond, Trip broke in again, his carefree smile never faltering. "Well, you know, she keeps coming back time and again. How many texts this week, Grey?"

Grey glared at Trip, but said nothing.

"Kelsey's a great person, if a little too enthusiastic." Avery shook her head, glowering. "Instead of being flattered by her attention, you make fun of her?"

Grey shot Trip a death stare before responding. "She's nice enough, just not my type."

"Too bad you didn't figure that out *before* you led her on and kissed her." She lit up with a flash of resentment. How had she been fooled into thinking he was different from most men? *Mr. Right doesn't exist.*

Trip's brows rose. "I came up with her nickname, Avery, not Grey."

Avery looked at Grey for confirmation. He held her gaze for two seconds then shook his head, silently confessing. Avery rolled her eyes and waved her hand. "Maybe it's time someone came up with nicknames for you two." Then she glanced at Trip. "Of course, I doubt your parents named you Trip."

"Gunner Lexington the Third, at your service." Trip bowed.

Avery's puzzled expression must have prompted Grey to explain. "Lexington the *Third* . . . triple . . . Trip."

"Ah," she nodded, unable to keep from grinning, "now that one's cute."

◆ ◆ ◆

So are you.

Grey wanted to wring Trip's neck for busting in when he had, and for outing the whole Boomerang thing. Avery might be grinning now, but she'd been offended by that nickname.

By him.

He liked the way she'd defended her friend, but her loyalty also meant she wouldn't hurt Kelsey by spending more time with him.

Probably just as well, considering the potential conflicts with Andy, and the fact Grey had neither the time for a relationship nor a burning desire to be devastated by love again. Given how long it had taken him to recover from a broken heart with Juliette, he'd be better off if he could just adopt Trip's attitude toward women.

"Well, I've really got to be going." When Avery looked at Trip, full of smiles and sunshine, something sharp twisted in Grey's gut. "Nice meeting you, I think."

"My outlook on this little town just got a whole lot better, A-ver-ee." Trip glanced at Grey. "Where are your manners? First you don't give her a towel, and now you aren't walking the lady to the door?"

"It's okay. I'm good." When Avery's eyes met his, she'd buttoned up all traces of emotion, like the heat that had been building between them today never existed. "See you on Monday."

"Thanks for the ride." Grey waved as she exited his apartment.

The second the door closed, Trip covered his heart with both hands and collapsed on the sofa. "Now I know why you're always in such a good mood when you come home from therapy. Even her voice is cute—so feminine. Wonder what it sounds like when it gets low and throaty?"

"Hands off, Trip. I mean it." His deadly tone brooked no argument.

Trip raised his hands. "Oh, this *is* good."

"Just lay off and stay away from her. Your Boomerang remark did enough damage for the rest of the year."

"Hey, Grey, you'd better be nice to me. After all, you're gonna need help getting rid of Kelsey, and I may be the only guy who can do it for you."

Grey shook his head. "You're a man with no shame."

"No, I wouldn't cross any lines. But—"

"But nothing. Seriously. If you end up hurting her friend, I'll be doubly screwed."

Trip tapped his hands on the arms of his chair. "I haven't seen you this worked up in . . . well, maybe never. You've got it bad for this girl."

"I like her enough to protect her from you. And whatever I might feel, I've still got my priorities." Grey held up his hand and ticked off his fingers. "My recovery, for one. Launching summer climbing programs, for another. And then, *maybe*, if she doesn't hate me when the dust settles between her brother and me, I'll figure out what to do about Avery."

"Well, looks like you've got it all worked out." Trip stood up and started to walk away, then stopped. "Of course, that's assuming no one else makes her their *first* priority." Then he whistled and wandered into his bedroom.

Grey filled an ice bag before slumping into the sofa cushions and turning on the television. Sure, someone else might catch her eye while he dealt with the fallout from the accident.

Time wasn't on his side, but he had no choice. It would be impossible to get involved with her and stay objective when it came to her brother. Even if he *might* be willing to risk his heart again, he couldn't afford to risk his entire future.

He twisted his bracelet, wondering what Juliette would think of Avery. His phone rang, rescuing him from his cloudy thoughts.

"Hello?"

"Grey, it's Warren. Wanted to give you an update. I have some good, if incomplete, news about Randall's assets. Apparently he and his sister own a house in town. Based on tax records, its market value is now probably somewhere north of five hundred thousand dollars. Once we win at trial and get a judgment, we'll file a lien against the property to secure payment. If Andy can't come up with the money, you can foreclose on the house."

"You said he *and* his sister own it, so how is that good? Can we even force him to sell it when she owns half?"

"The short answer is yes. They own the property as tenants in common, so any judgment lien can be enforced against his share of the house. It looks like their parents transferred the title to them a few years ago, so maybe they made an outright gift. In that case, Andy could get a bank loan or possibly work out some other arrangement with his parents' help. But that's his problem, not yours."

"If he needs to sell his interest to raise the money, it's his sister's problem, too." Grey scratched his head. "I'm not interested in making her pay for his mistake." Dammit, his feelings were already affecting his judgment.

"Grey, you're the victim. You're the one whose business is at stake. Andy's criminal behavior is the sole cause of any loss experienced by his family."

"Maybe, but it doesn't feel right. It's complicated." Hadn't Grey identified Bambi as being a complication the instant he'd seen her? "Let's hope he has some other assets, so I don't need to hurt his sister just to get what I need."

"I'll get back to you once I have a full report."

Grey pitched the phone onto the coffee table. Business loans, living expenses, therapy and medical bills, new programming and marketing budgets—real obligations that were piling up quickly.

If only Avery's interests weren't tangled with her brother's. Then again, if her parents were rich enough to give their kids a house, maybe they had money to cover their son's debts, too.

Adler was right about him deserving adequate compensation. This injury limited every part of his life right now, and disrupted his sleep to boot. And as much as he couldn't allow himself to even think it, it could keep him from the out-of-bounds ski areas for quite some time.

Grey laid his head back and closed his eyes, recalling the unspoiled minute of his day when he'd held Avery's hand in the park. That had been nice.

Uncomplicated.

Real.

Maybe, if he were very careful and brave, he could end up with everything he needed *and* everything he wanted.

Chapter Five

The sun was peeking over the trees when Avery turned onto her street, her feet padding along to the beat of an old Justin Timberlake song. She entered the house whistling, thanks to the invigorating four-mile run and the fact she'd be working with Grey today.

"You're awfully chipper." Andy sat at the counter, drinking coffee and reading the paper. "Mind sharing your secret?"

"Spring is finally arriving. Mom and Dad have gone back to Arizona for a while." She set her phone and earbuds on the counter and poured herself some water, conveniently omitting any mention of Grey. "Life is good."

"Maybe for you." Andy raised his coffee mug toward her, silently requesting a refill.

Frowning, she refilled his cup and sighed. Andy's legal troubles were never far from his thoughts. "Sorry, I didn't mean to be insensitive."

"It's okay. Not your fault my life's a mess." He scrubbed his hands over his face. "Just got a lot on my mind. If I'm convicted of the felony, I'll lose my job as a ski instructor, which I understand because of the background checks they do to protect clients. But I didn't think these charges would cost me my off-season job, too."

"You won't be painting?" Avery picked a strawberry off his plate and popped it into her mouth. Surprisingly juicy for this time of year, so she stole another.

"Rob's wife is a MADD volunteer. She doesn't want him to keep me on the payroll."

Avery's eyes closed briefly.

"I'm sorry. I know things look bleak now, but it will get better."

"Before or after I go to jail?" His sarcasm failed to conceal his anxiety.

Instinctively, she reached out and stroked his arm. "Can't your lawyers negotiate a reduction of the charges?"

"Not yet, apparently." Andy slid off the stool and took his empty cup to the dishwasher. After staring at the drain for a few seconds, he looked at Avery, his brow furrowed. "They're telling me to go to AA, and to talk to kids about the dangers of drinking and driving. So, I'll do that and hope Grey Lowell doesn't want to see me fry."

"He won't go to the DA with guns blazing." Avery gulped the rest of her water.

"Why not?" Andy turned toward her, his eyes scanning her face. "You think he's your friend now because you're his PT?"

While she wouldn't admit it aloud, she couldn't ignore the truth. She did feel friendship and more for Grey, and she suspected it was mutual.

"A little bit, maybe. Just trust me; he's not the type who's out for blood." Avery pictured Grey's intense gaze, which made her body thrum. "He's a 'live and let live' kind of guy."

Andy stepped closer and narrowed his eyes. "You're blushing. What exactly is going on between you and Grey? I thought Kelsey liked him."

Only because Avery didn't tell her about "Boomerang." She'd considered it, but chose not to humiliate her friend. Yet, despite Avery's gentle dissuasions, Kelsey continued to hold on to hope.

"Nothing's going on! You know I can't get involved with a patient." Avery ran her fingers through her ponytail. "We're friendly. He's a good guy. He's got a lot riding on his recovery and I want to help him."

"You know I rarely agree with Dad, but I've gotta admit, I'm not sure it's a good idea for you to be involved with Lowell until the business between him and me is finished." Andy turned one palm upward. "Show some loyalty, for God's sake."

"You're part of the reason I decided to work with him." Her hands went to her hips. "If I can help him recover more quickly, it'll reduce his damages. In fact, maybe you should consider offering to help him out, too. That might go a long way with a judge."

"Lowell probably doesn't want much to do with me." Andy shrugged. "Despite your *opinion*, he could make things worse for me with the DA. Plus, my lawyer says the only reason Lowell hasn't filed the civil suit yet is because his lawyer can't assess damages until they can reasonably determine the full extent of his recovery. So it's not a question of if, but when. You and I both know that means trouble for our whole family."

"He won't take the house." The words sprang forth without a moment's hesitation. Why, she couldn't say. Intuition? Or was she turning into Kelsey, making major assumptions based on her gut, or worse, her heart?

"How can you say that? He's got a business to keep running, Avery. A business he can't participate in as long as he's hurt. Trust me, that's more important to him than his 'friendship' with you."

She scowled, unwilling to acknowledge Andy's warning. Was it really too much to ask to be able to enjoy one or two days of peace?

"I don't want to talk about this anymore. You're ruining my good mood." Her stomach growled, so she grabbed a banana yogurt and spooned it into her mouth. "Stop borrowing problems. Let's take things as they come. In the meantime, try to enjoy the peace and quiet here for a change."

"About that." Andy's expression turned sheepish. "I should warn you, I spoke with Matt yesterday."

"Did you?" She threw the empty container in the trash. Her spoon hit the sink with a resounding clang. "Why?"

"He'd gotten wind of the accident. Wanted to check and see how I was doing."

"I can't believe you didn't tell him to go to you-know-where. Really, Andy, where's *your* loyalty?"

Andy's forehead creased before he wrapped one arm around Avery's shoulder and kissed the top of her head.

"He acted like a jerk, but he was my friend for five years before you two got involved—against my advice, if you recall. Right now I'm a little short on friends, so I wouldn't mind reclaiming one." He stepped away and leaned his butt against the counter. "Besides, you never seemed all that broken up when he left."

At the time, Avery had put on a brave face so no one, most especially not Matt, could see how deeply she'd been hurt. But she'd privately broken down when, despite her best efforts to make him happy, Matt suddenly turned away from her and into the arms of some other woman. When he'd upended the future they'd been discussing. When he'd confirmed all her worst suspicions about men and relationships.

"I'm your sister. Aren't you mad at him on my behalf? He humiliated me in front of the whole town."

"You know I hadn't spoken with him since. But we talked about it yesterday, and right now I know how it feels to screw up and need forgiveness." Andy rubbed his jaw, as if weighing his next words. "He's sorry, Avery. In fact, he asked whether you were involved with anyone. I got the feeling he misses you. He's not happy with Sasha What's-her-face."

Sasha Grossman. Only child of a wealthy movie executive from Hollywood. A twenty-two-year-old girl who looked like the quintessential Californian. Silky blond hair, perfect tan, double-Ds. Not that Avery didn't have a nice figure, but Sasha's body—long, leggy, lean— resembled a supermodel with a boob job. Plus she was loaded and happy to spend her money freely on Matt. She'd booked him as her private instructor for the week. Unfortunately for Avery, the bumps Sasha enjoyed with Matt weren't located on the slopes. Given Matt's track record, perhaps Avery shouldn't be surprised he'd tired of his young plaything already.

"You better have told him I'm having the time of my life." She placed her hands on the counter and leaned toward him. "You tell him I'm being pursued by a dozen guys or something."

Andy chuckled. "Or something, all right. Of course, if I'd have known Grey Lowell gets you all hot and bothered, maybe I'd have mentioned that to him."

"I am not hot and bothered!" Avery wadded up a napkin and tossed it in her brother's face to cover her lie. "There's nothing romantic going on between Grey and me."

"Well, Matt will be delighted to hear it." Andy grinned, goading her.

"I couldn't care less what Matt thinks or does." She crossed her arms.

"I hope that's true, because he's coming back soon."

"How soon?" Avery rubbed her forehead to stave off a headache.

"Couple of weeks."

"Raspberries!" She stomped her foot. "Well, that's just fan-freakin'-tastic."

"Raspberries?" Andy shook his head, unlike Grey, who hadn't judged her dislike of cursing. "You've really got to get over your thing against swearing, or come up with better fake curses. You're not twelve, Ave."

Unable to think of a snappy retort, she stuck her tongue out and trounced off to her room to shower before meeting Grey—er, going to work. Work, dang it.

◆ ◆ ◆

Grey arrived at therapy in a shitty mood. The miraculous recovery he'd counted on wasn't happening. Throughout his years of skiing, he'd broken a collarbone, suffered two concussions, bruised ribs, and torn a rotator cuff. That rotator cuff hurt like a bitch, but this knee worried him more than anything.

When Avery came to the reception area to get him, he didn't greet her with his typical smile. "Let's get started. I feel like I should be stronger than this by now."

Avery's eyes widened. "Grey, you're doing great. You're still compensating a bit with your good side, but that's not uncommon this early in your recovery. You need to be patient and trust the process."

Grey loathed being lumped into the "average" recovery zone.

Avery proceeded to put him through the paces, working on gait education to minimize hip hikes and drops, doing a series of lateral box steps with TheraBand resistance, quad work on the TRX.

Throughout the exercises Grey's mood fell further, but not because of his knee. Normally Avery gave him one hundred and ten percent of her attention. Normally she was hands-on, touching him to correct his body alignment. Normally he enjoyed being the center of her universe for the hour they spent together.

Not so today.

Today she maintained physical distance. Her manner remained polite but impersonal. At times, she seemed almost distracted.

"What's up with you today?" Grey's direct question surprised him, but didn't seem to affect her.

"Nothing." She crossed her arms while intently watching his knees and hips as he completed a set of lunges. "Focus on your balance, Grey. You're still compensating."

"Am not." He watched her worry the hell out of her lip. Something he'd be happy to do for her if she'd let him. In fact, he'd like to drag his mouth all over her hot body, watch desire light up the gold flecks in those blue eyes, and confirm his suspicion she'd be as forward in bed as she was everywhere else. *Quit it.*

"I'll grab the video and prove it."

Avery went to get the camera, but Grey suspected she'd also walked away to shove aside whatever was bothering her. She might think she'd fooled him, but she hadn't.

While she set up the tripod, she casually asked, "So, how's your friend Trip?"

"Fine." His stomach dropped. Why was she asking about Trip?

"How many new hearts has he broken since I met him?" Her teasing voice and curiosity tunneled under Grey's skin. *Jesus, does she have the hots for Trip?*

"Why? Are you volunteering to be one of his next victims?" Okay, maybe his voice snapped a little more sharply than he'd intended.

Avery's brows shot up. "Touchy subject?"

Grey concentrated on his squats, refusing to look at Avery until his insides stopped flopping around. He forced a casual smile when he finally met her eyes. "I'm not a dating service. If you want info on Trip, you'll have to get it some other way."

Avery hid her face behind the camera. "Just making small talk."

Grey frowned, feeling stupid and exposed. He ran through the series of planks they'd incorporated to improve core stabilization.

Didn't she feel *any* of the tension he felt in her presence? His entire body ached with need whenever she came close. Every brief touch provided him a little relief from his yearning. Her withholding, physically and emotionally, felt like some kind of punishment, though for what, he couldn't say.

Neither said much during the remaining exercises. When he rolled onto his back, he pressed his palms against his eyes. Dammit. He'd been acting like a baby for the past twenty minutes.

He opened his eyes once he felt her standing over him. She reached down. "Up you go."

Although he didn't need help getting up, he'd never turn down an opportunity to grab hold of some part of her body when offered—any part would do. Once upright, he forced himself to release her hand. She mindlessly rubbed it with her other hand.

"Let's take a quick look at this footage so I can show you how you're compensating."

Grey grunted an acknowledgment, mostly because he'd become distracted by the scent of her skin. The light aroma made him guess she wore some kind of fragrant body lotion instead of perfume. An image of her slathering creamy lotion on her damp skin after a shower made him groan—aloud.

"Does your knee hurt?" Her concerned expression made him feel doubly asinine.

"I'm fine." He waved her off. *Idiot, get a hold of yourself. The girl is off-limits.*

She pulled an extra chair beside hers, and then hooked the camera up to the computer. Initially he concentrated on the monitor, but then he began noticing everything else about her having absolutely nothing to do with his therapy.

Her forehead creased in concentration. Her slim fingers pointed at the screen to illustrate whatever she described. Her hair fell across her face, forcing her to push it behind her ear—the one with two earrings, by the way. One little gold hoop and one small pink gemstone. He could almost feel the scrape of metal as he imagined capturing that little hoop with his teeth.

Avery's dimples deepened whenever she spoke, giving her a perpetually flirtatious appearance. He could barely keep from running his hand along the length of her thigh. Then, in the midst of his sexual fantasy, a horrible thought resurfaced.

What if she really was interested in Trip? She wouldn't be the first. Grey had no more right to stop the two of them from dating than Kelsey had to stand between him and Avery.

That recognition prompted a genuine pang of empathy for how bothered Kelsey might be by his pursuit of Avery. He didn't like to hurt anybody, especially not a girl who'd been nothing but nice.

"Are you even paying any attention to me? You look about a million miles away." Avery elbowed him. "What's going on?"

Not paying attention? I'm paying too damned much attention to you.

"Nothing." Grey looked at his feet. *Complications!*

Avery sat back into her chair. "This probably—this *definitely*—isn't my place, but I'm guessing you're worrying about your business. Kelsey says you have plans for expanding Backtrax by offering summer climbing tours. Since you won't be able to participate for a while, that's another financial blow, isn't it?"

Grey raised an eyebrow. "Yeah."

Avery pursed her lips and rubbed her hands over her thighs. Her tight expression radiated anxiety. "Are you planning to sue Andy?"

Aw, shit. He didn't want to have this conversation. Definitely not here or now. He pushed back in his chair. "We shouldn't be discussing legal stuff, Avery. Let's keep this"—he gestured between them—"separate from all of that, okay? We have to avoid all the conflicts of interest, right?"

"Just tell me why you wouldn't accept the insurance payout."

He noticed the additional creases marring her forehead. "Because twenty-five grand doesn't cover my losses. Medical bills, lost wages and tips, extra business expenses because I had to hire a replacement, and more."

"Twenty-five grand?" Her eyes widened in surprise. "That's all the liability coverage Andy carries?"

"It's the state minimum." Grey couldn't even criticize the guy, considering he'd lived most of his life by the same philosophy when it came to car insurance.

"Well, how much do you need?"

Grey crossed his arms, closing his eyes so he didn't have to see the panic in hers. How had he thought he could keep his personal feelings out of this mess?

"Listen, we really can't discuss this." He leaned forward, resting his elbows on his thighs. "It's not personal. I'm not trying to hurt anybody. Not you. Not even your brother."

"That's what I told him." The relief exuding from her grateful smile pierced straight through his heart. "Thanks for proving me right."

Hell. She'd clearly misunderstood him. He didn't want to hurt anyone, but he wouldn't roll over and lose everything either.

Absent some miracle, he knew he'd probably have to go after Andy's interest in their home. Despite his good intentions and near-desperate sexual desire, this friendship—or whatever this was—with Avery was as doomed as a sandcastle on the beach.

Chapter Six

Chaos—the only word that adequately described the scene at the Sterling Canyon Annual Tent Sale. Each late-April after the slopes closed for the season, all the retailers pitched canopies along Main Street, dragged out their remaining stock, slashed prices, and let the customers go crazy. By midday, the entire Sterling Canyon population milled around in a disorganized frenzy, scoping out that perfect deal.

"Ave, I'm gonna go home." Andy cast a quick glance over his shoulder at old Vanessa Cartright, who had just sneered at him and was now whispering something to her husband.

Throughout the weeks following the accident, Avery had discovered the locals had divided into three groups.

The smallest group—those who were standing by Andy—could be counted on her fingers and toes. Then there were those who weren't particularly eager to see him punished, but who salivated over the latest gossip and were quick to point out how lucky he was that nobody died. And finally there were those who jumped at the chance to openly criticize and ostracize him for his mistake.

Avery threaded her arm through Andy's, placing her body between him and Vanessa. "Don't let that old bag bother you. Besides, you promised to help me find a new pair of skis." She tweaked his nose, hoping to force a laugh, then rested her head against his shoulder.

"It doesn't make me feel better when you treat me like a baby." He shrugged free. "I'm taking off."

"Fine. No more babying. I drove, and I'm not ready to go home." She grabbed his hand. "Besides, your lungs and ribs are healed now, so no more excuses for lazing around the house. Sooner or later you need to start walking around town with your chin up."

"Now you sound like Dad." His observation caused her to bat him on the shoulder with the back of her hand, which only made him grin. "Knew that'd getcha. But you can't control me or my feelings, Ave. I'm going to walk home."

She looked at his Merrell hiking shoes. "That's a long walk."

"I can use the fresh air." He bent down and kissed her cheek. "See you at home."

Avery drew a deep breath and exhaled slowly as he walked away. She shook her head and then ducked into Gary's Gear to look for new skis for next season. An attractive pair of green Atomics caught her attention. She plucked them off the makeshift wall to see if they were long enough.

While holding them along her body to determine if the tips were at about the same height as her nose, she felt someone approach. She braced to deal with a pushy sales person, but it was Grey's voice she heard. "I doubt those are what you're looking for, Bambi."

Like a reflex, she grinned and turned to face him. Only two weeks earlier she'd stormed out of his apartment, relieved his insulting nickname for Kelsey had weakened her growing crush. Sadly, that feeling had only lasted until their next therapy session. Now she was back to battling against her attraction every minute they spent together.

Even dressed in old gray sweatpants and a faded Whistler hoodie, he looked handsome. She raised her brows in question. "Why do you say that?"

Grey took the skis out of her hands and put them back against the wall. "You grew up here. You've skied all your life, right?"

"So?" She chafed at the way he'd swooped in and taken over.

"You ski the whole mountain?" His hands rested on his hips.

"Yes."

"Ever go out of bounds?"

"Not often." When he grimaced, she said, "I've got to be careful. An injury could affect my ability to work." The minute she heard her words, she felt idiotic. If anyone understood how a serious injury could mess with one's profession, Grey did. Fortunately, he let the comment pass.

"Regardless, that particular Atomic is for beginners. The radius is too short for you, and there's not enough rocker for the times when you might need it."

"But it's the prettiest pair and it's half price." Her protest made him roll his eyes. "Hey, Atomic makes a good product."

"I know, but that's not the right ski for your needs." Grey studied the other skis still available, his silvery eyes focused, thoughtful, serious. Eventually he picked out a red set of K2s. "Now *this* ski is perfect for someone like you. A medium-length radius, rocker/camber/rocker combo, and a strong core reinforced with bamboo. It's even got skin grommets built into the tip and tail in case you want to hike up a ridge."

"But that red clashes with my ski outfit." She heard Grey laugh, like Matt used to do when he disagreed with her decisions. Her body lit with heat, making her snippy. "What's so funny?"

"Normally you aren't afraid of throwing different colors together." He held out both hands to fend off the light punch she threw his way. "Come on, Avery. You know gear isn't about fashion. *This* is an all-mountain ski that will do everything you need for your level of skiing. I promise, I wouldn't steer you wrong."

His sincerity softened her attitude, making her realize she'd overreacted. Grey wasn't Matt.

"You have no idea what level I am." She gestured between them. "We've never skied together."

"Maybe we'll remedy that next season." He watched her closely, as if willing her reaction to confirm that he would, in fact, ski again. Of course, all she could think about was the idea of skiing *with him,* which made her flush. "In the meantime, I can tell you're athletic. Your brother's an instructor. And the fact you *ever* go out of bounds tells me you're technically an intermediate to advanced skier, probably the latter. But if you don't trust me, ask your boyfriend when he comes back."

She felt her eyebrows pinch together until she realized he must've seen her with Andy. "You mean the blond guy who just walked off a few minutes ago?"

"Yeah."

"First of all, I don't need *any* guy's help making decisions. Secondly, that particular guy is my brother, not my boyfriend."

Grey practically got whiplash when he snapped his head around, as if he might still catch a glimpse of Andy. "Huh. I pictured him different."

"Different how?"

"Well, he doesn't look like you, to start. And he doesn't look like a jer——" Then he stopped, chagrined. "Sorry. He looks like a normal guy."

"He *is* a normal guy." She felt the heat rise to her cheeks again, this time for less pleasant reasons.

Grey shoved his hands in the front pocket of his hoodie. "I'm sorry if I offended you. Give me a break here. If he's a monster in my head, it's because he's caused me a shitload of trouble."

A beat or two of silence passed as each of them emotionally withdrew. Andy might as well be a concrete wall dividing her from any fantasy she harbored about Grey.

"You don't need to swear to make your point. I get it. But he's just a regular guy who made a bad mistake. One he's very sorry about, and one he'll be paying for, too, probably with his freedom."

"Truce." Grey held up his hands to reveal two fresh lollipops, one of which he handed to her. She took his response as a sign he disliked conflict. He stuffed a lollipop in his self-conscious grin, and redirected the conversation. "So, you want these K2s?"

"Maybe." She pulled at her ponytail, unwilling to let him think he'd made the decision for her.

"Stubborn girl. Bet you'd take them if I told you not to." His tone rang with admiration instead of scorn.

Rather than confirm or deny his claim, she changed the subject. "So, what are you here looking for, anyway?"

"Considering picking up a bunch of cheap facemasks, gloves, and other stuff that gets ruined or lost easily."

"No new skis? The prices are amazing."

He shrugged, looking uncomfortable. "Not in the budget this year."

Of course not. Once again she'd shoved her foot in her mouth. "Well, if you were buying a new pair, which would you choose?"

Without hesitation, he beelined to a set of black skis, one of which had a red tip. "These beauties." He lifted the Volkl V-Werks BMT 94s off the wall. "Light as air, full rocker, carbon center." He whistled. "Even at half price they're still over five hundred bucks. Right now it'd be a stupid waste of money I don't have, especially since these are big-mountain skis, and no one can promise me I'll be skiing in the backcountry again." He set them back, staring longingly.

"Avery the woman" wanted to combat his worry, to make him the promise he wanted—needed—to hear. But "Avery the PT" could *not* make recovery promises she couldn't absolutely keep.

Her increasing emotional attachment to Grey was exactly why that code of ethics existed. One major reason why she should *not* spend time holding his hand in parks, listening to him play piano in his apartment, or hanging around with him outside the clinic. Personal feelings compromised objectivity.

Knowing the difference between what she wanted to do and what she should do gave her the strength to say nothing, even though it gutted her.

As if sensing her discomfort, he sighed. "I've got to meet up with Trip. See you next week, Bambi." He turned to go, then glanced over his shoulder. "Whatever you do, do *not* buy those K2s." He winked before weaving through the open cardboard boxes and folding tables strewn throughout the tent.

She noticed him favoring one leg. Something else they needed to work on next week. Just before she lost sight of him, she spotted Kelsey approaching him. Another person Avery didn't want to see hurt because of something developing between her and Grey.

After they'd disappeared, she stood there at a loss for a minute. She'd come today looking for a new pair of skis yet no longer wanted any, not even the K2s Grey had just tried to trick her into buying with his silly attempt at reverse psychology. She walked back to the Volkls he prized. Lifting them up, she gently slid her hand over them, almost as if she were massaging Grey's leg instead of the smooth, lacquered surface of the ski.

Everything about her interactions with that man skirted ethical lines. Yet here she stood, once more pushing aside the tiny voice reminding her not to become personally involved with her patient. Some secret, unfamiliar, scary, wonderfully daring part of her flouted the rules where Grey was concerned.

Maybe she couldn't make a promise about his recovery, but she could provide encouragement and incentive. Her financial concerns paled in comparison to the red-hot need to give him hope. Decision made, she unwrapped the sucker he'd given her, stuck it in her mouth, and smiled.

◆ ◆ ◆

"You seem distracted." Trip flung a pencil at Grey from across the desk.

"Sorry. You know I hate this spreadsheet shit." Grey leaned back in his chair, hands behind his head. "I'm frustrated."

"Because of the numbers?" Trip leaned forward.

"No." Grey clucked. "Well, partly. I've always hated paperwork, but the skiing part of this business made it tolerable. Being up on the mountain, stomping big air, working with clients. That's what I love. Not this shit."

"But you gotta do this stuff, Grey."

"What if this is all I ever get to do from now on?" He leaned forward, elbows on his knees, head hung low. "Dammit, that's depressing."

"Don't think that way. Attitude is half the battle. It's only been a month since your surgery. You've got a long road ahead of you, but you'll get there."

"Meanwhile Andy Randall is walking around town, able-bodied." Grey looked up at Trip. "I finally saw him today with Avery at the tent sales."

"Awkward." Trip sat back, crossing his legs at his ankles.

"I didn't meet him. Only saw him from a distance. Waited until he took off before speaking with Avery."

"Again I say, awkward."

Grey shrugged. "Sometimes when I think about how he's screwed up my life, I want to see him pay for it so bad. But she loves him. Not only has she said so, but I saw it in the way she looked at him, talked to him. She's hurting over what's happened, over how it's affecting him, over how he'll handle jail. And as much as I think he deserves whatever happens, I don't like seeing her upset. And then, at the same time, I have to acknowledge the fact that I'm not the only one facing an uncertain future."

"Don't beat yourself up for feeling victimized. Sure, he's looking at serious charges, but *you* didn't cause his trouble. He brought that on himself." Trip narrowed his eyes. "As for Avery, I know you've got a little crush on her, and I get it, but don't get sidetracked."

Grey waved his hand in the air. "I know what's at stake. I just wish I had a crystal ball. If I *knew* I'd fully recover, I'd be a lot more patient and forgiving."

"I've skied with some of the best athletes. The toughest guys. You're one of them, Grey, so don't get soft on me now. If anyone can overcome this injury, it's you."

Grey smiled. "Guess some part of all those cheerleaders you've seduced has rubbed off on you."

Trip grinned, slow and easy. "Can you blame me for liking girls with spirit . . . and pom-poms?"

"On that note, I'm taking Shaman out for a walk." Grey pushed out of the chair. "See you in a while."

◆ ◆ ◆

Normally his walks with Shaman cleared Grey's head. Not today.

Today he kept focusing on how his knee ached from the dankness. How worried he was about his future. How pretty Avery looked in her pink fleece earlier. How impossible it was to see her and not want to stay close to her. How grateful he was that Andy had turned out to be her brother instead of her boyfriend.

When he and Shaman entered the apartment, Trip was lying on the sofa watching golf on television and drinking a beer.

Grey tossed his keys on the coffee table. "You locked up downstairs?"

"Yep." Trip chugged another gulp.

"Any calls or new climbing tours booked?"

"Nope. But we had a visitor." Trip shot a look toward the corner of the room, to where the Volkls Grey had admired earlier now sat propped against the wall.

He blinked. It had to have been Avery, but it couldn't have been her. But it *had* to be. His heart thumped hard against his ribs.

"Pretty sweet gift from your therapist." Trip sat up. "I tried to grill her a bit, but she didn't say much. Something you want to tell me?"

Grey shook his head as he walked over to the skis and tested the flex again. "I don't understand." He twirled back toward Trip. "Avery bought these? For me?"

"Bingo." Trip turned down the television. "Seems you've been holding out on me."

"No. I'm as shocked as you. Aside from the rainy day she drove me home, I've only seen her at the clinic. She's very strict about the whole ethics thing." For one minute, all the crap he'd been thinking about vanished, making room for a surge of hope and happiness.

Closing his eyes, he pictured her in that tent, imagined her debating the idea and defiantly grabbing these skis. For him. She'd done it for him, which made him feel like he'd just won a freestyle-skiing gold medal.

"Not so strict, it would seem." Trip came and stood near Grey, retrieving a small envelope from his pocket. "Helluva great set of skis, though. She left you this note."

Grey's heart pounded harder as he withdrew the small notecard from its envelope, straining, as always, to read the loopy scrawl.

Grey,
I'll do everything in my power to get you back on big-mountain terrain. I won't give up as long as you don't.

Avery

He felt his nose tingle, so he coughed and stuffed the card back in the envelope before slipping it into his own pocket. She hadn't made him a promise, but the skis proved she thought it possible.

Of course, he wanted to believe there was more behind this gift. That other feelings motivated her generosity. But that leap might only be wishful thinking. Wishful thinking that would probably result in heartache.

In either case, he couldn't let her spend that kind of money on him. Even if they were becoming friends, it was too much. And he didn't like the idea of her pity. "I can't keep these."

"You can't return them. *Final Sale* means final." Trip slapped Grey on the shoulder. "You two are quite a strange pair. This is going to be an interesting off-season, no doubt about it."

Grey placed the skis against the wall before he walked back to his room and closed the door. He sat on the edge of his bed, staring at his phone. Several minutes later, he dialed Avery.

"Hello," she answered. Just the sound of her voice made his heart speed up again.

"You never told me you moonlighted for the Make-A-Wish Foundation."

Her soft laugh made him wish she were sitting beside him so he could see her dimples.

"I guess you got my surprise."

"I did, thanks." He hesitated. "Much as I love them and appreciate your generosity, I can't keep them, Bambi."

"You have to keep them. I can't take them back."

"Then I'm going to have to repay you somehow. I don't mean to step on your gesture, but I'm not comfortable being a charity case."

"It's not charity. If Andy hadn't hit you, you'd have bought those skis today. I saw your face, read the worry written all over it. I bought them to keep you motivated. I bought them because it made *me* feel better, like I could make a small difference in this terrible situation my brother created. It's the first time I've felt good in weeks. Please don't take that away from me."

He let her words sink in. "Then at least let me take you out to dinner as a thank-you."

She fell silent on the other end of the line, causing his body to heat up with discomfort. "Grey, that's very sweet, but I can't date a patient."

"Who said anything about a date?" he covered. "Surely you can share a friendly meal."

"Oh." She hesitated again. "I think, given all the circumstances, it's best for now if we keep things more or less professional. If you want to show me your appreciation, just work hard and follow my instructions to the letter."

"Okay. We'll do it your way." He couldn't help but grin, despite being shot down. One of these days he would wrest that need for absolute control from her.

After they said good-bye, he tossed the phone aside, fell backward on his bed and rubbed his hands over his face. Week by week she'd been getting under his skin, chipping away at the wall he'd constructed years ago. The one he'd built to avoid the pain he'd suffered after losing Juliette. Lord knew it had been too long since he'd let his heart run wild. Just his luck Avery—the girl with so many complications—would be the trigger.

Lying there, he imagined what he would do if she were beside him. Grey had rarely been one to waste time fantasizing, but lately it was becoming a bad habit. Like all bad habits, he suspected it would probably end up biting him in the ass.

Chapter Seven

"Go on in. I'll wait out here for Emma." Avery patted Andy on the shoulder. "Good luck."

He shot her a sideways glance, his sandy-colored hair flopping over his brows. "I couldn't wait to leave high school. Can't believe I'm back here now, about to air my dirty laundry to a bunch of teenagers who aren't going to listen to me anyway."

"You don't know that. Even if you only get through to five of them, that's five kids you'll help save from trouble." She hugged him. "Em and I will sit up front for moral support. Don't forget, we need to zip out of there when you're done so I can run you home and make it back to the clinic for my four-o'clock appointment."

"I'll meet you back here, then." Andy kissed her forehead, then pushed open the glass door and disappeared.

After slumping onto a bench, Avery rubbed her hands together for warmth. She hadn't sat there for a dozen years. Unlike Andy, she treasured her high school memories—the days when she, Em, and Kelsey wandered these halls. Honors classes, football games, passing notes. Carefree fun.

When she looked around to check for Emma, she noticed Grey crossing the street.

Accustomed to seeing him in his gym clothes, her pulse stuttered and her mouth fell open at the Overland-catalog-model look he sported. Faded jeans hung low on his hips. He'd raised the shearling collar of his rugged lambskin leather jacket to keep away the chill. Unusually brisk early May winds ruffled his overgrown hair. The square lines of his jaw emphasized his masculinity.

Perfection.

Well, almost. She couldn't help notice the asymmetry of his gait. Concern about that problem took priority over questioning why he was at the school in the first place.

"Hey, Bambi." The right side of his mouth lifted into a coy smile. "I've never seen a woman frown so hard when staring at my . . . hips."

"Don't flatter yourself." She smirked to cover up the heat rising in her cheeks. Had she grown to like her ridiculous nickname, or was it simply the sound of his taunting, low voice that turned her on? "I'm staring at 'your hips' because you're still compensating with your good leg."

"Am not." He squared his shoulders and tucked his thumbs in his pants' pockets, drawing her attention once more to "his hips."

"Are too." Avery jerked her eyes up to his face then gestured in a circular motion with her hand. "Turn around and walk away from me over there, along the sidewalk. I want to see you from behind."

A lazy grin crept across his face. "I bet you do."

"On second thought, maybe there's not enough room on the sidewalk for you and your ego." She raised an eyebrow and made another circular sweep with her index finger. "Just go!"

Grey shrugged and turned. Oh yes, she did enjoy having a legitimate reason to stare at his tight little butt. Naturally, he decided to make a joke of her concerns and began swaying his hips like a woman as he strolled away from the table. On the third step, he grabbed his bad knee and leaned against the nearby bike rack. "Ooh."

Avery jumped up, dashed to his side, and grabbed his waist. "What happened? Did your knee give out?"

He spun on his good leg, laughing. "Gotcha!"

"You think you're a wise guy." She slapped his shoulder, although truthfully she didn't mind the excuse to be so close. Stolen moments like this were all she could enjoy.

"Just admit it." He caught her arm before she eased away. "You were enjoying the show."

His silver eyes glittered. Had his breathing turned a little ragged? She felt hers fall shallow. He held fast to her arm, almost tugging her closer. His focused attention made her girly parts tingle and tighten. Her mouth went dry.

"You're blushing," he said, still clutching her forearm.

"Let go." She tried wrenching herself from his grasp before she did something stupid like throw herself at him. And then, as if coming out of a dream, she remembered why she was there in the first place, which made her wonder about his plans. "What are you doing here, anyway? Meeting the athletic director to discuss teen climbing programs?"

He released her and shoved his hands deep into his jacket pockets.

"No." All traces of humor had fled his voice and eyes. "I came to hear what your brother has to say for himself."

His uncharacteristically somber tone and demeanor set off alarms. She tried to control her response, but felt her eyes grow wide with panic. "Are you planning to use his words against him in your case, or with the DA?"

"You're determined to suspect the worst, aren't you? Maybe I'm just curious to learn something about the man who messed with my life. Wouldn't you be?"

"I suppose." Avery pressed her lips together. "Why here and now? Andy's already nervous. Seeing you in the audience will only make it worse."

"Then I'll stay in the back, okay?"

Avery shrugged. "Guess I can't stop you."

"Would've been nice if you invited me to sit with you, Bambi. I thought maybe we'd started to become friends." When he turned toward the door, he glanced over his shoulder. "You know, you can't go staring at my backside again after refusing to keep me company." He winked and sauntered into the school.

Avery slouched onto the bench, holding her stomach. What if Andy said something to hurt his case? Grey had as much at stake as the rest of them, so she couldn't fault him for sharing whatever he might learn with his lawyer.

She dropped her head into her hands, but then Emma walked up and cleared her throat.

"You looked piqued." Emma tipped her head sideways. "What's going on between you and Grey?"

"What?"

"I couldn't help but notice the tension—the heat—between you and Grey." Emma straightened up and crossed her arms. "Are you two *involved*?"

"No." Avery sighed. "He's a flirt, but he's harmless."

"He likes you, not Kelsey?" Emma touched her fingers to her mouth.

"He most definitely is not interested in Kelsey." Avery huffed at Emma's surprised expression. "Oh, come on. You aren't really surprised, are you? They met in a bar months ago and shared one drunken kiss. He's never called or given any hint of interest since then. She's hanging on to some fantasy. Why is this one lasting so long?"

"Well, he is pretty gorgeous. She thinks he's nice, too."

"He *is* nice." And talented, gentle, sweet, sexy.

"Look at your dreamy face." Emma's eyes widened. "You really like him!"

Avery gave up the pretense, nodded, and then buried her face in her hands a second time. "What should I do? He's off-limits! He's my patient. He's probably going to end up taking Andy to the cleaners.

My entire family mistrusts him, not to mention all my own hang-ups about men. This stinks."

Emma sighed. "Don't forget Kelsey."

"Seriously?" Surely Avery misheard that last part. "If Kelsey and Grey had even gone on a single date, maybe I could see your point. But, assuming Grey and I wanted to date after he's done with therapy, why should I say no if he's never going to like Kelsey anyway?"

"Because a lifelong friend is more special than some new guy, especially one who belongs to a clique of men you mistrust."

Avery couldn't argue with Emma's logic. Maybe she and Grey would date a month or a year, but maybe not. And *maybe* wasn't a good enough reason to hurt a friend. "You're right. But I wish Kelsey would meet someone new."

"Well, yes, then she wouldn't be an obstacle."

"Too bad she didn't fall for Grey's friend Trip."

Emma's freckled cheeks pinked. "Is he a really tall, dark-haired guy?"

"You left out startlingly handsome." Avery tilted her head. "When did you meet him?"

"I saw him sneaking out of my inn early one morning last month while I was baking muffins. Later, I overheard two women talking over breakfast about their night. One was gushing about a ski guide named Trip who'd given her a night to remember, but took off without leaving his number."

"Yes, that sounds like him. Womanizing smooth-talker. Honestly, if I were ever interested in a one-night stand, he'd be perfect. He's so good-looking, even *I* might've fallen victim to his charm had I not met him through Grey." Avery scrunched her nose. "If only Kelsey had kissed Trip that night in the bar."

"Oh, brother, Avery. Keep him away from Kelsey." Emma chuckled. "She'd never be able to sort the silver-tongued lies from the truth."

"Good point." Avery's phone alarm beeped. "Oh, let's get inside. Andy's starting now."

On their way in, she'd noticed Grey seated on the aisle in the last row. Every nerve in her body burned with worry about how he'd interpret and use whatever Andy might do or say on that stage.

She and Emma managed to find two seats near the front left side of the old theater, which still had creaky seats and the dusty smell she remembered.

Her brother fidgeted in his chair while being introduced by Principal Winters. That old man probably wasn't overly surprised to see Andy—who'd been a bit of a class clown—end up in this position, she realized with sorrow.

When Andy stood in front of the microphone, he didn't say a word for at least ten seconds. She watched her brother scan the crowd and could almost see his mind decide to toss his originally planned speech.

"My name is Andy Randall, and I used to be like you: sitting in this auditorium, being forced to listen to speakers talk about stuff that didn't matter to me. I came here every day, played sports, chased girls, partied in the woods, and was satisfied enough with my B-minus grades. That was twelve years ago.

"Unlike my sister, I didn't go to college. I got certified as a ski instructor, worked odd jobs off-season, including painting houses, and pretty much continued living the life I'd gotten used to in these hallways. That's to say, I had fun, did the minimum that was expected or that I was capable of, and thought I was invincible."

Andy paused, glancing at the front row until he spotted Avery and Emma. Then he looked back across the wider audience. "A couple months ago I was drinking with some buddies after work, and then I got behind the wheel and tried to drive home. Didn't make it.

"It took hitting someone on a bike and plowing into a lamppost for me to learn I'm *not* invincible. I'm here today to try to prevent you from living with the guilt of hurting another person and messing with their life. From suffering the pain of lung surgery. And from facing felony charges, which, if I'm convicted, will limit my future job opportunities, my ability to travel to other countries, my ability to borrow money, among other things. And let's not ignore the shame I've brought on my family."

Avery's eyes stung while Andy continued to discuss, in detail, what happened that night, the impact on his family and the victim, and the stress and expense of dealing with multiple lawyers to defend against multiple charges.

When she glanced around at the kids, she noted most of them were paying attention and, despite the circumstances, felt a surge of pride for her brother. She'd be sure to tell him that later so that he could feel good about what he'd done.

At the end of the thirty-minute presentation, Avery craned her neck to look for Grey, and caught him ducking out of the auditorium.

"Em, I'm going to run to the restroom. Meet you outside."

She trotted up the aisle and dashed into the school lobby just as Grey was exiting the building. "Grey!"

He stopped, hesitating before turning around. She trod over to him, but then didn't know what to say.

He raised his brows in question.

"Did you get what you came for?" she finally asked.

"Uh-huh."

"Well, is that all you're going to say to me?"

"Apparently not?" He crossed his arms, as if preparing to fend off an attack.

"Did anything he said make a difference to your plans?"

"No."

She swallowed her disappointment, which landed in her chest like a twenty-pound kettlebell.

"Will it make you feel any better to hear that I respect what he said, and the way he's trying to help these kids stay out of trouble?"

She shrugged. "I suppose that's something."

"I'm sorry I can't tell you what you want to hear, but there's too much uncertainty at this point for me to make any major decisions."

She nodded, fully aware of the truth of that remark. Just then the auditorium doors blasted open as dozens of kids poured out of the theater. Avery saw the top of Andy's head and Emma's red hair in the throng.

Grey must've noticed, too, because he touched her forearm. "I'll see you at our next appointment, okay?" Then he whisked himself away from the scene before Andy and Emma met up with her.

♦ ♦ ♦

During Avery's drive home after work, she replayed Andy's speech in her mind. The recitation of problems both he and Grey faced, not to mention the potential adverse impact on her and her parents. Most troubling for her was the fact that she had no control over the outcome. Well, almost no control. She could do her best to help Grey achieve a full recovery, but that wouldn't keep Andy out of jail.

She entered her house thinking her mood couldn't slip any lower. She'd been wrong.

"Hey, sis, look who dropped by." Andy stepped aside to reveal Matt, who was sitting on her kitchen stool as if he'd never left.

Unfortunately Avery's knees softened, but she managed to steady herself by gripping the back of a chair. Unbelievable! Matt was here, in her house, hanging out like he had one hundred times before, yet nothing was the same.

He hopped off the seat, approaching her with open arms. When she glowered, his arms fell to his sides, but he kept smiling. "Avery. You look great."

Despite her irritation, she couldn't deny how handsome he was, standing there all long legged, broad shouldered, with his mop of curly blond hair.

Avery dropped her purse on the floor beside the sofa and stared at Andy, who conveniently had become absorbed by cleaning the kitchen. She heaved a bitter sigh and glanced at Matt. "I'd have expected you to have a darker tan, or at least be that fake-tan orange color to match your girlfriend."

Matt glanced at Andy for help. "Maybe I should go."

"Yes, I recall you being quite good at that." Avery waltzed into the kitchen with all the poise she could muster. Resentment simmered for allowing Matt to make her uncomfortable in her own home. "Actually, I'm shocked to see you, considering how eager you were to escape this 'backwater' town."

"Avery," Andy began, but Matt held up one hand.

"No, it's okay. I deserve it." He looked at Avery. "I'm sorry for how I treated you last year. You deserved better. I had my head up my ass—uh, sorry—I acted like a jerk. I never meant to hurt you."

"Actually, you did me a favor by showing me your true colors before we made any real commitments." Avery smiled her sweetest smile. "In fact, I should thank you."

Matt tipped his head sideways. "Andy, can I talk to your sister alone?"

Andy looked at Avery. "Sis?"

"What? *Now* you care how I feel about having him in our house?" At least Andy had the decency to look chagrined. "Oh, just stop. It's done now. I can talk to Matt for five minutes. You don't have to hide the knives."

Andy kissed her cheek and shot Matt a warning glance before shuffling off to his bedroom.

"What's so important you needed privacy?" she asked.

"Can we sit and talk like civilized people for a few minutes?" He nodded toward the couch and grinned his charming but futile grin. "Put down your weapons, Ave. I've already apologized."

Avery inhaled slowly. She *had* put him behind her last year. She *didn't* miss him. And she *didn't* want him to misinterpret her annoyance for a pang of regret. Whatever was causing her insides to explode, it was most certainly not the familiar scent of his cologne or the rasp of his voice.

"Is this the part where I act sophisticated and ask you about your new life with Sasha?" Crud. Not exactly exuding indifference.

"This is the part where I tell you I'm fairly miserable in LA." Matt shifted slightly closer, lowering his voice. "This is the part where you get to gloat because I've realized I walked away from a warm, intelligent woman for the worship of a spoiled, young nitwit. This is the part where I grovel for forgiveness."

Matt searched her eyes as if seeking some response other than her stillness.

Truly, his confession should have her doing backflips. No spurned woman's revenge fantasy topped the "I made a huge mistake when I left you" speech. Well, it would be a tad better if she had also already moved on with someone new. But, little details could be overlooked.

This was huge.

And yet, curiously, Avery felt only a minor flutter in her chest. Maybe she was really over him. Maybe she didn't really care. Maybe she hadn't merely been fooling herself all these months.

"I appreciate the admission, but it's too little, too late."

Matt didn't look surprised by her lack of enthusiasm. "I hope not. In fact, I was hoping we could spend some time together."

"Ha!" Avery laughed out loud. When he didn't smile, her eyes widened. "You're not joking, are you?"

"No. I want to rebuild my friendship with Andy, and with you." He smiled. "Who knows what could happen?"

He looked sincere, but her ability to believe in him had long ago crumbled.

"Why would I ever trust you again, Matt?"

"I know it'll take time, but let me earn it back. We could start as friends, like before."

"'Like before' isn't a good argument, considering how it ended." She crossed her arms, raising one brow.

"You know, a big part of what happened had more to do with wanting to try a different kind of life in a bigger town than with choosing between her and you." He leaned closer to Avery, reaching toward her but resting his hand on the cushion near her thigh. "Now I know the other pasture isn't greener. It's out of my system. I won't make the same mistake twice."

"Me either." She could recite the litany of things that, looking back, were wrong with their relationship, but what was the point? She simply wanted to end the discussion.

"You don't believe me?" He held her gaze.

"It doesn't matter why you left or what you've learned. If a house is destroyed, what difference does it make if it happened by fire or tornado? It's still gone. So, no, I don't think there's any hope for us."

"You hate me that much?" He actually looked hurt.

Avery thought about it, admitting to herself some nonsensical chamber in her heart would always belong to him, for better or worse. She couldn't risk allowing him to make inroads to that hidden place. "I don't hate you. I just don't see any good reason to let you back into my life."

Matt hung his head and blew out a breath. "You always told me never say never."

His hopeful eyes begged for a crumb of mercy.

"Well, that's true." Avery stood, restraining her fingers from tousling his hair. She'd always loved his hair. "But I wouldn't hold my breath if I were you."

"You can't stop me from trying."

"I promise, you'll be wasting your time." She sighed and shook her head.

Resentment served no one, especially not her. Life was too darn short to hold grudges, especially when she had picked herself up and moved on. By letting go of the hurt, she'd finally be freed from the past.

"I can accept you and Andy rekindling your friendship, because he needs all the support he can get. But don't mistake my courtesy for more than that, okay? We didn't work out before, and we wouldn't work out now."

She picked up her purse and stood to go.

"Andy says you're working with Grey Lowell."

"Is that a question?" She cocked her head.

Matt hesitated. "Is he the reason you won't consider giving me another chance?"

"You know I can't date patients." Avery hoped the truth wasn't too obvious.

"That's not a real answer."

"Well, it's the best you're going to get." With that, she strode to her brother's door, giving it a sharp knock before going into her own room, and closing her door gently behind her.

She belly flopped onto her bed and closed her eyes. In a few short months, her entire life had run off the rails. Her ex-almost-fiancé had returned to win her back, her brother faced bankruptcy and jail, and her heart couldn't suppress its increasing infatuation with the most unsuitable man in town.

What else could possibly go wrong?

Chapter Eight

Grey tucked his finger inside the collar of his shirt. It had been forever since he'd worn a button-down shirt and slacks. Heck, he was surprised he even owned a pair. "I wish I hadn't let you drag me out tonight."

"If anyone needs a night out, it's you—my treat. Besides, you should hobnob with the locals and other business owners." Trip waved his hand toward the businesses lining the street. "According to folks I've gotten to know, Mamacitas is *the* place to go on Cinco de Mayo. It won't kill you to try to schmooze a few of these guys."

"Schmoozing's your area of expertise." Grey opened the door to the restaurant, letting the sound of dueling guitars playing flamenco spill onto the pavement. "Why can't that be your job?"

"Because I'll be too busy schmoozing all the women." Trip winked and strode in front of Grey, hips swaying to the music.

When they entered Mamacitas, Grey's mouth began to salivate at the array of churros, flan, and chocolate-pecan pudding thingies on display.

"I know it's been a while, but you do still remember sex gives you a better orgasm than sugar, right?" Trip remarked before tipping his cowboy hat at the hostess.

Grey chuckled, although how he found any humor in his sorry sex life, he couldn't quite say.

As they followed the hostess through the restaurant, Grey noticed the upscale surroundings. Each table was topped with flickering candles inside glass-and-iron hurricane lanterns. Deep reds and golds on the walls and tables complemented the antique wood floors, exposed brick wall, and wavy glass windows. Flamenco music enhanced the festive environment.

Baskets of chips and salsa and guacamole, along with pitchers of margaritas of varied flavors and colors, were scattered among the tables, too. Although a lot of single people crowded the joint, there were several families there too.

One little girl in particular—with a devilish glint in her eye—caught Grey's attention. She'd tugged the fancy bows out of her hair and pulled at the collar of her embroidered cotton Mexican dress. The kind of spunky daughter he'd enjoy having one day.

He twisted his bracelet, letting the leather softly abrade his tattoo.

Years ago, he and Juliette had been in love and making plans. They'd even picked out kids' names and daydreamed about what kind of house they'd have. It had been perfect, until it had been cruelly stolen. A once-in-a-lifetime kind of love he'd been convinced he'd never feel again, or at least he had been convinced until recently. But the complications surrounding a relationship with Avery increased the risk of failure. Could he survive another slam to the heart?

"Where'd you go, Grey?" Trip set his menu down. "You look morose."

"Just an old ghost." Grey picked up the menu. Pricier than he ought to be considering, but he'd grown pretty sick of PB&Js and egg salad these past several weeks.

"Uh-oh. Boomerang at eight o'clock." Trip held up the menu like a shield before peering over its top. "Oh, but she's not alone. Looks like a double date with her friend Avery and two guys."

Luckily the waitress appeared before Trip picked up on Grey's bothered expression. "Can I get you gentlemen a drink?"

"Black currant margarita, extra strong, and extra sugar on the rim." Grey leaned back in his chair and tried to peek around the waitress to get another look at Avery without Trip noticing.

"I'll stick with a classic margarita, thanks," Trip said.

Grey recognized Andy, but who was the other guy? The athletic-looking blond with a too-broad smile pulled out Avery's chair. The guy stared at her like she was a special on the menu, for chrissakes.

Who the hell was the man drooling all over Bambi?

Whatever appetite Grey brought with him fled. Why couldn't he get past this infatuation? His hopeless fascination with his off-limits PT.

"Ghosts again, or is that scowl because your pretty PT might be on a date?" Trip pinned Grey with a knowing gaze. "This is going to be a long meal, isn't it?"

"Nope." Grey drummed his hands on the table, determined to move past his obsession. After the waitress dropped off their drinks, he said, "It's May. We need to book more climbing tours in the pipeline or things will be very lean this summer."

"You should update the website. Maybe start a blog or do some of that other social media stuff." Trip hesitated, as if waiting for Grey to shoot down his idea. "We need buzz."

"How much does it cost?"

"Don't know, but the payoff could be well worth it. And as long as you're grounded, you've got the free time to post blogs and tweet shit."

"Yeah, have the dyslexic guy write every day. Sounds like a great plan." Grey slammed back a swig of the sweet yet tart drink.

"Blogs and tweets are short and sweet. You've got spellcheck to help." Trip stretched one leg out from under the table. "It'll get the message out. Get people interested."

When the waitress delivered their meals, Grey and Trip temporarily dropped all discussion of work. Grey swirled one shrimp in the habanero-lemon cucumber salsa before stuffing it into his mouth.

"Oh yeah, that's outstanding." Grey savored the explosion of flavor.

Grey happened to glance across the room at the same time Avery noticed him in the restaurant. She blinked just like the first time he'd seen her. Too damn cute. Before he could stop himself, he grinned and waved his fork.

She smiled and waved back, which caught Kelsey's attention. When Kelsey turned toward him, her face lit up like the North Star. He noticed Andy peering at him as Kelsey excused herself from their group and made her way across the room.

"Now look what you've done." Trip failed to conceal his laughter.

"Hi, guys!" Kelsey stood by Grey, wearing some kind of ruffled wrap dress. Her long blond curls hung low, drawing further attention to her cleavage. "What are you two over here conspiring about?"

"I'm trying to convince Grey to invest in a new website and some social media." Trip wiped his mouth with his napkin and took another swig of his margarita.

Kelsey's face nearly broke apart. "Ohmigod. Yes! I did that with my real estate business and it really helped. Maybe I can help you get started."

Trip's look of surprise mirrored Grey's, but Grey couldn't imagine a worse-case scenario than working closely with Boomerang. Too many land mines.

"Maybe once I settle things with the accident we'll have extra money to invest." Grey cleared his throat, uncomfortably aware of her friendship with Andy. "Unfortunately, it's all moving at a glacial pace."

Kelsey's eyes darted toward Andy then she leaned toward Grey conspiratorially. "Well, I don't mind helping you out in exchange for your promoting me to wealthy clients interested in buying vacation homes."

"Well, that's mighty nice of you, Boo—er, Kelsey." Trip coughed to cover his near miss.

Grey couldn't help but smile at Kelsey's confused expression. The stiff drink had begun to loosen him up. Maybe working with her wouldn't be so terrible. It would give him a chance to prove they didn't have a future.

"That's a nice offer." Grey noticed Avery watching them with interest, which boosted his ego. "I'll think about it."

"So, Kelsey, who are you here with?" Trip asked.

"Oh, Avery and Andy, and Matt." She smiled, clasping her hands by her heart.

"Why the saucy look?" Trip flashed her one of his patented smiles. "Is Matt someone special?"

Grey felt grateful Trip's fishing expedition would ferret out the answers he wanted. Sometimes Trip's social skills really came in handy. Thankfully they were friends, because the guy would be a dangerous enemy.

Kelsey leaned forward again, this time in a secret-sharing manner. "Matt and Avery were almost engaged, but then he left her for one of his rich, young clients. Now he's returned to try and win her back." Her eyes glittered. "Isn't it romantic?"

Grey stared at her wistful expression, trying not to let his disgust show. Romantic? The guy was a selfish dick.

"What the hell's romantic about a guy cheating on his girlfriend and then trying to dupe her again?" Shit. He'd actually said it aloud.

Kelsey's brows lifted. "Who says he's here to dupe her? Can't someone realize his mistake and try to make it right? True love wins in the end."

"That's a bunch of horseshit, Kelsey." Grey pushed his empty glass across the table. "True love doesn't cheat."

"You sound just like Avery." Kelsey frowned and glanced at Trip. "Aren't there any romantics left?"

"Just you and me, it seems." Trip raised his glass toward her.

Kelsey graced him with an appreciative smile. "Well, my offer stands. I'm happy to donate a few free hours if you decide to work on those social media plans. You can check out my firm's site, Callihan's Peak Properties dot com, which also contains a blog and links to Facebook and Twitter."

"Thanks, Kelsey." Things would be so simple if only Grey were attracted to her.

"My pleasure." She beamed at him. "Bye!"

Grey watched her strut back to her table. From the corner of his eye, he noticed Trip assessing her, too. *Huh.*

"Who knew the girl had useful skills?" Trip finished his drink.

Grey didn't respond because he'd become distracted by Matt's fawning over Avery. The only thing keeping Grey from punching something was the fact Avery didn't seem to be thrilled by the guy's attention. If anything, her fidgety hands and stiff posture suggested she had little interest in reconnecting with Matt. At least not yet, anyway.

Trip glanced at Grey then Avery and back again. "Tick tock, my friend. Tick tock."

Chapter Nine

Avery buried her face in her hands, sighing. Problem solving had always been a challenge she'd enjoyed, but the current financial dilemma held no simple solution. She toyed with the small desk clock as it ticked away the seconds like a game-show timer running out.

Her savings account was rapidly dwindling thanks to floating Andy's share of their house payments and expenses these past months. If only her parents weren't counting on the monthly loan checks to supplement their meager retirement income. She couldn't indefinitely pay Andy's share of everything without causing significant disruption to her own life. And every dime spent bailing him out took away from the fund she'd been saving to try to start her own clinic.

If Grey won a big judgment, they were all screwed. Even if he didn't, Andy was very likely going to jail, possibly for a number of years. How would she manage to do this all on her own? She rubbed her temples. How dare she fret over money when her brother would be facing far worse concerns in prison?

Andy wandered out of his room half-dressed, hair still wet from his shower. He stepped closer and peered at the papers on the desk. "Whatcha doing?" His shoulders slouched when his gaze fell on the house payment check sitting beside her laptop. He averted his eyes as he walked into the kitchen.

She nibbled on her thumbnail. "Any luck with the job search yet?"

"Nope." He gulped a large glass of orange juice. "No one's interested in hiring a felon who could be carted off to jail soon. I'm a poor risk."

Avery's hand flattened against her stomach, as it did each time she was forced to confront her brother's future. In that moment, she resolved to find a solution without adding to Andy's stress. "I'm sorry."

"I know." His defeated grin weighed on her heart, fueling her near-desperate desire to restore hope and some sense of normalcy to his life.

Silence mushroomed around them. Once again Avery's fingers massaged her temples to cope with the stress she felt whenever she realized how little control she had over either of their futures. She watched her brother pick at the fruit bowl and rinse his juice glass.

Although she couldn't do anything about the criminal charges, surely she could facilitate some kind of employment. Maybe Emma needed help around her inn this summer?

The doorbell rang, interrupting her train of thought. She glanced at her watch. "Who's here at this hour?"

"Matt's driving me to my defense lawyer's office. He keeps trying to reduce the felony charges, but honestly, at this point, I'd live with them if we could just get the prosecutor to drop the jail time."

"Andy." Avery paused, unsure of how to comfort him.

He dismissively waved his hand. "Can you let Matt in while I finish getting dressed?"

He shuffled to his room while Avery retied her robe, smoothed her hair, and caught a glimpse of herself in the hall mirror. She groaned before trotting toward the door, calling out, "Coming!" after Matt knocked again.

"Good morning." She held the door partly closed, blocking his entry. "Andy's not quite ready yet. Give him five minutes."

"Can I come in?"

Avery rubbed one eye with two fingers. "Fine." She stepped aside to open the door. "You know, you've spent a lot of time with us these past ten days. I hope whatever your reasons are for sticking around town, they aren't about me."

"Everything isn't about you." Matt crossed his arms, having the gall to appear indignant. "But I do want to talk to you before Andy comes out."

Avery held up her hand. "I'm not interested in sharing confidences. If Andy has something to tell me, he can do it in his own time."

"What if waiting costs you your chance to save this house?"

Avery tilted her head. "Well, that certainly got my attention." She sat at the kitchen island instead of in the living room, having no desire to make things cozy. "What are you talking about?"

He looked a little too pleased with his victory. Determined not to beg him for details, she waited.

"Did Andy tell you much about the night of the accident?" Matt remained standing, his elbows resting on the counter. His blue eyes scanned her face and took a quick inventory of the rest of her, too, eyes lingering on the knot just below her chest.

She tucked the top half of her robe together for additional modesty. "You mean about how he didn't see Grey on the bike, or about the ice on the roads?"

His gaze moved back up to her face. "No, I mean about what happened *before* he got in his car."

She crossed her arms and legs, impatient with his Twenty Questions approach. "Only that he'd been out for drinks with his buddies."

Matt straightened up, glancing toward Andy's room before continuing. "Apparently those guys hooked up with a bachelorette party at the OS."

The "OS," locals' shorthand for the Outpost Saloon, was a decades-old popular hangout among the ski instructors and local ski bums.

Cheap drinks. No posers. The kind of joint she and her friends used to haunt to scope out the cute guys. Guys like Matt, in fact.

"Oh, what a surprise. A bunch of skiers hoping to take advantage of drunk women." Why Matt considered this news helpful, Avery surely didn't know. She uncrossed herself and began to slide off the stool.

"Hold up." Matt pulled out the stool next to Avery and sat down. "Apparently Jonah Barton was bartending that night and had the hots for one of the girls. He wanted to keep her at the bar, so he kept pouring everyone rounds of shots despite their increasing rowdiness."

Avery waited for the big revelation. When Matt said nothing, she flipped her palm toward the ceiling. "And?"

"Jonah served obviously drunk people more alcohol. Every bartender knows that's against the law. Insurance companies require bar owners to enforce it. So it's possible the OS could be held responsible for the consequences of Andy's accident."

Avery sat up straighter, intrigued but wary. "If that's true, why haven't Andy's lawyers already raised this defense?"

"It's not a defense to the criminal charges. And in Colorado, the intoxicated person can't sue the bar. But a third party can." Matt shook his head when she didn't connect the dots fast enough. "Grey Lowell can sue the OS. These cases are real long shots, but if Lowell gets money from the OS, maybe you won't be forced out of your house."

Avery's mind raced in several directions while processing the possibilities. "Why is Andy confiding in you instead of me?"

Matt shrugged, his expression softening in response to her distress. "Guilt and shame have him gun-shy. He's also worried exposing the extreme partying could actually hurt his criminal case."

Could it hurt Andy? Avery felt her forehead crease. She returned her attention to Matt, who seemed to be studying her reaction. If only it were anyone other than him delivering this news.

"So why are you breaking Andy's confidence?"

"Andy says you think Grey Lowell doesn't plan on taking your family to the cleaners. Unlike you, I'm not convinced that guy's a selfless hero."

Avery felt a smug, if inappropriate, sense of satisfaction when she heard the jealous bite in Matt's voice. "I never said he was a hero, but Grey isn't the bad guy either. And if he did have a case against the bar, his lawyer would've already pressed it."

"They haven't filed suit yet, so they haven't taken Andy's deposition. All they have is the police report and some eyewitness testimony from the scene of the accident. As far as I know, Grey and his lawyer have no idea what went down that night beyond *where* Andy was drinking. But you can tell Grey."

Avery sat back and crossed her arms again, watching Matt, whose eager grin reminded her of a puppy begging for a treat. "What are you hoping to gain from this, Matt? Because you telling me sure isn't going to sit well with my brother."

"I'm just trying to be a good friend. You deserve the truth, especially if it keeps you from losing the house I know you love. And I'm convinced Andy will start feeling better once it's all on the table."

The pair engaged in a silent showdown. She could hug him for his help, but she couldn't afford to let him slip behind her defenses. Thankfully, Andy showed up before she said anything further.

"I'm all set." Andy, now fully dressed in khakis and a button-down shirt, smiled at them, unaware of what they'd been discussing. He glanced around the room and then teased, "Hey, no broken glass. Are you two friends again?"

Matt stood, his expression blank, and nodded at Andy. Unfortunately, her brother's poor joke provoked a flash of anger that short-circuited Avery's patience. Before outing Matt for breaking Andy's confidence, she glanced at him apologetically, although he knew her well enough to have predicted she'd tackle this news head-on.

Turning to Andy, she quipped, "I didn't have time to throw anything. I was too intrigued by a story about a certain bachelorette party."

She noticed Andy blanch before he scowled at Matt, who braced for an argument. No matter how much she might like to see Matt tossed out on his ear for *other* reasons, she wasn't about to let her brother attack him for telling her something Andy should've admitted weeks ago. "Andy, why didn't you tell me this sooner? More importantly, why didn't you tell Grey?"

Andy closed his eyes, breathing out through his nose. "Because I'm worried about my criminal trial."

"How does the bartender's recklessness hurt your criminal case?" The cobwebs cleared from her brain, allowing rational thought to prevail. "The blood tests are conclusive, so the lawyers and judge already will know exactly how drunk you were. There's no hiding from that evidence."

"I don't know, Avery. I'm not as smart as you, okay?" Andy's hands were on his hips as he began pacing behind the sofa, head bowed. "I'm scared. I don't want to be in jail for one day, let alone years. Telling everyone I'd been throwing back endless shots probably won't help my cause. Besides, Jonah didn't force those drinks down my throat." Andy paled as he raked his hand through his hair. His green eyes creased with worry when he looked at Avery. "If Grey files a suit against the OS, everyone in town will start talking again. They'll say I'm trying to blame someone else for my mistake. Mark and Cindy have been decent to me since this happened, but if their bar gets dragged into this mess, I'll have two more enemies."

"Hey, if Jonah was reckless and broke the law, maybe the OS *should* be sued. Surely *it* is more responsible for the fallout than the victims. At the very least, Jonah's behavior contributed to your accident. He should've stopped pouring shots or called you a cab. He did neither. Now Dad, Mom, me, even Grey, we all stand to lose, and none of us have any blame in this situation." Avery shook her head, fueled by a fire in her gut. "I know you're scared. But you've got to face what's coming and let the chips fall. The people who love you will stand by you and help pick up the pieces. Jeez, you know this, Andy. I know you know this."

Avery wiped away the tear streaming down her cheek. Now that she'd unleashed her repressed anger, her heart ached to see her brother shaken and ashamed. She glanced at Matt, bewildered by the mix of gratitude and irritation his presence stirred.

Before either man uttered another word, she hopped off the stool and ducked into her room.

Once safely inside, she leaned against the door, pressing her cheek and palm against the cool wood. Her body trembled slightly while she drew deep breaths to slow her heart rate. Andy and Matt's rising voices penetrated the walls, prompting her to crack the door open to eavesdrop. Maybe it was wrong, but curiosity grabbed hold of her.

"What an asshole move, Matt. I can't believe you threw me under the bus just to score points with Avery."

"I told you to tell her over the weekend. It's Wednesday. How long were you going to let your sister worry? Don't be mad at me because you've been too much of a chickenshit to do what's right."

"Back off, man. You can't judge *me* after the way you dumped her and took off. Now, suddenly, you're back using every trick to win her forgiveness?" From where Avery stood, it sounded like Andy banged his fist against something hard. "Don't destroy my relationship with my sister just to fix your own."

"I know I fucked up last year. It's why I can't sit back and watch her suffer just so you can put off coming clean." A brief silence ensued. "Believe it or not, I'll always love Avery, and I've always been your friend, too. I know you, Andy. In the long run you'll feel better once you do the right thing, even if it seems impossible right now."

Avery's heart hammered against her ribs as she quietly closed the door.

If Matt was right, this information might help her family and Grey. She didn't believe in frivolous lawsuits, but it sounded like Jonah's recklessness broke the law. Heck, he intended to get that poor woman fall-down drunk in order to get her into bed, and to hell with the danger he created for others.

She hugged herself, wondering whether or not Mark and Cindy had been nice to Andy simply to make it more difficult for him to speak up. She hoped not. Then again, anything was possible when livelihoods were at stake.

Avery mulled over her options and decided she'd grill Andy this evening, in private. Feeling more settled, she pushed off the door and finished getting dressed for work.

◆ ◆ ◆

By the time Grey finished therapy two days later, Avery's stomach acids had practically stripped her stomach of its lining. Previously, he'd asked that they not discuss his legal issues. With the exception of the one time she'd asked him about Andy's insurance settlement, they'd worked together without discussing the lawsuit. Today, however, she'd break that streak.

She had to risk it. Had to persuade him to investigate the claim against the OS. Long shot or not, the outcome *could* be a win-win for both of them. Yet the fact that she'd never previously taken an "ends justify the means" approach pinched her conscience.

He sauntered toward her wearing his impish grin, towel wrapped around his neck, looking relaxed and happy. His trusting manner intensified the hideous brew churning in her stomach. She could barely look him in the eye.

After swiping a handful of Jolly Ranchers from reception, he threw one into his mouth and pocketed the rest.

"Have time for a quick lunch, or do you survive on Jolly Ranchers alone?" She shook her head at his sugar addiction.

"Lunch?" He flashed a crooked smile then snapped her thigh with his towel. "Think we can manage a friendly lunch without breaking all the rules?"

She slapped his shoulder, wishing his boyishness weren't so attractive. He stood so close she could smell the potently sensual combination of sweat and musk-scented soap. She stepped back, feeling off-balance.

Sexual tension gripped her body. The thin sheen of perspiration highlighting his rippling muscles did nothing to weaken the sensations. With each small movement, his deltoids and traps flexed, sending her body temperature through the roof.

Honestly, she'd always had more control over her hormones. Maybe she shouldn't be his therapist any more. Richard Donner had returned last week, so Grey could switch now. But she would miss him. And, despite this schoolgirl nonsense in her head, she knew she hadn't compromised his physical therapy. She'd given Grey the best, most aggressive therapy possible.

"A simple yes or no, please," she said, and forced a smile. While she couldn't deny wanting to spend time with him outside the clinic, today she had an ulterior motive.

The lawsuit. Hopefully he'd realize the benefit to both of them and be grateful she'd decided to ignore his request.

"Where to?" he asked, and once more she was struck by the sudden softness those gray eyes could display.

"Coyote Deli? We can take sandwiches to the park."

"Okay. Sounds great." He held the door open for her and then followed her to the deli wearing a heart-melting grin. In that moment, she suppressed a sudden urge to kiss him. The way he easily broke through her defenses surprised her—discomfited her, too.

Twenty minutes later they were sharing the same park bench where they'd held hands weeks ago, finishing their subs and learning more about each other. Unlike a lot of guys she knew who liked to boast and tell stories, Grey proved to be an attentive listener.

Avery'd just finished telling a story about the time Emma had dragged her to the eldercare center where she volunteered on Sundays. While visiting residents, they'd found Mrs. Cooper crying on her deceased husband's birthday. Intense emotional upheaval always made Avery uncomfortable, but Emma had gently handled Mrs. Cooper's grief by getting a cupcake from the café, singing "Happy Birthday," and saying a group prayer in her husband's honor. By the time they'd left her room, Mrs. Cooper was smiling.

"Emma sounds like a real sweet girl. A true friend, too." Grey smiled.

"She's both, unlike me." Avery grimaced.

"Why do you say that?" Grey's expression grew more serious.

"*Sweet* isn't a word I'd use to describe myself. I'm too blunt, too . . . driven, maybe?" Avery shrugged. "I don't know; I'm just not soft and approachable like Emma."

"I think you're probably a very good friend. *Blunt* is just a harsh word for honest, and honesty takes courage. Honesty and courage are important in any relationship, friendly or otherwise." He crumpled up the tissue sandwich wrapping and stuffed it into the paper bag. "And you don't have to be soft to be sweet. It was sweet when you drove me home in the rain, and when you bought me those skis. It was sweet when you asked me to join you for lunch despite the whole 'ethics' situation."

Avery's guilty conscience must've shown all over her face, because Grey's expression transformed from hopeful to concerned.

"What's wrong?"

"Nothing." She knotted her fingers.

"Avery." He reached over to untie her fingers, his typically friendly expression turning anxious. The instant he touched her hands, her body reacted with a flash of heat. "You look like you're about to give me bad news. Is this about my knee? Did you ask me to lunch to soften the blow?"

Avery inhaled slowly. "No bad news. In fact, I think it's good news. But in the spirit of courageous honesty, I need to discuss something you've declared off-limits."

He held up his hand, shaking his head. "Not the lawsuit, Bambi."

"Wait, it's not what you think. It's not about you and Andy, at least not directly." She watched Grey's shoulders tense as he folded his arms in front of his chest. The warmth in his eyes was replaced by an impatient stare—one brow cocked—issuing a "proceed with caution" warning.

She drew another deep breath before plunging ahead. "I'll just get right to the point. Have you and your lawyer discussed suing the Outpost Saloon?"

Grey's brows gathered. "No."

"No, you haven't discussed it, or no, you won't talk to me about it."

"No, we haven't discussed it."

"Oh." The bloom of renewed hope unfolded. "That's probably because he doesn't have all the facts about what happened before Andy got behind the wheel. I just learned some details that might give you grounds to sue the bar."

Optimism continued to blossom when he didn't cut her off. Maybe once she told him the story, her suggestion would resolve everything. And maybe then something more than friendship could develop between them. The unbidden thought temporarily distracted her until Grey cleared his throat.

When he remained silent, she relayed the story about the bachelorette party, Andy's friends, the delinquent bartender, and then explained the laws against knowingly serving intoxicated people more alcohol.

Grey stared at her, saying nothing. She met his silence with an exasperated flailing of her arms. "Grey, this gives you another source of recovery—one I assume has adequate insurance."

Her heart raced as she awaited his response. But Grey didn't smile with relief. In fact, she detected no reaction whatsoever. The flowering hope she'd embraced withered. The chirping birds and buzz of insects grew louder as she felt his physical and emotional withdrawal.

Grey's eyes narrowed. "You surprised me today, A-ver-ee."

Apparently not in a good way, according to his tone. "How so?"

"Seems this friendly lunch was just a ruse to butter me up so you could break our agreement about not discussing legal matters."

His distrust stung, even if he was at least partly correct. However, his opinion had to take a backseat to saving her house and her parents' retirement fund.

Then Grey frowned and glanced at his feet, speaking softly. "I'm disappointed you let me believe this lunch was about friendship instead of just being straight with me or, better yet, having your brother contact me. Makes me wonder if you really want to help me or are just trying to save yourself and your family."

Her throat ached when she swallowed. "Why can't it be both— helping my family and you at the same time?"

Grey studied her, holding her gaze. "Do you believe the bar is more responsible for my injuries than Andy?"

"Not *more* responsible. But it seems to me it might be *equally* responsible. The law might agree, too. And now you have *two* potential sources of recovery. Isn't that what's most important to you?"

Grey should be thrilled about the possibility of recouping his losses without forcing her out of her home. Yet her whole approach sat like a jagged stone in his gut. For the past thirty minutes, he'd been riding a high, believing they were taking a step away from a professional relationship and toward something personal. Then reality smashed his hopes. Nothing caused his brain to shut down as fast as wounded pride.

"Did your brother send you to talk to me?"

"No." Avery wrinkled her nose. "To be honest, Andy didn't even tell me the story."

Grey tilted his head. Something was off. "Then how'd you find out?"

"His friend Matt."

Andy's friend, my ass. When Avery blinked at him with those pale eyes, a hot streak of misplaced anger scorched him. "You mean *your ex,* Matt, don't you?"

At least she had the grace to blush when busted for her continued attempt to share only what she wanted him to know to suit her own agenda.

So Matt was playing her white knight, using whatever he could to get back in her good graces. This whole suggestion was really his chess move, not hers.

He rubbed his hand along his jaw. "So your brother was going to leave you twisting in the wind?"

She glared at him, the gold streaks in her blue eyes flaring to life. "He wouldn't have let it go indefinitely. He's just terrified that 'bachelorette party boy' won't play sympathetically to a judge handing out a sentence. And he's not eager to make more enemies in town by dragging others into his mess."

"But *you* don't mind that second part." Grey tipped his chin.

Avery pushed off the bench, thrusting her index finger toward him. "You know what, you can drop the attitude. I'm giving you important information that can help you. And no, I don't feel bad about looking out for myself and protecting what's mine, especially since *I* didn't do anything wrong. I'm not suggesting anything illegal or unethical, either."

She took a step closer and pointed in the general direction of the OS. "That bar owes a duty to the public. Its bartenders shouldn't be overserving wasted patrons to increase their chances of getting laid, and then letting those same customers go home without calling a cab. If a judge concludes the OS has some liability here, that's not my problem, and honestly, its not Andy's either. And I'll gladly defend my position to anyone who thinks otherwise."

Grey glanced at the ground again. Everything she said was true. No doubt he'd call Adler and discuss it with him. He had no wish to hurt Avery, but he wouldn't go after someone else just to spare her.

And what if Andy cooked up this story to throw the blame elsewhere and she simply bought into his lies? What if Grey ran down this rabbit hole and ended up with nothing except a whole bunch of ene-mies in town?

Then again, as a business owner, Grey carried liability insurance and was prepared to deal with lawsuits by injured skiers despite all the waiv-ers and assumption-of-risk notices his clients signed. The OS should be equally prepared to face the consequences of its negligence, assuming the bartender was negligent.

All Grey knew for sure was that he had a lot of questions and no answers. Best thing to do was say as little as possible until he had all the facts.

He studied her—that prideful streak on full display, from her tipped chin to the fists on her hips. Of course, she had as much right to protect her future as he did his, the realization of which dulled the sharp edge of his anger.

All along she'd reminded him of the boundaries between them, but he'd kept hoping for more. Not very fair to hold it against her when she'd only been honest, but his mixed-up feelings sucked. He wasn't sure what to do about any of it, but knew he had to get away from her to figure it out.

"Well, I'd better get going." He stood to leave. When Avery grabbed hold of his wrist, he felt the heat travel all the way down . . . there. Clearly, even when she made him angry, throwing her to the ground and kissing her seemed like a good idea.

"Wait. Are you going to talk to your lawyer?" Although her sub-terfuge today had hurt, her hopeful eyes tugged at his heart, weakening his resolve to maintain objectivity.

"I've repeatedly asked you to stay out of the middle, Avery." Grey placed his hand over hers, allowing himself to savor the satiny texture of her skin. "Please."

"I can't!" She yanked her hand away from his. Tiny lines etched around her eyes and mouth revealed her frustration. "Just because you refuse to discuss it doesn't mean I'm not still in the middle."

"What do you want from me?" Grey's arms reached upward then slapped against his sides.

"I want you to acknowledge my point. I want you to promise you're going to look into what I've told you." She fell back against the bench, deflated, tapping her toe against the ground. "I want you to act like a friend."

"Well, which is it then, Avery? Friend or patient?" Grey stared at her, thinking about all the times she'd suddenly withdrawn from their flirtations just when he thought he'd made progress. "Or is it that when you need something from me, I'm your friend. Otherwise, I'm just a patient."

"That's not fair, Grey." She frowned. Her voice grew soft. "You *are* my patient. It's complicated."

Complicated.

"Exactly!" He scrubbed his hands over his face. "I don't want you to suffer for something you didn't do, but I'm in a tight spot. I can't afford to make my decisions based on how they affect you, Avery. I've got to follow my *lawyer's* advice, not yours, especially when our needs don't necessarily align. What happens if I don't sue the OS? Will your anger compromise our work together?"

Her misty eyes made him feel like a prize ass. But he didn't have much income right now, and his dwindling bank balance put him at risk of missing a business loan payment in the near future. He had to secure his finances, no matter what.

"If you don't trust me, maybe you should be working with a different PT." Avery's voice faltered just a bit before she regained control of her emotions.

If her words hadn't carved him up like a field skinner blade, he might've admired her moxie.

Maybe she was right. This was probably exactly why things like her stupid code of ethics existed.

From the outset he'd let his interest in Bambi persuade him he could have it all—a full physical recovery, a legal victory that didn't hurt her, and some kind of relationship. Obviously his beliefs had been nothing more than wishful thinking.

Damned fool.

He let the silence stretch for a minute, hoping she couldn't hear his thundering heartbeat. "I'm going to leave now, before either of us says something we regret."

She stayed on the bench, fingers gripping the edge of the seat, as he turned and walked away.

Chapter Ten

Grey massaged his thigh and knee, dismayed by the fact he still felt discomfort—sometimes pain—despite all the work he'd been doing. The other day's confrontation with Avery hadn't helped matters either. The indignant look in her eyes had haunted him all night as he'd alternatively battled feelings of disappointment and hope.

Shaman rounded the block as they returned to Backtrax. He glanced at his watch, sighing. Time to meet with Kelsey to discuss social media. For months he'd been trying to gently discourage her interest. Now Trip was forcing him to ask for her help.

Of course, Grey couldn't argue with Trip's logic. Kelsey's site looked professional, active, and proved she was an accomplished local businesswoman. Grey could probably learn a thing or two from Boomerang. *Shit.* He had to stop calling her that before it slipped out and hurt her feelings.

Shaman barked and copped a squat just as Grey's phone rang. His lawyer's name flashed on its screen as he fished for the plastic bag in his pocket.

"Hey, Warren."

"Grey. I got your message about the events precipitating Andy Randall's accident. Sounds like we might have grounds for a third-party Dram shop claim against the Outpost Saloon."

"Dram shop?"

"That's what we call the statute that establishes liability in cases where a person suffers injury from a drunk driver after said driver has been served by a negligent bartender. Colorado's statutory cap on those claims is one hundred and fifty thousand dollars, but these cases aren't easy to win. If we find solid evidence, I'll send a claims notice to its insurer and see if it offers a settlement."

"Anything is better than what I've got now, which is nothing."

"It's tough to be patient with the pace of the legal process, but hang in there. I'll make sure you're compensated fairly. However, you should consider the backlash you might suffer if you file a claim against another local business owner in this small town. I'm not suggesting you refrain. Just giving you forewarning. Do you know Mark and Cindy Suttner?"

"Not personally." Grey didn't want to kick up a lot of dust in the community but, on the other hand, the majority of his business came from tourists. Over time, he and Trip would work to repair any short-term blowback from the locals. "Frankly, I can't let anyone's opinion factor into my decision. I need money to protect my business."

"I agree. In the end, you should pursue all avenues of recovery."

"So you'll follow up and keep me posted?"

"I'll be in touch."

Grey pocketed his phone. When Shaman sniffed his calves, Grey tickled him under his jaw. Then, after bagging the dog poop and tossing it in the nearby trash can, he walked home.

He arrived at the office five minutes late for his meeting with Kelsey. Kelsey, however, seemed more than content to have been amused by Trip, who'd seated himself on the corner of Grey's desk.

"Morning, Kelsey." He noticed her plunging neckline and high heels.

The woman was curvy enough without needing to call extra attention to her chest. He tried to keep his eyes up. "Sorry I'm late."

"No problem." She glanced at Trip and grinned, flipping her long, blond hair back. "I had ample entertainment."

Trip tipped his cowboy hat at her and grinned. "Glad to be of service."

"I thought you were going to investigate some intermediate rock-climbing areas we could use for touring groups," Grey said to him while unleashing Shaman.

"I am." Trip pointed to his bag of gear and rock-climbing shoes. "Just waiting for Jon to pick me up."

"Could you take some photos for me?" Grey walked into the small office bathroom to wash his hands, then returned. "When you get back, let's go over the mountain safety lecture we're giving tomorrow at the high school."

"Sure." Trip turned and smiled at Kelsey before rising off the edge of the desk. "Something tells me you're gonna need a lotta luck convincing Grey to embrace technology."

"Don't underestimate me." Kelsey gently swayed, her hands clasped together in front of her hips. "I'm nothing if not persistent."

No one would argue that claim. Grey noticed Trip swallow a smartass remark before turning away from her and grinning at Grey. "You two have fun, now."

"Bye!" Kelsey called out just as Trip escaped through the office door. Then she turned her full attention on Grey. "So, did you look at my site?"

"Briefly." Grey crossed to his desk and punched in his password, praying he could get through this meeting without a lot of discomfort. "I've been a bit preoccupied, but what I saw looked nice."

"Thanks. I try to strike a balance between professional and personal. Selling real estate requires both." Kelsey pulled a chair right next to him, overwhelming him with a sweet-smelling perfume. She reached into her mammoth bag to retrieve a thick manual. It landed on his desk with a thwack. Patting its cover, she said, "I used this to get started. And if you don't have your own photos, you can use Photobucket or other sites to buy images."

Grey shoved the manual away. "That won't work for me, thanks."

"Why not?" She pushed it toward him again. "It's a little intimidating at first. It just takes time to play around and get comfortable."

He stared at it then looked at her. "I can't learn that way."

"Why not?"

For better or worse, Grey preferred not to share his dyslexia with the world. People could be cruel, or try to take advantage of a perceived weakness. Kelsey didn't seem the type to do either, but she also didn't seem like the most discreet girl in town.

"If I have to read my way into this, it'll never get off the ground. Either someone can show me, or I'll eventually pay someone to do it."

Kelsey sat back, her head tipped slightly, assessing him. "Okay. Well, I taught myself how to do a lot of the basics. So, I can show you how to rework some of your site and set you up on Tumblr, Instagram, Facebook, and Twitter."

Boomerang really was relentless, in the nicest way, of course. What puzzled him most was why this attractive, friendly woman would waste her time pursuing him rather than accept any number of offers she must receive from other guys. Was she crazy or just plain clueless?

"Why do you continue to be so thoughtful when I haven't been exactly encouraging?" Grey held up a finger. "And don't say you just want access to my wealthy clients. Be honest."

Kelsey swallowed before meeting his eyes. "It's no secret I like you, Grey. You're a nice guy, and that's not so easy to find around here. I know you've been busy getting your business on track and dealing with your recovery. I thought this would give us an opportunity to get to know each other better." Her hopeful, open smile nearly killed him.

"That's what I've been afraid you'd say." Grey leaned forward, grabbed her hand, and looked her in the eyes. "Kelsey, you're beautiful, kind, and obviously talented, but I don't want to mislead you. All I can offer in exchange for your help is those real estate leads and friendship. Nothing more personal."

"How can you be so sure when you haven't even given me a real chance?" Her lips pursed into a childlike pout.

Grey glanced away, gauging how honestly he should respond. "Because I'm interested in someone else."

"Really?" Her eyes widened as she pulled back. "I've never seen you with anyone in town. I haven't heard any gossip either."

"Well, she doesn't know it yet. At least, I haven't told her directly." He grimaced. "It's complicated. I don't really have the time for a relationship right now, so I'm waiting to pursue it . . . her."

"Is it someone I know?" Kelsey's expression turned curious. *Shit.* He did *not* want to tell her about Avery before he told *Avery.*

Fortunately, he was saved by a call on the business line. "Hang on." He held up a finger before picking up the receiver. "Backtrax."

"Is Grey Lowell available?"

"Speaking."

"Mr. Lowell, this is Richard Donner. You'd left me a message about physical therapy."

Fucking bad timing. Grey closed his eyes, swiveling away from Kelsey. "Mr. Donner. Thanks for getting back to me so quickly."

"In your message, you said you underwent ACL surgery in mid-March and have been in therapy since then?"

"Yes. I've been in therapy two, sometimes three, times per week, but there may be some conflicts with my current therapist. Plus I'm not making as much progress as I'd expected, so I thought maybe I could come talk to you about your approach. See if it might be a better fit."

"Why don't we set up an appointment for tomorrow afternoon at three?"

"Perfect. I'll see you tomorrow. Thanks."

Grey hung up the phone and braced himself for Kelsey's questions before spinning back around. Stunned outrage radiated from every pore on her face.

"What the heck are you doing? Avery is the best PT for miles around." She leaned forward, jutting out her chin. "You aren't switching because of me, are you? Do I make you so uncomfortable you can't even work with my friend?"

"No, Kelsey. It's got nothing to do with you." Grey rubbed the area above his knee. "I thought Avery and I could work together and keep the situation with her brother separate. But it's not working out so well. It's complicated."

"Complicated again? Maybe you *make* things complicated." She shoved at his good leg. "If you want your knee to be one hundred percent, you should stick with Avery. Seems pretty simple to me."

"I appreciate your concern, but I think this might be best for everyone."

Kelsey shook her head, sighing, then bent over to heft her bag over her shoulder. "I don't understand you at all, Grey Lowell." She glanced at the manual on his desk. "I'll leave that for you and Trip. You need to upgrade your site and work on social media to build a clientele. Looks like I'm not the person to help you, though. I wouldn't want to add any more *complications* to your life."

Grey heaved a sigh. "Understood. Thanks for trying, anyway."

He walked her to the door and watched her get into her car. Her frustrated and confused expression would've been humorous if his mood weren't so heavy.

Back at his desk, he flipped through the manual, trying to read several pages. Predictably, neither the techniques of tracking with his finger or using a blank sheet of paper to block out text seemed to ease the eyestrain. The letters jumbled up too easily. He slammed the book against the desk, knowing his reading frustration wasn't really what had him upset.

Starting over with another therapist seemed daunting. Even that, however, was a lie. The truth was, he couldn't imagine not seeing and working with Bambi each week. But given their last conversation, he'd run out of options.

◆ ◆ ◆

Avery pulled behind the Weenuche Inn. Emma's great-grandparents had named the eight-room bed-and-breakfast after the Ute tribe native to the area. The authentic woven baskets and clay pots they'd originally displayed still decorated the main lobby and dining areas of the hundred-year-old brick building.

Avery knocked on the back door before waltzing into the kitchen. "Emma?"

Emma emerged from the walk-in pantry carrying a large sack of rice, her fiery red hair piled atop her head under a hairnet. "Hey, didn't expect to see you. I assume you're not here to help me prepare dinner."

"Uh, no." Avery smiled when Emma swiped the back of her hand across her forehead and uttered *phew.* "Hey, no need to emphasize how happy you are to avoid that potential disaster."

"Sorry, couldn't help it." Emma grinned then dropped the bag on the counter and grabbed a measuring cup. "So what brings you here at this hour?"

"Well," Avery began, taking a seat on the top rung of the stepstool beside the counter. "I was wondering about your off-season plans for the place."

As the words left her mouth, she couldn't help but draw a parallel to her passive-aggressive approach with Grey yesterday.

"What do you mean?" Emma poured six cups of chicken stock into a pot, more focused on her meal prep than on Avery.

"Do you still use the slow summer weekdays to spruce up the place, make repairs, and such?"

"Sure. We need to repaint a few guest rooms, address one bathroom's plumbing, and . . . well, the list is long."

"Did you already line someone up to do it all?" Avery held her breath, hoping Emma hadn't already signed any contracts. Okay, okay. So she did meddle a little. But only to help the people she loved. Her interference very rarely hurt anyone, and never with intention.

"Not yet." Emma frowned. "We're a bit behind schedule this spring."

Maybe Grey had a small point, though. She *should* be more direct. "Can I ask you to consider a favor?"

"Sure." Emma laid out a cutting board and knife then returned to the pantry.

"Could you offer Andy the chance to do some of that work?" Avery called after her. When Emma came out of the pantry looking surprised, Avery hastened to add, "He's handy. He can do basic plumbing, although he's not licensed. And he's got four years' experience as a house painter."

"Isn't he working for Rob?" Emma frowned with concentration while she peeled and chopped the onion she'd retrieved.

"No. Rob's wife blackballed him since the accident." Avery sighed, setting her hands on either side of the stepstool. A stab of guilt needled her for spilling her brother's secrets. "He's having trouble finding work because of the likelihood of him going to jail this summer."

Emma paled. "That's awful. How's Andy taking it?"

"Probably not as well as he's pretending." Avery walked over to stand beside Emma, who looked almost as unhappy as Avery felt. "I wouldn't put you in an awkward position if I didn't think he'd do a good job. And I know the opportunity would help him both financially and emotionally."

"Of course I'll help Andy." She touched Avery's hand. "He's like a brother to me."

"Great, Emma." Avery hugged her friend, relieved. "One last request. Could you pretend this was your idea? You know how proud men can be."

"Sure." Emma smiled then approached the sink and rinsed two tomatoes. "I'll call him tomorrow."

"Thanks!" Avery picked her purse off the counter, preparing to leave Emma to her cooking. Then Emma piped up again.

"Before you bolt, tell me what's going on with you and Grey?"

"Nothing." Avery waved her hand in an ineffective attempt to erase her memories of their recent argument. "We had a big argument last time we were together. I'm not looking forward to our next therapy session."

Emma winced and twisted her lips. Her expression looked uncomfortable.

"What?" Avery narrowed her gaze, noting the pink flush in Emma's freckled cheeks.

"I guess you haven't spoken with Kelsey today."

"She left me a voice mail, but I haven't played it yet." With everything going on, she'd forgotten Kelsey had planned to help Grey today. She fought the streak of envy tearing through her chest at the suspicion perhaps Grey had changed his mind about Kelsey. He had, after all, kissed her when they'd met, which meant he found her attractive. And Kelsey wasn't shy about using every tool in her considerable arsenal to her advantage.

Emma set down the tomatoes and wiped her hands before sharing what she knew.

"Apparently while she was at Grey's this morning, she overheard him making an appointment with Richard Donner."

Avery's heart dropped to the floor, just like her purse. "What?"

"He claimed to want a second opinion." Emma scrunched her nose. "I kinda suspected something else happened between you guys that sent him running. Guess I was right."

"I can't believe it." Avery slumped back onto the stepstool. Grey was planning to fire her? "I knew he was mad, but to quit working with me? And to contact Donner without telling me first?"

Although the circumstances were wildly different, Grey's betrayal humiliated her much the way Matt's had last year. And it hurt, too.

She'd begun to trust Grey, to believe him to be different, only to be proven wrong again.

Worse, this time she'd failed personally *and* professionally.

"I was surprised, especially considering what I witnessed between you two at the high school." Emma leaned over the counter. "Could Grey have heard about Matt coming back into your life?"

"That wouldn't matter." Avery waved her hand. "And Matt is not back in my life. Not now or ever again."

"Because you don't care about him anymore?" Emma crossed her arms. "Or is your pride keeping you from forgiving him?"

Good question. Truthfully, she guessed it was a little bit of both.

"I won't lie. Some part of me will always feel *something* for Matt because, despite everything, I can't pretend we never shared any good times. But nothing's going to happen."

"At least not as long as Grey Lowell is an itch you haven't scratched."

Avery stomped her foot then lifted her purse onto her lap. "Grey has nothing to do with Matt."

"Well, something drove him to call Donner." The diced onions sizzled when Emma tossed them into the hot skillet. "It's for the best, really, considering your family situation, Kelsey, and your own feelings for him."

As angry as Avery was that he'd embarrassed her by contacting Richard Donner, she still wanted Grey to have the best treatment and a full recovery. In her mind, that required retaining *her* as his PT.

"It's not for the best, Emma. I can't believe Grey would jeopardize his recovery like this." Avery hopped off the stool. "He's being an idiot."

"Maybe, but it's his choice." Emma began slicing the tomatoes. "Nothing you can do about it."

We'll see about that.

Chapter Eleven

Avery drove along Grey's street while speaking with Kelsey on the hands-free phone. "He didn't say anything else? Not to Richard or you?"

After leaving Emma's, it had occurred to her that Grey might've switched because his lawyer planned to file the lawsuit against Andy this week. She prayed she was wrong, because that meant she'd run out of time to find another solution.

"No. He told Mr. Donner he wanted a second opinion, and then told me things weren't working out with you because of complications surrounding the accident." After a brief pause, Kelsey added, "I told him he was an idiot."

"I bet that went over well." Despite the lump in her throat, Avery grinned at her friend's loyalty. Then remorse for her own disloyalty to Kelsey's feelings for Grey grabbed hold.

"Yesterday I would never have said it. Once he told me I've got no shot, I just didn't care if he got offended."

"Really?" Avery parked her car in the lot next to Grey's building, carefully choosing her next words. "He told you you've got no shot?"

"Mm-hm. Apparently he's involved with someone else." Kelsey snorted, then her breath caught. "Hey, have you seen him with anyone in town, or seen any woman hanging around before or after his therapy?"

"No." Jealousy gripped her with shocking force, whisking away her guilty conscience. All these weeks she'd thought he'd been interested in her, but apparently, she'd misjudged that, too. Had he really been seeing someone else? "Guess he didn't offer a name?"

"Nope. Actually, he didn't say *involved* exactly. He said he's *interested* in someone else. Said it was *complicated*. Apparently he hasn't told her yet." Kelsey blew out a breath. "He likes that word . . . *complicated*."

"Well, I'm sorry if you're disappointed." The clarification shot a bewildering but welcome wave of relief though Avery. Maybe she hadn't misread him. But, given the disloyalty and "complications," did it matter? She stared out the window, noticing the streetlights flicker as dusk fell. "At least he was honest with you. Now you can move on."

"Yeah, I guess. Still sucks, though." Avery could almost hear Kelsey shrugging. "Oh, well. Listen, I'm going to scoot over to a yoga class. Wanna meet me?"

"Not this evening, thanks. I've got some things to take care of. Talk to you later."

Avery turned off the ignition and sat in her car, hoping for wisdom to strike. Or, at the very least, a little clue as to why she'd driven over to Backtrax. She'd be a big, fat liar if she pretended she came merely because she'd never lost a client before, although it *was* part of her motivation.

Instinctively, she knew her feelings went deeper. Went someplace she'd locked away because of her family and Kelsey and her difficulty trusting a man with her heart—a skier, no less.

Perhaps none of that mattered anymore. Even if Grey had a little crush on her, he'd coldly stormed off the other day and called Donner. He'd felt betrayed, which might've poisoned whatever affection he'd developed. He could just be using the "other woman" excuse to let Kelsey down gently.

Not that Avery should care. From day one she'd known to keep her distance from Grey, to ignore her romantic fantasies in favor of accepting reality. So why did his retreat wrench her heart?

Avery stepped out of her car debating what she would say once they came face-to-face. She glanced at the unlit apartment windows. If she lived there, she'd probably keep the lights off too rather than stare at all the beige-and-brown decor. Of course, if she lived there, it would be repainted and redecorated within the week.

She walked around to the office entrance, which was lit by a small desk lamp. Her eyes scanned the empty space. Grasping the door handle, she held her breath then tugged. Luckily, it was unlocked and swung open. A single alarm chirp rang out, prompting her to call, "Hello?"

"Back here." Grey's voice drifted from the narrow hallway.

Avery inhaled one long breath before taking those next few steps. Her stomach clenched as if she were about to enter her dad's study for a reprimand. When she reached the door, she lightly tapped on the doorframe. "Hi, Grey."

Grey nodded while keeping his expression blank. His messy hair and tired eyes made him appear a bit haggard.

"You don't look very surprised to see me." Avery pointed toward the extra chair next to his desk. "Mind if I take a seat?"

He gestured with his hand. "Go ahead. And no, I'm not *very* surprised to see you. Only a little surprised." Grey crossed his arms in front of his chest, withdrawing from her again. "I assume Kelsey told you about my appointment with Richard Donner."

She drummed her fingers on his desk, staring at him, waiting. Of course, he remained silent. She leaned forward, unable to disguise the hurt in her voice. "Why, Grey? Why did you betray me by quitting and going to Donner behind my back?"

"Betray you? You're the one who suggested it, if you recall. I'm not even sure I'm *switching* therapists, but at this point I think it deserves a little consideration."

"We were arguing." Avery waved her hands in the air. "You had to know I didn't really mean it."

He rested his elbow on the desk then set his chin on his fist.

"No, Avery. I didn't know. *I* don't say things I don't mean." Grey sat back, fiddling with a notepad on his desk.

"Would you tell me if you were filing your lawsuit soon?"

He nodded, his scowl seemingly aimed at his own thoughts rather than at her. "It doesn't matter, anyway. All the circumstances worked against this going smoothly," he said, gesturing back and forth between them. "I don't like fighting with you. And honestly, this gets you out of sticky situations with your whole code of conduct. So if Donner's good enough to take me through the rest of my therapy, it's best for both of us to part ways."

He'd made a reasonable case, but she couldn't—wouldn't—accept it.

"So that's it. One argument and you're out?" She sat up straighter and threw her hands up in frustration. "Are you really willing to compromise your recovery? I'm not saying Donner's bad. He's fine. Conservative. Old school. Honestly, he's simply not as knowledgeable or up to date as I am. That's not an empty boast, just the truth."

"Gotta love a woman who knows her worth." Grey grinned, then his silvery eyes dimmed to dull pewter. "Don't worry. I can build on what we've started and incorporate anything else he recommends. It's not ideal, but it's better than this pressure cooker."

Avery didn't know what to say. She needed a minute to think, and let her gaze wander around his office to buy some time. Scattered across his desktop were a half-eaten bowl of ramen soup, two chewed-up lollipop sticks, a napkin, a glass of water, and his computer with a GoPro camera attached via USB.

"Is that your dinner?" It popped out of her mouth before she had time to censor herself.

"Yes."

She then noticed a bunch of crushed-up ramen soup and Tootsie-Pop wrappers in the trash can. "Is that your dinner every night?"

"Lately." He grimaced while tilting his head and studying her.

She almost asked why, then it hit her. Ramen soup was dirt cheap. His financial straits really were dire if he couldn't even afford decent groceries. Suddenly she felt about two inches tall.

"Grey, I'm sorry."

"About my dinner?" His crooked grin looked too cute. Those darn sexy lips of his made it impossible for her to stay focused.

Now was not the time for another Grey Lowell fantasy.

"No. About breaking my promise to butt out of your claim against Andy. I promise, I won't do it again. So please reconsider switching. I honestly believe I'm the better therapist to get you back to one hundred percent."

Grey leaned forward, his elbows on his knees, head bent down. "It's not just about you butting out. Working with you is messing with my head."

"Why? I just promised not to pressure you. Believe it or not, I do know you were the victim of my brother's stupid choices." She bit her tongue to keep from mentioning the bartender's negligence. "The thing with the OS, well, I only thought I'd hit upon a legitimate solution for both of us."

"I appreciate that, Bambi." The corners of his smoky eyes crinkled a bit when he looked at her. "Still, it doesn't change anything."

"Why not?"

"Because you don't have to say anything for me to feel pressure." He sat back and ran both hands through his wavy hair. "I already hate the fact I'll have to hurt you to get what I need. The more time I spend with you, the harder that fact becomes. If I had never gotten to know you, this all would've been so much easier. Now it's all fu—it's all messed up."

"Gee, Grey, it almost sounds like you *do* think of us as friends, despite your recent behavior." She smiled, hoping to ease the tension in the room, and gently kicked his foot.

"Of course I do." He rolled his chair closer to her and grabbed her hand. "I like you. I like you a lot."

Heat shot up her arm and spread throughout her chest as his thumb brushed against the back of her hand. When she panicked and tried to pull away, he gripped her hand tighter. "Grey?"

He was staring at her as his other hand brushed back her hair. His touch set off a spark of energy that pulsed throughout the room. They both held their breath for a second, eyes locked on each other.

"Screw it," he muttered before pulling her into a powerful kiss—one she felt down to her toes the instant his hot mouth claimed hers. A low rumble resonated in his chest as he tried to get closer to her despite their awkward positions in the chairs.

For several exhilarating seconds, she allowed herself to be swept away by the taste and smell of him. By the commanding way his tongue tangoed with hers. By the rising temperature in the room and shivery sensations overwhelming her entire body as he buried his hands in her hair.

Kissing Grey was every bit as hot as she'd imagined, and that heat shot straight through her abdomen and in between her legs.

One of his hands ran down her neck and back, pulling her closer. His chest heaved. Low sounds rumbled deep in the back of his throat as he got carried away and took her right along for the ride, crushing her to him.

Weeks and weeks of pent-up desire burst forth, causing her resolve to falter. She dug her hands into his thick, wavy hair, kissing him as she'd done so many times in her dreams. Then danger signs flashed in her mind, causing her to exert gentle pressure against his chest. "Wait."

He kept his forehead pressed to hers, allowing his breathing to slow down. He held her there, cupping her neck, his thumbs gently rubbing her jaw. "Sorry. That wasn't planned . . . or particularly gentle."

"It's not that . . . I just . . . I don't . . ." She fumbled, unsure of her feelings.

Grey reluctantly withdrew his hands from her face, letting them slide down her arms until he grasped her wrists. "I know. You can't get involved with me because of your family. At least not until things are settled. And the way things look now, chances are you probably won't want anything to do with me once that's resolved." He kissed the back of her hand. "This is why I shouldn't keep working with you. Look at how I lost control. I'm sorry if I upset you."

"I'm not upset. I mean, I am upset, but not because you kissed me." She kept staring at his hands.

Grey released her and rolled his chair back a foot or two. "I think this is what they call an impasse."

"You know, it's not just the lawsuit." Avery sighed rather than kick something or laugh or cry. "There's Kelsey to consider, and, well, you're a skier."

"Kelsey knows I'm not interested in her. And what's skiing got to do with anything?" His perplexed smile caught her unaware.

"I've sworn off them." She watched his smile fade.

"Why?" He narrowed his eyes. "Because of that idiot, Matt what's-his-name?"

Oh, great. He *had* heard the gossip.

"Not just because of him, although he hammered the final nail." When he kept staring at her, she shrugged and brushed her fingers against the ends of her hair. "I've lived here my whole life. I've watched two generations of ski pros use women and then leave them behind. It's hard enough for me to accept the compromises required of relationships, so I'm not too keen on doing so for another skier."

"Well, I'm not one of those guys, Avery." Grey's defiant attitude triggered a need to defend her position.

"Really? You're thirty-something and single, best buddies with a notorious Casanova, kissing girls like Kelsey in bars and then leaving them hanging." *Shoot.* She wished she could retract that petulant last remark.

Grey started twisting the leather bracelet at his wrist. "You don't know anything about me, or why I'm single."

She could hear the cooling tone in his voice, all traces of passion and playfulness disappearing. Yet his words didn't sway her. "That may be, but, after Matt, I'm not eager to take chances . . ." her voice trailed off.

Avery didn't want to insult him. She simply didn't want to get her hopes up only to have her life turned upside down again. And everything about Grey seemed destined to break her heart.

"If you think I don't know something about heartache, you're wrong. And if you think I can't commit because I ski, well, that's just stupid. I know what it is to love someone with your heart and soul. To feel so connected, you think you can't breathe without them once they're gone. To face that truth and have to fight your way back to the living." He pushed the bracelet back and traced the tattoo on his wrist with his finger.

Avery could see it clearly now. A single name.

Juliette.

She glanced back at Grey. His expression had never looked so bleak, nor had his voice sounded as desolate. Appearing lost in his own memories, he uttered, "To believe you'll never find that kind of love again."

Avery held her breath, her heart rate reaching its maximum training zone. Grey kept his head bowed, his focus on the tattoo. She was about to reach out and touch him when she heard heavy footsteps approaching.

"Grey, you back here?" Trip's deep voice called out.

Grey snapped out of his trance, his eyes murky. He cleared his throat. "Yeah," he said, just as Trip entered the small office.

"Well, hello there, m' lady." Trip smiled when he saw her. "What brings you by after hours?"

The glint in his eye might have been charming at another time, but the mood in the room swallowed everything. He apparently sensed his misstep. "Everything okay?"

Grey stood, mindlessly twisting the bracelet. Without really looking at either Trip or Avery, he said, "Sorry. I've got to get some air."

Before anyone uttered another word, he shot out the door.

"What just happened?" Trip cocked his head. "Did you give him bad news about his knee?"

Avery shook her head. "Who's Juliette?"

Trip whistled and folded his arms in front of his chest. "How'd she come up?"

"That's not important. What do you know about her?"

Trip sank into Grey's chair and scrubbed one hand through his glossy, black hair. He scowled, apparently debating with himself, while drumming his fingers on the desk. "Juliette's his story to tell, not mine."

Trip's surprising loyalty made her happy even though it meant she'd have to work harder for the story. At least Grey's trust in his friend wasn't misplaced.

"You interrupted us just when he was about to tell me."

"Sorry."

"She was the big love of his life?" Avery wanted confirmation of her assumption.

Trip held her gaze and nodded.

"So, why aren't they together? Why can't they reconcile?"

"He doesn't like to talk about it. I'm not comfortable being in the middle of this discussion, Avery. Sorry." Trip stood and Avery followed suit.

"Wait. Why? Is he embarrassed? Did she cheat on him or something?"

"No. Don't even suggest something like that unless you want to see him go ballistic." Trip started to step around her. "I think it's time for you to go home. Talk to him tomorrow."

Avery followed him down the hallway and to the front office. "Hold up, Trip. I'm not out to hurt Grey. I'm just trying to understand him. Why isn't he with Juliette anymore?" She grabbed his arm. "Please, tell me."

Trip's expression—normally a mash-up of flirtation and devil-may-care glibness—turned stony. Avery released his arm and moved toward the door, defeated.

Just as she stepped outside, Trip stepped into the doorway. "Tread lightly."

Avery spun around, hopeful he'd changed his mind about talking. Nope. Trip shook his head to indicate he'd say no more. He locked the door and disappeared up the interior stairwell.

She stood on the sidewalk, unable to move. A light spring breeze rustled the branches of trees budding with new leaves. Yet the cool evening air offered no relief from the pressure building in her lungs.

Was Grey upstairs, or had he gone off to walk and think? She turned and looked around. The sky had grown dark, blanketing the sidewalks in shadows, so she couldn't see beyond the block.

Dragging herself to her car, she replayed everything from the discussion about Richard Donner, to their heated kiss, and finally the agony in Grey's eyes when reminiscing about his beloved Juliette.

She shouldn't have stormed his office demanding answers, and she sure shouldn't have presumed to accuse him of being some kind of playboy.

Her eyes stung as she put the car in reverse. When she pictured Grey twisting that bracelet around and around, her throat ached.

The devotion in his voice when he spoke of Juliette had forced Avery to acknowledge an uncomfortable truth. At thirty, she'd still never experienced that level of commitment—of love—not even with Matt, with whom she'd been considering a future.

Perhaps she was incapable of loving that deeply. Maybe Kelsey had a point about her not understanding squat about romance. Had Matt sensed these deficits? Was that why he strayed? All these years she'd blamed men for the fact she couldn't make a relationship work without losing herself. Now she had to consider an alternative.

Maybe men weren't the problem. Maybe *she* was.

When she arrived at home, she sat in the car for an extra minute, her fingers pressed to her lips. Lips that had been burning up less than thirty minutes ago, but no longer tasted like grape-flavored sugar.

Grey had been open and honest with her tonight about his feelings. Since they first met, he'd treated her with the same direct respect, despite the fact she'd done nothing to really earn it.

And how did she reciprocate? By protecting her own interests and downplaying her feelings. Her hand slammed against the steering wheel several times. *I'm a coward.*

Chapter Twelve

Grey managed to avoid bumping into Avery for the next several days—making it the shittiest week he could remember since the accident.

A dozen times or more he'd thought to call or stop by the clinic. But he'd made a fool of himself when he'd run off after getting choked up over Juliette, and he didn't know what to say about that. He'd come off as a lunatic if he confessed to the complicated mishmash of guilt and desire, fear and need. Yet with each passing day, desire and need were winning out.

He exited Richard Donner's clinic following his first serious therapy session with the older man, cutting through a narrow alley to get to the center of town.

He turned the corner onto Main Street and yanked open the door to Higher Grounds, where he found Trip waiting at the corner table.

"Bought you one of your girly coffees." Trip pushed a salted caramel mocha toward Grey.

"Thanks." Grey let the girly comment pass, seeing that Trip had picked up the tab for the seven-dollar beverage. A small luxury for some. Huge for him lately. He stretched out his legs and took a sip. Sweet Jesus, that tasted wicked good. "You said you had some good news?"

"Yeah. I'm hoping it will break this downward spiral you've been in lately."

"That'd be a welcome change." Grey leaned forward, waving a "come-here" signal with both hands. "Lay it on me."

"Earlier today I convinced the Western Colorado Council of Boy Scouts to use our outfit for weekend camping and rock climbing leader-ship-development programs for their Majestic Mountain District troops. That's over one thousand kids—huge pool of potential customers." Trip grinned. "Since I'm sure we'll kick some ass with those boys, I bet we can count on repeat business in upcoming years. I think you'll be able to afford to hire Jon on a part-time basis to help manage those trips."

For the first time in days, Grey felt a burden lifting off his shoul-ders. "That's the best news I've had in weeks, Trip. You've really gone above and beyond."

"I know. I'm awesome." Trip chugged his black coffee. "You really couldn't have hired a better employee. Oh, but please, don't grovel."

"Okay, I won't." Grey snickered. Yet he couldn't deny how Trip had really been pulling through for him since the accident. "At the risk of increasing your oversized ego, you've been a great friend this year."

"I know how you can repay me. Come out on Wednesday night."

"What's Wednesday night?"

"Ladies' Night at On The Rocks. Sure to attract a nice crowd." Trip outlined an hourglass shape with his hands then settled back in his chair. "Maybe Avery will show up."

"I doubt she wants to see me." Grey sighed at the memory of how he'd bolted from his office a few nights ago. That, and the fact he'd switched therapists.

"Do you want to see her?"

"Doesn't matter what I want." Grey absentmindedly stirred his coffee.

"I guess with that shitty attitude, you're right." Trip then leaned for-ward. "I've no idea why you'd want to saddle yourself with a girlfriend, but apparently you do. It's pretty obvious she's attracted to you. So get your head out of your ass and man-up. Nothing can be worse than this mopey thing you've got going on. Better to have it fall apart than to never take a shot."

"This from the love guru?" Grey quirked his brow and finished his drink.

"Just one of many names women have given me over the years." Trip's gaze followed a cute young woman from the front door to the counter. He returned his attention to Grey and flashed a big smile. "And not even the best one."

Grey laughed aloud. "Your modesty must be the big attraction."

"Not the biggest, if you catch my drift." Trip winked at the cute girl as she walked past their table. "So are you in on Wednesday?"

"Sure, I could use a night out." Grey's phone vibrated on the table. He looked at the screen. "It's my lawyer. Mind if I take it?"

"Not at all. I think I'll see if I can catch up to the filly who just walked out the door." Trip stood and nodded. "See you at home."

"Hey, Warren." Grey stretched his neck from side to side, hoping for more good news. "What'd you find out?"

"Got the evidence we needed."

"So, it's fair to hold the OS responsible?" Grey straightened, hope coursing through his body.

"It's not frivolous. But for its bartender's reckless disregard, Andy wouldn't have been as intoxicated when he left the bar, and probably wouldn't have hit you. That's the whole point of the Dram shop law." Warren cleared his throat. "I sent a claim notice and hope to hear from its insurance company fairly quickly."

"That's great news." Perhaps this could help clear the way for him and Avery. "Keep me informed."

"I'll get back to you soon."

Grey set the phone on the table and finished his sweet drink, which had turned a bit cold. As he stood, the text message tone went off.

Meet me at our bench at five thirty.

Grey's heart pumped a little harder upon reading Avery's message. God, he missed seeing her.

"In the park?" he wrote, confirming where she meant.

Yes.

He checked his watch. Fifteen minutes. He had no idea what to expect from Avery, or what he would say. Should he apologize, pretend the kiss never happened, kiss her again? Naturally that last option sounded best.

He strode out the door and walked several blocks, arriving at their bench ahead of schedule. Stretching out his bad leg, he rubbed gently behind the knee. Each day the pain receded a bit, but occasionally a tightness or sharp ache flared. White clouds rolled across the sky. A squirrel dashed up a nearby tree, birds chirped, spring flowers were blooming. A damned Disney movie going on all around him, taunting him with the promise of a fairy-tale ending.

Within five minutes, Avery arrived carrying a large manila envelope. Grey couldn't help but smile. Although she still sported her black-and-white work attire, she was wearing a lime-green Windbreaker, blue-and-banana-yellow sneakers, and a fuchsia-and-green headband.

She took the seat beside him. The breeze ruffled her hair, carrying the minty scent of her shampoo through the air.

"Thanks for coming, Grey."

"No problem." His gaze dipped to her mouth. A bolt of energy shot through him as he remembered their kiss. Had she relived it twenty times a day like he had? "What's up?"

"I understand why you've decided to work with Richard. Given *all* the circumstances, I can't honestly argue it's the worst decision." She crossed her ankles, looking at her feet. Then she turned and looked him in the eye. "Still, I'm concerned about your recovery." She handed him the packet she'd brought with her. "I've written out the rest of the program I'd put together for you, including depictions, timelines, and so forth. Supplement Richard's therapy with them. And if, at any time, you change your mind or you have any questions or concerns, *please* call me."

"Thanks, Bambi." Grey smiled at her thoughtful gesture then held the envelope up. "This goes above and beyond the call of duty. Told ya you were a good friend."

"I owe you at least that much. I'm not very proud of my recent behavior." She shook her head, waving her hand in the air to brush the past aside. "Why don't you read through those papers quickly in case you have any questions?"

Grey folded the envelope in half and shook his head. "I'll look at it at home." He didn't want to read in front of Avery, Miss PhD, and have her watch him struggle with a skill she took for granted. Plus it would take him forever if he tried. "If I have any questions, I'll give you a call. And you don't owe me anything, by the way. In fact, I owe you an apology. A couple, actually."

"Me? For what?"

"For starters, the way I treated you the last time we sat on this bench. I should've thanked you for that information instead of shutting you down—and by the way, I'm filing a claim against the OS. And the other apology is for throwing myself on you the other night and then taking off like a two-year-old. That was badly done, and I wouldn't blame you for being uncomfortable."

"I'm okay. Let's call it a draw. Maybe now that we're not working together we can be friends." She bounced her knee for a minute in awkward silence, avoiding his gaze. Her infamous backbone seemed to melt like hot butter the instant things got personal. "And I realize this thing with the OS doesn't clear Andy, or mean that you won't still press your claim against him." Avery sighed and shrugged. "Who knows, though? Maybe everything will work out for both of us."

"I hope so." Grey meant it. He wanted it so much. Wanted her. Wanted everything to be settled so he could move forward without making promises he couldn't keep.

"Grey?" Avery chewed on the inside of her cheek, as if she was debating whether or not to continue. "I'm sorry about stereotyping you. And I'm really sorry it pushed you to recall painful memories."

Instinctively, he gripped his bracelet. He glanced at Bambi and saw her pretty gold-and-blue gaze home in on his wrist. No doubt she was chewing off her tongue inside her mouth, which made him chuckle. "Go on, ask."

Her gaze snapped to his, eyes wide and wary. "Really?"

"You want to know about Juliette, right?"

"Only if you want to tell me." She bit her bottom lip.

Grey rolled his shoulders once and sat back. He hated talking about Juliette, especially when it wouldn't clear all the obstacles between him and Bambi. However, he needed to prove he could be trusted with a woman's heart. If there was one promise he *could* make right now, that was it.

When he finally started speaking, he stared at a distant tree and let the memories rush to the forefront, playing like a movie montage of his early life. "I met Juliette when I first moved to Truckee, during the fall of seventh grade. We shared the same bus. I noticed her right away because she was cute, but I didn't talk to her at first. I was kind of a shy, scrawny kid, and I had trouble in school."

He felt himself scowl at the memory then decided to trust Avery with the truth. "I had . . . have pretty serious dyslexia, so I didn't do real well in class, or reading aloud, and so on. Unlike the kids who liked to pick on me, Juliette befriended me. We started sitting together on the bus, and she'd try to help me with homework. One thing led to another, and by Christmas we were 'going steady'."

Grey smiled at the recollection of how nervous he'd been when he'd asked her, and of all the awkward and exhilarating firsts that followed throughout the years: holding hands, kissing, "I love you's," and sex. "She was gentle and kind and everything good. That was it for me. We spent the next six years dating—were pretty much inseparable. After high school, she went to a local college hoping to become a teacher, and I started working half the year at Squaw Valley as a ski instructor, and the other half year as a waiter."

Grey glanced at Bambi, whose rapt expression momentarily made him grin.

"So you broke up when she went to college?"

"No." Grey twisted his bracelet, frowning. "I saw her every weekend during the school year, more often in the summer. When we turned twenty, we talked about getting married, but decided to wait until she finished school, mostly because we didn't want her parents to freak out. They thought she should date around. Guess they believed she could do better than me—find a guy with a good education and less risky future. My parents loved Juliette and would've been supportive."

Grey sat back and let the heaviness fill his chest as the worst moments of his life came rushing forward. Avery waited patiently, which surprised him. He looked at her, his throat tightening. "Juliette was with me at my parents' house one weekend. My folks had gone to visit my aunt in Reno. Anyway, we'd watched a movie and gone to bed. Fooled around. Nothing unusual. Then she suddenly complained of a sharp pain in her chest and between her shoulder blades that radiated down her back." Inadvertently, his own hand began rubbing his sternum. He envisioned her blond hair against her cheek, the pained look on her face. Remembered the gut-wrenching sound of her concerned whimper. "She wasn't one to make a big deal out of nothing, so I took her to the emergency room. By the time we got there, she was dizzy and disoriented. I called her parents, but it was too late. When they'd arrived, she'd already died from a burst aortic aneurysm. No one even knew she had one until then."

He heard Avery gasp yet he couldn't look at her. He bent over, elbows on his knees, and looked at the ground. "The doctor said it wasn't my fault, but it haunted me for a long time. Had I been too aggressive that night in bed? Had I pushed her too hard to be active on the slopes and hiking trails over the years because that's what *I* loved to do? How had we missed the symptoms? So many questions. So much grief. But nothing—no answer—would bring her back."

A gentle breeze wafted through the air, lifting the edges of Grey's heavy bangs. He traced her name over his wrist. "After we buried her, I couldn't stand to be in Truckee anymore. So I took off for Utah, then kept running. Kept moving."

"I'm so sorry, Grey." Avery's eyes were teary. "That's devastating."

Rolling his shoulders to ease the tension, he straightened up and sank back into the bench.

"It was. For a long time, I had no interest in women. Of course, eventually I realized I couldn't live the rest of my life without them either." He grinned when Avery blushed. "I got the tattoo to remember Juliette and the love we shared, but I hide it because the loss still hurts even after all these years. I've dated around, met one or two women I remember more fondly than the rest. But, as you know, it's not easy to fall in love."

"No, it's not."

"Anyway, that's my story." Grey rubbed his forehead and sighed. Retelling—no—reliving that nightmare always wiped him out. He peered at Avery, who looked flushed. He'd come clean, now it was her turn. "So, how about you? Are you going to give your ex another chance?"

"No." Avery shook her head, looking a bit surprised by his question. Grey was thankful to hear her certainty. "I'm not interested in 'Matt and Avery 2.0.' Our relationship was nothing like what you shared with Juliette. I've never had anything like that, actually. Never felt so connected or certain or . . . or loved. You're lucky."

"Guess I am." He sure hadn't felt lucky when she died, but he was grateful for the years they had shared. Telling Avery about Juliette had been a calculated risk, but the payoff could be worth it if she were willing to take that plunge with him. He dipped his head to force her to look at him. "For a long time I felt hopeless, like I'd never recapture that magic with anyone else. Lately, though, I've been more optimistic."

She didn't blink. Her lips parted slightly, her chest rose and fell with each breath. Time slowed. *Kiss her.* But this time he wanted to do it right. His heart thumped hard as his hand reached across the bench toward her and he slowly leaned in, but then she flushed and shifted away.

"Thank you for sharing Juliette's memory with me. Obviously she must've been quite special to have won your heart so completely." Avery's forehead wrinkled as she looked away. "What woman could compete with that history?"

Someone completely different from Juliette but equally compelling, just like you.

"Avery—" he began, sensing from her quick rise off the bench that his past was scaring her away instead of pulling her close.

"I'm sorry," she stammered. "I've got to run, Grey." She jumped up and started walking backward. "Call me if you have any questions about those exercises."

And then she was gone.

Chapter Thirteen

"What's got you whistling?" Avery tossed her keys on the counter and grabbed an iced tea from the refrigerator, wishing for ten minutes of privacy—like, ever. Just ten minutes alone to think about why she abandoned Grey on that bench.

"Started working at Emma's today. Feels good to have something else to think about besides the lawsuits." Andy joined her in the kitchen and dug his hand into the M&M'S jar on the counter. "And Emma's such a softie. Nicest boss I've ever had."

Avery poked his chest, latching onto a welcome distraction. "Don't you dare take advantage of her."

He slapped her hand away, looking appalled. "I'd never do that. I can't believe you'd even say something like that."

"Sorry." Avery stroked his arm. "I was half teasing."

Andy nodded and tossed back his fistful of chocolates. The whispers and gossip had taken a toll on her already-sensitive brother's self-esteem. Maybe now that he had a purpose and some ability to contribute to household expenses again, he'd start feeling better.

"What do you want to do for dinner? Eat in, order takeout?" She scanned the refrigerator again, looking for something resembling food. Milk, OJ, iced tea, blueberries, lettuce, eggs, and a big hunk of Manchego cheese. Not a lot of options.

"Chinese takeout? I'll share some sesame chicken and spring rolls," he said after scooping a second handful of candy and closing the lid. "By the way, brace yourself. Mom and Dad are coming to visit again soon."

"Oh." Avery sighed at the thought of spending more time under the same roof with her dad. "When?"

"Not sure. I think Mom's trying to squeeze in a 'nice' trip before the criminal trial."

Criminal trial. The words still sliced through her heart like a Chinese star. She shouldn't be wasting her time whining about *her* future happiness when Andy's was in jeopardy.

Avery hugged her brother, fiercely proud of him for having the courage to take responsibility, to get a job, and to joke with her when he must be terrified. "I still think your lawyers will work out some kind of last-minute plea bargain."

"We'll see." He patted her back and then eased away. "I'm going to shower. Got a little sweaty from moving furniture and sanding crown moldings. Whoever painted the place last time just layered paint over old caked stuff. Awful job. Can't believe she paid for such crappy work." He shook his head as he meandered toward his room.

Avery sank into the sofa and ordered their dinner, then turned on the television. Anything to keep from thinking about her family's troubles or Grey's tragic love story.

A loss like that—and the way it happened—well, no wonder he's always touching that tattoo. Although she'd been curious to learn more, she'd been too overwhelmed and afraid to pry. *Juliette.* Such a pretty name. Was the girl as pretty? Grey hadn't mentioned anything about her appearance other than noting she'd been cute when they'd first met.

Would he really have gotten married so young, to the only girl he'd ever dated? It seemed incredible, but she'd known of other people marrying their childhood sweethearts. Especially in small towns like Sterling Canyon and Truckee.

Grey's eyes had taken on a dreamy quality when he'd talked about Juliette.

Kind and gentle and everything good.

Avery considered herself a decent person, but doubted anyone would ever use such words to describe her. For better or worse, she took more after her dad with his can-do approach, controlled emotions, and lack of romanticism. God, that unwelcome realization stung.

She closed her eyes, trying to envision a thirteen-year-old version of Grey—scrawny and bullied because of a learning disability—and the sweet girl whose compassion had captured his heart. Talk about a romantic. Grey might rival Kelsey in that department.

Any woman who got involved with him now would be competing against a ghost—a saintly ghost, if Grey's tone of voice conveyed how he thought of Juliette.

Although he wasn't a cad like so many other skiers she knew, he remained equally unattainable. No way could she live up to his expectations of love. That kind of love only comes around once in a lifetime.

For her, maybe never.

Until today, that admission had never, ever caused an aching longing.

Andy reappeared and flicked the top of her head as he passed behind the sofa. "Dinner here yet?"

"No."

She watched him set up plates and flatware at the island. Domestic, like their mom. Somehow that gene had passed her by, too. In fact, most of her mother's genes, including her soft heart, went to Andy.

"Hey, I heard Jonah got fired today." Andy's expression turned grim as he folded napkins. "Add him to the list of people whose lives I've wrecked."

Whether her hopelessness about Grey or her dawning recognition of similarities with her dad had worked her into a tizzy, she couldn't say. But it didn't matter, because Andy's remark tipped her over the edge. Fueled the need to regain control of her life, and the lives of those she loved.

"Stop it." Avery stood and approached the kitchen. "*Jonah* ignored the fact that you were all getting bombed. He lost his job because of what *he* did. You have more reason to be angry with him than the other way around. If he had done his job properly, maybe you wouldn't have gotten in that accident. He could have called you a cab. Not to mention what could've happened to all the other really intoxicated people he let walk out the door that night."

Andy shrugged. "Maybe. Guess we'll never know. Bottom line, I was drunk and I tried to drive. I hurt someone, too. That's all on me."

"And you're taking responsibility. Your license is suspended. You're facing criminal prosecution. You *don't* need to add feeling guilty about Jonah to the list, okay?" As usual, feistiness resuscitated her previously flagging mood.

"Okay, boss." He grinned while filling two water glasses and setting them at the table. "So, what's going on with you and Matt? You must be feeling grateful toward him, because Grey's suit against the OS could mean we won't lose this house."

"There isn't any guarantee." Avery sat at the island. She had no idea what kind of expenses Grey had racked up, or how much income he'd lost, but given his current diet, she assumed they were significant. As for Matt, well, that was a nonstarter. "And PS—Matt's help now doesn't erase the past. I don't hate him, but I don't love him. Maybe I never really did." She picked at the napkin, avoiding her brother's contemplative stare.

"Yeah, I kinda thought that might be the case." He drummed his hands on the counter, antsy.

"Really?" She sat back, surprised by his remark. "You *never* thought I loved him?"

"You weren't all that devastated when he left. Your pride took a hit, for sure. Man, you were pissy. Stunned. A little dazed. But you never seemed heartbroken." He reached across the island and tickled her arm. "Then again, you've never been a girl to fall apart over a broken heart."

She felt herself glowering as she slapped his hand away. "If that's true, it's partly your fault!"

"My fault?" Andy pressed his hands against his chest as he laughed. "How so?"

"How many times did you warn me that guys were only interested in one thing? That I shouldn't trust them? You made me so wary."

"I was trying to protect you in *high school*, Ave. And believe me, I wasn't wrong about horny teenaged boys."

"Well, your honesty killed any romantic dreams I might have had." Okay, so maybe she'd overstated a tad.

"You're actually pouting. That's pretty funny, sis." Andy tilted his head, studying her. "If you want to blame me, go ahead. 'Cause it couldn't possibly be anything *you* did or didn't do. Not like overthinking every step of a relationship might kill the passion, right? Keeping a lid on your emotions wouldn't make the other person feel you're not all in, would it? Being like Dad and viewing compromise as a four-letter word might not make you the easiest partner, would it?"

Thankfully the doorbell stopped the discussion, because Avery didn't have any quick comebacks to Andy's remarks.

She tossed her wallet at him, pointing toward the door. Once he'd gone to pay for their dinner, she rubbed her temples.

Had Avery fought so hard against turning into her mother that she'd somehow ended up becoming just like her dad?

◆ ◆ ◆

Four nights later, Avery parked around the corner from On The Rocks. Somehow she'd let Kelsey rope her into Ladies' Night. One drink. One drink was all she'd promised.

Kelsey thrived on flirtatious banter with random men. In contrast, Avery had never been comfortable in that environment. She'd preferred something more personal and, well, *elevated*, for want of a better word.

She checked her hair and makeup—what little she wore—in the rearview mirror before walking into the bar.

The din of rambunctious chatter competed with the DJ's tunes. She elbowed her way through the crowd toward the bar, where she expected to find Kelsey surrounded by at least three men.

Only two. Surprising.

"Hey!" Kelsey waved, flashing a gigantic smile. She'd dolled up tonight, sporting a snug pair of jeans and sparkly wrap top. Kelsey had quite the bombshell figure. Sexy and feminine, if somewhat curvier than contemporary ideals. The two men standing beside her clearly admired her assets. "Saved you a seat. Meet Dylan and George, from Montrose."

"Montrose? What brings you two all the way down here midweek?" Avery slid into the barstool next to Kelsey, feigning interest.

"Working construction on some big shot's vacation home just outside of town."

"Which one?" Kelsey asked. "Might be one of my former clients."

"Mitchell Westwood. Ten-acre ranch property."

Kelsey's eyes lit up. "Yes, I sold Mitchell that old ranch house. His wife is sweet. So they're starting the remodel?"

"Tear down and new construction. Six-thousand-foot post-and-beam project."

"Wow, should be stunning." Kelsey leaned closer to Dylan, or George—whoever.

Avery paid for her half-price martini and surveyed the scene, paying little attention to her friend and the two men whose attention remained rather glued to Kelsey's chest. As she scanned the room, she happened to catch sight of a very tall, dark-haired man in a cowboy hat strutting through the door. *Trip.*

Her pulse kicked up a notch when she noticed Grey just behind him, looking almost as out of place as she felt. His intentionally disheveled, wavy hair hung sexily across his brows, partially obscuring his eyes. His lips were the only soft thing amid the sharp, masculine lines of his face. Even when set in a firm line, their fullness drew her eye.

The last time she'd seen him, she'd run away. Each time he'd tried to get close and open up to her she'd basically shut him down. Part of her wanted to dive-bomb into his arms. But the bigger part cowered, because she feared both failure and success. Rejection would hurt, no doubt. But she'd bounced back from rejection before and could do it again.

What scared her more was how she'd not only bent ethical rules for Grey, but now her affection for him also had her dismissing major family conflicts, and being dishonest with one of her dearest friends. Once again, she'd begun to lose her identity for a man. How'd she let herself go there again?

She turned toward the bar and gulped her martini, her heart beating a little too fast. Straightening her shoulders, she tamped down the butterflies in her gut and donned a smile for Kelsey and the guys, who were still discussing Mitchell Westwood's project.

◆　◆　◆

As soon as he entered the bar, Grey knew he'd made an error. Instinctively, he lowered one hand to shield his bad knee from getting kicked or shoved by the throng. Fortunately, Trip's size and appearance tended to part the crowd, so Grey stayed in his friend's wake and made it to the bar without injury.

Trip ordered a pair of IPAs and then faced the crowd with his elbows resting on the bar. "Not bad. Not bad at all for a Wednesday night."

Grey grunted, knowing Trip's laser-like eyesight would quickly identify his prey. "Ah, and the entertainment factor just jumped by about twenty degrees."

"Why?" Grey craned his neck to try to see what Trip did, but he couldn't compete with the five-inch advantage.

"Boomerang's down there at the end of the bar with two guys and your Avery." He nodded to his left. "Shall we go have a little fun?"

Grey shook his head, unwilling to interrupt Avery and Kelsey while they were with other men. "You've got to stop calling her Boomerang."

"You named her."

"I know. But it was rude, and I don't want anyone to hear us use that name again."

"Naturally." Trip stroked an imaginary beard and tossed him a sideways glance. "So are you gonna go after the girl, or are you gonna be a pussy?"

When Grey refused to respond to the insult, Trip began walking away.

Grey grabbed his arm. "Where are you going?"

"*I'm* not a pussy." He shrugged free of Grey's grip. "Stay here if you want."

"Hey." Grey reached out again, but Trip twisted away and cut through the crowd with Grey on his heels. "Dammit."

"Well, look at what I found, Grey. The prettiest girls in town." Trip smiled, ignoring the men who looked pissed about the intrusion, and turned to Grey. "I told you it would be worth coming out tonight."

"Trip." Kelsey's smile faded as she turned and coolly glanced at Grey. She then made a big show of looking all around him. "So, Grey, is your mystery woman here tonight?"

Grey noticed Avery's eyes widen and her cheeks flush. She took a huge swig of her drink and looked like she was trying to blend into the background.

"Kelsey." Grey waved at her then met Avery's eyes. "Avery."

"Hi, Grey." She only managed to eek out two whole words for him. When she turned toward Trip, her expression relaxed. "Trip. Imagine seeing you here on Ladies' Night."

"Where else would I be?" Trip inserted himself between Kelsey and Avery, effectively boxing out the other guys.

"Hey, man," one protested.

"Sorry." Trip casually swigged his beer. "Didn't see you there."

"Trip, Grey, meet George and Dylan, from Montrose," Kelsey supplied, helpfully.

Predators, not dates.

"Montrose?" Trip shook his head while making a tsk-ing sound. "Sorry, guys. We can't let out-of-towners poach our favorite girls." Trip waved his beer over the crowd. "Don't worry, though. Lots of other women here."

Grey had to chuckle when Avery choked on her drink, her eyes bulging at Trip's audacity. Kelsey couldn't seem to decide between being flattered or angry, but in either case, she maintained indifference toward Grey.

George or Dylan, Grey wasn't sure which, tipped up his chin. "Hey, asshole, why don't you mind your own business?"

Trip raised one brow and set his beer on the bar, straightening every inch of his muscular stature, and set his hands on his hips. He smiled while looking down—way down—at the guy, then wrapped an arm around Kelsey's shoulders. "This here gal is my business, aren't you, baby?" Trip brushed a kiss on her temple, which seemed to snap her out of her confusion.

Kelsey slapped him on the shoulder and shot him a puzzled glare. "Hey!"

"Aw, come on." Trip tugged at her hair. "You can't stay mad forever."

Before Kelsey could utter another protest, George and Dylan waved in disgust and walked away.

"What in the heck are you doing?" Kelsey eyeballed Trip like he was a lunatic, which Grey thought might just be true.

"Just goofin' around. You girls weren't seriously interested in those two yahoos, were you? Trust me, they were just looking for a quick . . . y'know." Trip smiled and finished his beer.

"Unlike you." Avery smirked, rolling her eyes.

"You've got a sharp tongue, sweet PT. Surely you can think up better uses for that particular body part than taking me down a peg or two." Trip glanced at Grey with a mischievous expression, ignoring Avery's snorted response, and then returned his attention to her. "Come on, girl, you look like you want to dance."

"No, I don't." Avery shook her head.

"Sure you do." Without waiting, Trip grabbed her hand and dragged her toward the dance floor. As they brushed past Kelsey, Grey heard Avery muttering something about Trip being crazy.

He didn't have a great vantage point from where he and Kelsey stood, so he stretched his neck to watch them cut through the crowd. Although he knew his friend wouldn't make a pass at her, jealousy still took root as he watched Trip twirl Avery and hold her close. She may have protested at first, but now she was smiling and joking around with him.

Grey stabbed his fingers through his bangs. *That should be me.*

"Oh. My. God." Upon hearing Kelsey's incredulous voice, he turned toward her. "It's *Avery.*"

"Huh?"

"Avery is the girl you like. The *complicated* situation." Kelsey crossed her arms, frowning. "Just look at you staring after her, all moony-eyed."

"I'm not moony-eyed, for chrissakes." He chugged his beer and surreptitiously searched for Trip's cowboy hat.

"I can't believe this." Kelsey shook her head, appearing somewhat crushed, which made Grey feel bad. "Have you told her yet?"

Grey shrugged one shoulder. "Sort of."

"She didn't mention it to me." Kelsey narrowed her eyes and turned toward the dance floor. "Wonder what she's waiting for?"

"She's a good friend, Kelsey. Your feelings are one of the reasons she shot me down."

"Shot you down? Really?" Kelsey played with her necklace and shifted on the stool. "So, she's a good friend for turning you down, which

I suppose means you think I'm not a good friend if I don't tell her not to worry about my feelings."

"I don't know you well enough to know if you're a good friend." Grey set his empty bottle on the bar. "Guess I'll know soon enough."

Kelsey's pointed stare gave nothing away. Dammit. He shouldn't have said anything. Now Kelsey would blindside Avery, a development that would not win him any points.

Before he could do any damage control, Trip and Avery rejoined the group.

"Brrr, it's chilly on this side of the bar," Trip quipped when neither Grey nor Kelsey did more than grunt at their return.

Avery tapped Kelsey's shoulder. "What's going on?"

"Nothing." Kelsey faked a smile.

Avery's brows rose then she looked at Trip and shrugged.

"Looks like you need a turn to dance, little lady." Trip clasped Kelsey's wrist and practically yanked her off the stool. "Come on now, but watch that top. We don't need you spilling out of it and starting a frenzy on the dance floor."

"What did you just say?" When she beat against his shoulder, he just laughed and weaved her through the crowd.

"Does that approach really work with women?" Avery mused aloud as she watched them disappear.

"Surprisingly well." Grey grinned and stepped a little closer. They stared at each other, she apparently as tongue tied as he. *Get a grip, Grey.* "Want another drink?"

Just then some loudmouth chimed in. "Watch out with that one, man. If you get a Randall too drunk, you could end up getting sued or fired."

Avery's attention snapped toward the booming voice, her jaw tensing. But Bambi's spine stayed ramrod straight as she looked that guy dead in the eye. "Jonah."

Oh, hell. The bartender—make that ex-bartender.

"Where's your brother? Too chickenshit to show his face in here?"

Jonah smirked. "Come to think of it, he'll probably have a hard time getting service in any pub in town from now on."

If Grey was reading Avery's expression correctly, she was about to lay Jonah out with a zinger. One day that pride of hers would land her in a heap of trouble. Still, he found it kinda hot. Unfortunately, right now Grey didn't have the physical stability to properly defend her.

"Just like you'll have a hard time getting a *job* at any pub in town." She pinned Jonah with a pitying stare. "I guess your sex life will suffer, too, now that you can't give away free booze to loosen up your targets."

Oh, Jesus.

Jonah's face turned tomato-red when his pal laughed at Avery's retort. The big man lunged toward her, looking as if he might punch her in the face.

"Hey, pal, cool down." Grey stepped between them. "Do us all a favor and walk away."

Jonah shoved at Grey's shoulder. "Who the hell are you?"

Protect the knee. Count to ten.

"Grey Lowell." Grey held one arm out to protect Avery from getting caught in the middle of a scuffle. "I'd suggest you don't touch me again, if you know what's good for you." Where the hell was Trip when he needed backup?

Jonah's hands shot up in surrender, but his voice dripped with sarcasm. "I'd kick your ass if I didn't think you'd sue me afterward, fucktard."

"Fucktard?" Grey glanced at Avery, whose forehead creased with concern. If Avery hadn't been in harm's way, he'd have gladly clocked the asshole. Harnessing all his patience, he simply crossed his arms and stared at the jerk.

"Pussy," Jonah finally said before backing away and storming off. Grey really didn't like being called a pussy, especially not by two different people in a single night, dammit.

Behind him, Grey heard a whoosh of relief rush from Avery's lungs. He turned around. "You okay?"

She nodded. "Andy warned me Jonah got fired. I should've been better prepared. Shouldn't have baited him."

"You sure don't pull any punches." He noticed her withering now, as the adrenaline ebbed from her system.

She nodded, not nearly as confident as she'd appeared moments earlier. "I shouldn't be here. I should go." She dug in her purse and threw a couple of dollars on the bar. "Can you tell Kelsey for me?"

"Hold on a sec." Grey clutched her forearm and she stilled. "Hang out with me a while."

She shook her head. "I need to go. I didn't want to come in the first place."

"Me neither, but I'm glad I ran into you." He smiled, hoping to coax her into staying. Her defeated, torn expression warned him he'd already lost the battle.

"I'm sorry, Grey." She turned and bolted toward the door.

Grey watched her snake through the crowd, checking to make sure Jonah wasn't lying in wait to get her outside. He scoped the dance floor, but couldn't locate Trip's cowboy hat. When he looked back toward the door, he caught sight of Avery slipping outside.

Two seconds later, his feet started moving. He exited the bar, glancing left and right. No sign of her. He jogged—gingerly—left for a block and saw her vivid-blue Jeep parked on the side street. "Avery, hang on!"

She looked up while unlocking her door. As he approached, he noted how flustered she appeared. Shaky almost, as if she'd depleted all her energy holding herself together in the bar.

"Hey. Hey, settle down." He rubbed her arms. "Everything's okay."

"Andy predicted the backlash. I thought I could handle it, but Jonah's anger scared me."

He stepped within inches of her, his body strung tight with desire. "Come here." Pulling her into a hug, his own body unwound a bit as he fitted her against his chest. He heard a little sniffle as her shoulders trembled. He whispered against her ear, "You've got one helluva backbone, Bambi."

Despite the precipitating events, that minute on the sidewalk seemed heavenly. When she started to ease away, he tightened his hold. "Shh."

"I'm all right now." She managed to pry herself ten or twelve inches away from his chest, but he refused to release her. "What?"

He stared at her wide eyes and parted lips, and lost all grasp of rational thought.

"This," he said, gesturing between them. He took her hand and placed it over his heart. "Tell me you don't feel this, Avery. Feel the way my heart beats so fast when you're near, like it's trying to pound its way out of my chest just to get closer to you." He heard her breath catch. "The way my skin gets so prickly and hot, just aching for you to touch me." He snuggled closer until his good knee nestled in between her legs. "The way everything in me wants to grab hold of you whenever I see you."

He trailed his finger along her neck to the spot where her pulse throbbed as hard as everything in his body. "I think you feel it, too. Let's stop fighting it."

When she didn't move, he leaned in and captured her lip with his, gently sucking on it before he kissed her. It was better than before, because this time he could press his entire body up against her. She didn't even seem to mind him pinning her against her car. After snatching the car keys from her hands, he set them on the roof without breaking their kiss.

Her hands weaved into his hair and he felt her moan in his mouth. Good God, he nearly passed out there on the sidewalk. "Avery."

His mouth trailed along her jaw and around her earlobe, finally catching those little earrings in his teeth, before continuing down her neck. She shivered and kissed him back with intensity. He got so hard, so fast. Her thighs locked around his leg, like she needed the same relief he did. *Yes!* "Come home with me now." His voice rasped like it came straight from his lungs.

He kissed her again, long, slowly and deeply. *Can't. Get. Enough.*

"No." Her answer came too quickly. She gently pushed him away. "I can't."

But he had her. He could feel her yearning, just as strong as his own. "Please," he begged before leaning in to steal another kiss.

He felt her melt into him again. So close. His hands roamed her waist and down behind her hips, grabbing hold and tugging her against him. *I want this woman.*

"Grey, stop." She was panting when she pushed him away again. "You know this isn't right as long as the lawsuits are unresolved. And, well, I don't want to hurt Kelsey."

"Kelsey's a big girl, dammit. I never dated her. The control you're giving her is plain childish." He stopped when Avery's fist landed on her hip. "What's with the look? Because I swore? Because I said it's ridiculous Kelsey has anything to do with us?"

"At the very least, I'd need to talk to her first."

He sighed, preparing for her to tense up once he confessed. "She already knows."

"What?" Her eyes widened immeasurably. "When?"

"She guessed the truth when you and Trip were dancing. So I admitted you were the girl I'd been talking about, and I told her she was one reason you shot me down."

"Oh you did not!" Avery looked up to heaven, grabbing her skull with both hands. "Great. No wonder she looked so uptight when I returned from the dance floor." Then she rested her hands on his arms and looked away. "Doesn't matter. The bigger problem is that you're still suing my family."

"I'm suing your brother." He tipped her chin to meet her eyes.

"Same thing."

"No, it's not. Honestly, the more I think about it, the less important that seems to be. If your parents gave you the house, why can't Andy borrow against its value to pay any judgment?" He cupped the back of her neck with one hand.

"What gave you the idea my parents *gave* us the house?" She crossed her arms, looking ready to read him the riot act.

"There's no mortgage." He squeezed her hip with his other hand.

"They *sold* us the house and loaned us the money to do it. We kept it informal, but they're relying on that money for their retirement."

"I didn't know." Grey scrubbed his hands over his face, unhappy with this new information. "Listen, I'm slowly building new summer business, and it's possible the Outpost's insurance company will offer a decent settlement. If that comes together, maybe I'll be able to make ends meet without needing too much from Andy."

He blocked out the possibility he might never regain full use of his knee, which would devastate him personally and professionally. He stared at Bambi, unable to stop his hands from reaching for her again. *She might be worth it.*

She placed her hands on his chest, which felt so good his eyelids fluttered. "Really?"

"Maybe," he said. Before she could protest, he pulled her into another kiss, savoring every second. Fortunately, she didn't fight him this time. He cradled her face then broke their kiss just long enough to say, "Stay with me tonight. I don't want to let you go."

"I can't."

"Why not?"

"Normally I date someone for at least a month before sleeping over." She glanced away for a second, as if she anticipated some kind of smart-aleck remark.

"Why?"

She looked him square in the eyes. "If he's willing to wait, I know he really likes me."

"I already really like you." As far as he was concerned, he'd already waited more than three months for her, clearly meeting her test.

"Then prove it by respecting my boundaries. Besides, I won't hurt Kelsey. I'd need to speak with her first." She looked at his bracelet and frowned, looking like she wanted to say something then thought better of it. "And let's not forget, you quit working with me to maintain objectivity. A relationship would put more pressure on you, not less."

Grey slapped the top of her Jeep. "I'm getting to the point where I don't care about the lawsuit."

"You won't feel that way in the morning."

"Don't you ever lose control?" He bent his head and kissed her neck. "Just let go and trust me, Avery. I'm not going anywhere."

He heard a sexy little sound in her throat just before she eased away. "I told you, I don't want to get hurt again, Grey."

The honesty of her statement stopped him. She was telling him something important, and he had to listen.

"Neither do I, but I'd rather take a chance than pass it by." He reached up and brushed her hair back with one hand. "How about you give me one date? If it doesn't go well, I'll back off."

She caught her lower lip between her teeth, looking up at him with her big blue eyes. He held his breath, promising God whatever he wanted if he just made this one thing go right.

"Let me talk to Kelsey first." She let her hands slide from his chest down to his waist.

Lower, please.

"Deal." He grinned and yanked her close again. "Can we seal it with a kiss?"

Chapter Fourteen

"I have something to do after work today. Can you hitch another ride home?" Avery asked Andy as she pulled up to the inn, where she saw Emma sweeping the front steps.

"Sure." Andy's gaze seemed fixed on Emma as he barely mumbled a good-bye before exiting the car. He stopped to speak with her—head awkwardly bowed, thumbs tucked in his belt loops—and then he ducked inside.

When she threw the gearshift in drive, Emma held up a hand and jogged toward the car. "Hang on!"

Avery stuck her head out the window. "What's up?"

Emma's expression turned gossipy. "So, what did I miss last night? I meant to come, but dinner ran late here with one couple. By the time I'd cleaned up, I'd lost all motivation."

"You're better off, trust me."

"Better off because it was lame, or because something bad happened?"

"When is Ladies' Night *not* lame, Emma?" Avery rolled her eyes upon remembering the Montrose guys whose attention never left Kelsey's cleavage.

"Come on, Grumpy. We've had some fun there." Emma reached through the window to give Avery's shoulder a little push. "Just give me the short version."

Avery adjusted her sunglasses, hoping Emma didn't notice the heat creeping into her cheeks as she recalled Grey's kiss. "Honestly, I didn't stay long. Jonah showed up drunk and confronted me about getting fired 'because of Andy.' He was really pissed. Scared me a bit."

"Let me guess—you didn't back down." When Avery shook her head, Emma grinned and shook *her* head. "How'd it end?"

"Grey got him to back off, and then I ran out of the bar and went home." Knowing how Emma felt about her interest in Grey, Avery decided not to share the details of the hot make-out session.

"Grey rescued you?" Emma tilted her head as if to summon more information, but then resorted to a direct question. "Has Kelsey really given up on him?"

"Seems so. Unfortunately, while I was dancing with Trip, Grey told her he has feelings for me."

Placing a hand over her mouth, Emma winced. "How'd she take it?"

Avery shrugged one shoulder while caressing the steering wheel. "Not really sure. We haven't talked about it." She paused for a moment before looking directly at Emma, suddenly compelled to be honest. "The more I learn about Grey, the more I want to know. Now that we don't work together, I want to see where things could lead. I know you probably don't approve, though."

"I don't disapprove of him, you know." Emma leaned into the open window. "I just don't want *any* guy to mess up our friendships."

"I'm meeting Kelsey for lunch today to feel her out." Avery sighed and raked her hand through her hair. "It's probably a pointless exercise since I'll likely end up getting hurt one way or another."

"If he's so nice, why do you assume you'll get hurt?"

"Well, there's a good chance my family will hate him if they end up bankrupted. And, what if he's not as great as he appears? I've been fooled before, you know." Avery tried to ignore the sense of foreboding amassing around her like mist.

"You won't get hurt," Emma announced. "You'll go in with your eyes open, like always."

Like always. "Eyes wide open" hadn't proven to be the best recipe for romantic success. Still, Avery didn't know how to let go of her need to protect herself and her heart. In every other aspect of life, she had confidence and faith that things would turn out well. But not when it came to love.

"We'll see." Avery patted Emma's hand. "Gotta go to work, Em. See you later!"

She drove to the clinic resolutely *not* thinking about Grey or Kelsey or Andy. *Yeah, right.*

◆ ◆ ◆

At exactly noon, Avery watched Kelsey enter Boxcar Cantina looking stunning in a pair of beige linen slacks and lightweight, coral-colored sweater. Classic Kelsey maneuver—donning a killer outfit after a setback or romantic disappointment.

Squaring her shoulders, Avery waved while preparing for what she anticipated to be an awkward conversation.

"You look super!" Avery rested her chin in her hands. "I'm glad you're here so we can order. I'm starving."

Kelsey slung her purse around the back of her chair before sitting and pulling up to the table. After avoiding eye contact for a few seconds, she gazed at Avery and sighed. "Look, Avery. I know why you invited me to join you for lunch. This is about Grey, right? So let's just skip to the heart of it. I liked him. He didn't feel the same. He likes you. You two left together last night. Now you feel guilty about hurting my feelings. Am I close?"

Good gravy. Avery hadn't expected Kelsey to fire the opening shot. Although a bit shaken by the surprise, she quickly regrouped.

"Sort of, but last night wasn't what you think." Avery sat back, resisting the urge to cross her arms and become irritated about having to defend her relative innocence. "Jonah got in my face about his getting fired. He was nasty, and fairly aggressive, so I took off. Grey followed me to my car to make sure I was okay, and then I went home *alone*. You know my rules."

Kelsey pressed her lips together while thinking. The waitress stopped by to take their order, temporarily interrupting Avery's explanation. After the waitress left them alone, Avery continued, "But you're right. I do want to talk about him—or, more to the point, about him and me."

Kelsey held up her hand. "Just stop. I know I can be a baby sometimes, and I won't lie and pretend it isn't a huge bummer that he rejected me because he wants you, but we aren't in high school anymore. I hope I've grown up a little bit since then. I'm certainly not going to stand in your way if you want to date him, although I'm a little surprised you do considering how, when *I* was interested in him, you were firmly *anti*-skier."

The subtle taunt made Avery frown despite Kelsey's otherwise levelheaded attitude about the situation. Had she been hypocritical? She fiddled with her silverware for a few seconds.

"Thanks for being understanding." Avery dipped a blue corn chip into the fresh guacamole. "I know what I've said about skiers and maybe I'll regret this, but I've gotten to know Grey and I think he's different from the others."

"Which is what I said from the get-go, if you recall." Kelsey's "told you so" expression would have been comical if the situation weren't so awkward.

Avery nodded then leveled a pointed stare at her friend. "You did. However, your opinion was rooted in a first impression and a crush, not from months of getting to know him."

"Don't get testy just because I've got better instincts than you." Kelsey crossed her legs and sipped her water while Avery tried not to choke on her chip or begin to enumerate all the examples of poor judgment her friend had exhibited through the years. "Listen, I don't want to get into an argument. I'm fine. It's not going to be a problem between us. All I ask is one favor."

"Dare I ask?" Avery grimaced as she reached for another chip. "What favor?"

Kelsey leaned forward with one hand on the table. "Since I'm being so gracious and all, don't blow it by being so closed-off. If you're going to go for it, then really go for it, okay? Try to be a little romantic. Seriously. We aren't getting any younger."

Avery studied Kelsey. For the most part, her friend looked pretty much the way she did every other day, excepting the extra glam. But there was a new glint in her eye—a determination Avery hadn't seen in the past.

"What happened last night after I left?" Avery narrowed her gaze, suddenly attributing Kelsey's generous outlook toward another possibility. "Did something happen between you and Trip?"

"No." Kelsey scowled and adjusted her sweater.

Avery waited for an explanation, but Kelsey fell suspiciously quiet.

"No? Why not?" Avery leaned forward. "Did you end up reconnecting with those guys from Montrose?"

Kelsey paused while the waitress delivered their food, maintaining a pensive silence as the waitress set their meals on the table.

"I left soon after you did. Something did happen to me, though. I'm not sure I can explain it exactly. I was dancing with Trip—" Kelsey broke off to sample her taco salad. "And by the way, that guy is the world's biggest flirt. Too bad he's so shallow, because he's flippin' hot. Anyway, while he was laying on the charm, I noticed all the other guys in the bar doing the exact same thing with other women. For the first time, I saw the futility of it all. I mean, really *saw* it.

"How many nights did I waste hoping to make some kind of

genuine connection with some guy I met in a bar—like with Grey—and worse, the hours I've wasted practically begging for crumbs of attention. The sudden revelation made me a little queasy." Kelsey paused and then tilted her head as if about to deliver sage advice. "Let's face it, few people ever find love at a ladies' night."

"Wow. I'm not sure what to say." Inside, Avery danced a happy jig in thanks for her friend's epiphany.

Kelsey waved her fork at Avery, her eyes intently studying her lunch as she speared another bite. "Nothing *to* say. Bottom line, I'm changing my whole MO. I'm thirty. It's time to get smart. Use my head." She nearly poked her skull with her fork. "Time to find a good guy who values me. One who isn't just out for a couple of weeks of fun with me and my girls," she announced, peering at her ample breasts.

Avery felt a huge smile spread across her face until she thought about how using her own head hadn't been any more successful than Kelsey's former tactics. "I bet something in between your old approach and mine is probably best. Can't hurt to try something new."

"Oh, yeah, something new is right. Talking to those construction guys about Mitchell's project made me think about all the clients I've met through work. The single older men and divorcees have never been on my radar, but older guys treat younger women well. It's high time I dive into that pool and see what happens."

"Gold digger!" Avery teased before sipping her iced tea.

"There's that, too. Heck, I could be a trophy wife." Kelsey winked. "I'm not saying I'd go after someone for money, but I think it's time I considered the whole package, not just the wrapping, y'know?"

Avery lifted her glass, feeling lighter than she had a mere hour ago. "To unwrapping the package!"

"Cheers!" Kelsey clinked her glass with Avery and they both chuckled.

Grey sat at his desk, rubbing his palm against his chest to douse the fire stirring every time he thought of kissing Avery—thoughts which were occurring nonstop since last night. Then again, pent-up desire proved to be a powerful motivator. In order to have her, he needed to settle these lawsuits as soon as possible, which meant he had to power through the spreadsheets, no matter how painful.

He stared at the columns of numbers he'd amassed: medical expenses and rehabilitation costs, his own wages, and extra salary expenses on the books for replacement guides. And that didn't even include intangibles like pain and suffering, time spent in therapy instead of focusing on building Backtrax, and on and on.

"What's got you by the short hairs?" Trip entered his office, chomping on an apple.

"I'm trying to figure out the minimum settlement I can accept and still guarantee making the loan payments so I don't lose the business."

Trip frowned and sat across from Grey. "Is it really that bad?"

"Take a look." Grey passed the worksheet to Trip. "I knew I'd never get rich in this line of work, but I don't want to lose everything, either."

Trip pushed his cowboy hat back a bit, his brows pinching together as he concentrated on the numbers.

"Okay, that's a bit grim. However, I think you've underestimated the income side of the equation. Next ski season business will pick up, especially if you improve your social media presence." Trip stretched out his legs. "I keep telling you not to micromanage the money. Think long-term."

"I need to get through the present in order to have a 'long-term.' This injury has affected my ability to build the business these past few months. And thirty percent of whatever I get from Randall or the OS goes to my lawyer. I hate this. All I want to do is ski and climb and have a good time with clients. All this other shit sucks." Grey chucked his pencil at the worksheet.

"Didn't you keep any of your inheritance for personal use?" Trip tossed the apple core in the trash and leaned forward.

"Not much. I needed to apply most of it toward the purchase price of Backtrax in order to qualify for the small-business loan. I only kept about fifteen grand in my personal account." Grey scrubbed his hands over his face. "I've dipped into it a bit, but am trying to save it in case I need it to cover a loan payment or two if the business account runs dry before I recover any money from Andy Randall. Problem is, that could happen before next winter unless we drum up a lot more business in a short time frame."

Grey scratched the back of his neck and blew out a long breath. Had he not been sidelined in February, he'd have some extra funds to buy a couple of snowmobiles and maybe upgrade the snowcat, too. Now those things would have to wait. "If only this accident happened two years from now, after I'd reserved more capital, it might've been less problematic."

Trip cleared his throat. "Listen, if you really get into a squeeze, I might be able to come up with some extra cash."

"Oh, really?" Grey grinned. "You got some sugar mama I don't know about?"

"Something like that." Trip's typical teasing tone was noticeably absent.

"Cryptic." When Trip didn't respond to Grey's prompt, he dropped the subject. "Well, thanks for the offer. But setting aside your sugar mama, I think if I can clear about one hundred grand, I can make it all work."

"That's not right, Grey." Trip pointed at the wage-and-tip column. "Avery advised you to sit out a full year, which means you can't count on skiing this coming season, at least not until late spring."

"I've got to be back on the mountain come Thanksgiving or the expenses jump." Damn it, he couldn't entertain another ski season without more income and tips. Granted, guides barely broke the poverty level in terms of wages, but something was better than nothing. "If I want to stick to my plan of taking as little from the business as possible for the first three years, I can't afford to pay another guide *and* take an income for myself."

"The worst thing you could do is be shortsighted and end up blowing your knee out again."

"I'm the face of Backtrax. I've got to get back out there to buddy up with the customers. I can't just throw in subs and hope to build repeat business from behind a damned computer." Grey kicked the desk.

Trip stood and paced, his forehead creased with concern. "Listen, I know you don't want to hear this, but you've got to consider what happens if your knee never fully recovers. What if this injury takes you off the big mountain slopes permanently? Don't you want to be compensated for that possibility, too? It's not just about the nuts and bolts of your actual losses. We're talking about your entire future. Don't be so quick to lowball the money you need to cover yourself."

Holy shit! Never cutting freshies in backcountry chutes would be like losing an arm. Grey didn't even want to entertain that thought.

"The most I can get from the OS is one hundred and fifty grand, which—best case—translates to one hundred grand in my pocket. Andy Randall's got nothing but the twenty-five grand insurance policy." Grey inhaled slowly, trying to stave off the headache at the base of his skull.

"I thought your lawyer said Randall's house would sell for more than half a million bucks."

"Yeah, but I'd be screwing over Avery. She doesn't deserve to be stuck in the middle of this nightmare." Grey looked at the ceiling. "It'd screw her parents, too. Apparently they didn't just *give* their kids the house. They just never formalized the loan with documents. If I get a judgment lien, they'll be screwed, too."

Trip whistled. "Just 'cause it sucks for them doesn't mean it's your fault."

"Doesn't matter if it's not my fault." Grey unwrapped a grape sucker. "If I hurt her family, it'd pretty much kill any relationship we could have."

"I know you like her. Hell, you may even be halfway in love with her despite never having been on a single date." Trip drummed his fingers on the desk, shaking his head in apparent dismay. "Bottom line, you've made no promises and have no commitment to or *from* her. You've got to look out for yourself. Don't ignore the worst-case scenario or you could end up with nothing—no business, no money, and no Avery."

"Did someone mention my name?" Avery popped her head in the doorway, surprising both Grey and Trip.

Trip bowed and tipped his hat. "Look how pretty you are—like a daffodil and ball of sunshine mixed together."

Grey rolled his eyes at Trip. He grinned as he rose from his chair, scanning Avery's yellow-and-white ensemble. Yellow must be her favorite color, because she wore it often.

"Thanks, Trip." She glanced at the papers spread out on the desk. "Am I interrupting something important?"

"No, ma'am." Trip stepped toward the door. "I was just getting ready to head out."

"Should I warn all the single women in town?" She playfully punched his bicep as he passed by.

Trip folded his hands in prayer. "Please don't." Then his expression transformed to something more sober. "But do remind Grey of the importance of not pushing that knee too early."

She nodded as he exited the office. Grey liked her smile. Liked the waves of energy she threw off when she talked. Liked the way her eyes reflected her intelligence. Damn, she was pretty perfect.

He waited, frozen in place by a mix of wonder and surprise at her visit, rolling the remains of his Tootsie Pop around his tongue. "What's up?"

"Is this a bad time? Kinda sounded like I interrupted something serious."

Grey waved his hand and threw the bare lollipop stick aside. "It's fine. We were just having a difference of opinion on things related to the business."

"Oh, sorry." Avery grimaced. "Trip's right about your knee, though. The more time you take to build strength without pushing it, the better."

"Appreciate your advice, but ultimately it's not your decision." Grey stood and stepped closer, somehow refraining from grabbing her waist and pinning her against a wall or chair or other object in the office. Her cute smile made him stupid, and made the crotch of his jeans feel a little snug. "I'm happy to see you, though. Did you come by for any particular reason?"

"Well, I brought you a present for rescuing me last night." Avery reached into her purse and pulled out a bag of lollipops.

Grey chuckled. "Thanks. I can never keep too many of these around." He set the bag on the corner of the desk. "Anything else?"

Her cheeks turned a darker shade of pink as she tugged at her ear-lobe. "I wanted to let you know I spoke with Kelsey."

Hmm. She came by instead of calling. A good sign. He stepped a little closer and reached out for her hand, twining his fingers in hers. "And?"

Her gaze drifted from their clasped hands to his face. "And if the offer still stands, I'm up for that date."

"That's good news." Grey felt his smile nearly splitting his face.

"You look like you just won the lottery."

"I feel like I did. I'll take you and a bag of lollipops over cold, hard cash any day of the week." He raised her hand to his lips and then wrapped his other arm around her waist.

"You're still optimistic about the outcome of these lawsuits, right?" Her hopeful expression gutted him, but he didn't want to risk her pulling away because of her family. Trip might've tossed Grey's rose-colored glasses in the trash, but his heart was caught in a vise of anticipation, so he shoved his friend's warnings aside.

"I'm optimistic about a lot of things," he deflected, then leaned in and kissed her. He felt her smile against his mouth, so he pulled back. "What's so funny?"

She licked her lips. "I'm wondering if you'll always taste like grape candy?"

"Count on it." He lowered his head and planted another kiss on her lips. "Just think of me as a different kind of sugar daddy."

"Funny you should use those words. Apparently that's exactly what Kelsey is looking for now."

"Really?" Grey rocked back on his heels. "Actually, I can see that working out well for her."

Avery's mouth and nose twisted up for a second. "I'll choose to interpret that in a positive light."

"Interpret it any which way you like. All I care about is this, here. So don't make any plans for Saturday." He grasped her waist with both hands again.

"The whole day?" Her expression grew curious as she tentatively rested her hands on his shoulders.

"And night, if you'll hold that open for me too." He squeezed her waist.

"What did you have in mind?"

"At night?" He grinned when she slapped his shoulder.

"You've clearly forgotten my one-month rule."

"Hey, can't blame me for trying." He had blocked it out, dammit. Another month would feel like an eternity. "I want to check out a potential bouldering site. Thought maybe we could go hike in the afternoon, then I'll take you out for a proper dinner."

"Now I understand Trip's remarks." Avery's forehead creased a bit. "Your knee isn't ready for heavy-duty hiking, Grey."

"This wouldn't be *real* hiking. We'll take the van as far as we can, and then go slowly. I'm told the trail to this particular spot is fairly flat and clean, so the worst that will happen is I'll get a little sore. No risk of turning an ankle or twisting the knee."

"Promise we'll turn back if the terrain is too risky for this stage of your recovery."

Frickin' stages of recovery. Being held back angered him, but not nearly as much as being deemed fragile or feeble did. "I've been working hard to rebuild my strength."

"I know. Still, there are limitations in the healing process. You're not superhuman."

"That's where you're wrong." He yanked her up against him. "And I can prove it."

This kiss was more demanding—almost savage. He wouldn't allow her to see him as some kind of pathetic project. Some weakling who needed to be coddled and protected. He was a man, dammit. A strong man who knew what he wanted and how to get it. Who knew what she needed and how to give it.

He felt the instant she submitted. Her body softened, and her hands found their way into his hair, which sent tingles fanning out over his scalp. He moved his mouth along her jaw to the sensitive spot behind her ear and then down along her neck. She arched into him.

He kissed her again, walking her backward until her back hit the wall. She gasped, but he didn't stop. He grasped her wrists and pinned them over her head, pressing his body against hers until they both shuddered.

With the aching need in his body, waiting another month to have her fit the definition of cruel and unusual punishment. He released her wrists so he could fondle her body, her breasts. But he'd barely got the feel of her in his hand when she pushed him away.

"Whoa, slow down." She swallowed hard before meeting his eyes. "I want to see where this leads, but I move slowly. It's a self-preservation thing, you see."

He wasn't sure if she was afraid he'd break her heart because he'd prove to be the player she feared, or because he'd end up forcing her out of her home. Either way, he understood her hesitation. Couldn't even blame her, really. He'd be wise to follow her lead in that regard or they could both end up in a lot of pain.

"Okay, Bambi. I'm in no rush." *Liar!* His raging hard-on protested. "So how about Saturday. Is it a date?"

"It's a date as long as you promise to be honest about how your knee is feeling." And there it was again—her concerned scowl.

Between her worry and Trip's warnings, Grey's good mood began to tank again. Maybe he did need to brace himself for the possibility of being permanently sidelined by this damned accident.

"I have a question for you, and I want an honest answer." He stepped back and crossed his arms. "Will I be able to ski again by winter? And I'm not talking about slopes at the resort. I mean *my* kind of skiing."

Bambi blinked at him and chewed on the inside of her cheek. "Don't you think I would make promises if I could, not only for your sake, but so you could also settle things with Andy? No one can know if you'll be able to put the extreme stress on your knee required for leading hardcore ski tours, let alone know when. But I remain hopeful it can happen."

No promises. No certainty. She'd hedged with him as he'd hedged with her about the lawsuits. Turnabout was fair play, he supposed.

Hopefully their insidious optimism wouldn't act like water, slowly undermining the foundation of their relationship.

Chapter Fifteen

By noon on Saturday, Grey and Avery had hiked to a clearing alongside a narrow trail following the river, about one hundred yards from an outcropping of twelve- to twenty-foot-high boulders. Ideal for climbing without ropes and harnesses, and for perfecting specific moves at a safe distance from the ground.

Shaman scampered around the area, barking and sniffing under the brush. Although the sky was virtually cloudless, the shaded area felt cooler than the sixty-four degrees predicted. Grey noticed Avery rub her hands over her biceps for warmth.

He dropped his pack on the ground, unzipped it, and removed a lightweight jacket. "Here." Smiling, he draped the fleece over her shoulders. "I know it isn't pink or lime-green or yellow, but it'll keep you warm."

"Thanks." She slipped her arms into its sleeves. He grinned when she then unwittingly held them up to her nose and inhaled. *She likes me.* "I'm surprised you didn't make fun of the color of my Merrells, too."

"A lot of purple." He handed her a fresh bottle of water.

"Grape! Your favorite flavor." She stuck one foot out, wiggling it around.

"Careful, Bambi, or I might come over and suck on your toes," he teased, stepping closer.

She shook her head. "I'm ticklish."

"Good to know." He bent over, reaching back in the pack to retrieve a blanket and several small Tupperware containers.

Avery sat cross-legged on the blanket and glanced at the boulders. "So this is where you'll teach bouldering?"

"Seems so." Grey quickly surveyed the area. "It's easy to access. Should be a good training spot, and then when things progress, we could begin heading up that way," he motioned farther down the canyon, "to access some switchbacks and reach better terrain—good walls with views."

"Who will sub for you this summer?"

"I can handle bouldering, for God's sake." Grey sensed an oncoming lecture, so he cut her off. Plus, he'd hoped to avoid discussing the obstacles between them, like his recovery. "I don't need you and Trip to babysit me and my knee. I've got to be involved with the clients. I can't build relationships sitting in my office."

"I'm just looking out for your long-term recuperation. That's all."

He drew a deep breath, looking at her with a sheepish grin.

"Sorry for snapping at you." He popped the lid off a container of fresh berries and set it between them. "I hate being seen as an invalid. I'm already at a disadvantage here, with your being a PhD and my being an undereducated, dyslexic ski bum."

Avery straightened up, tilting her head slightly. "Do you actually think I look at you that way?"

He shrugged while opening another container filled with a brown rice-cranberry-pine nut-chicken salad, then passing her the last two containers: one with olives, feta, tomatoes, and cucumbers, the other with hummus and pita chips. "I know a girl like you has a lot of options."

"A girl like me?" Avery began to load up her plate.

"A girl like you." He stretched himself out on his side, propping his torso up on one arm. "Pretty, smart, ambitious, confident, with a hint of smart-aleck."

Avery glanced away, appearing embarrassed by his compliments. When she finally looked at him, a shy grin appeared.

"First of all, thank you for this excellent spread. Not at all what I'd expected given your lollipop fetish." Avery bit into a big strawberry and held up her index finger. "Secondly, thanks for the high praise, but obviously my exes didn't quite see me as a great catch, so consider yourself warned."

"Their stupidity is my gain." He stuffed an olive into his mouth. When he licked the oily dressing off his lips, he saw Avery's gaze linger on his mouth. *Easy, Grey.*

"I see you as an entrepreneur, not a ski bum." She hugged her knees to her chest. "I envy you, actually. I've been saving up for four years to start my own clinic, so one day I can be my own boss, too."

Determined to keep this date light, Grey ignored the reminder of their uncertain financial futures, and teased her. "Like Donner?"

"Only better." When she winked, Grey chuckled.

"Naturally." Setting his empty plate aside, he nudged closer to her and brushed his fingers along her thigh. "Did you like growing up here?" He waved his arm over the surroundings.

"I did." She glanced around at the new grass, budding trees, and river. "I love it here. In fact, my reluctance to leave is part of what came between Matt and me."

"Huh. Again, his stupidity is my gain." Grey didn't really want to hear about her relationship with Matt. "So you want to stay in your hometown. Do you like living with your brother?"

As soon as the words were out, he regretted bringing up Andy and their home. *Idiot!*

She glanced away, obviously uncomfortable talking about Andy or their home with him. "We get along really well, actually." She ran her hands up and down her calves. "Although, if I'm being honest, that's probably because he's usually happy to go along with whatever I want. He's more quiet and sensitive than me. In that way, he's a lot like my mom."

Grateful for a chance to move away from that hot topic, he picked up on her last comment.

"So are you like your dad?" He watched her expression swiftly turn to a deep frown.

"Not willingly." Her lip curled.

"Oh, really." He popped up higher on his arm, eager to dig into the crack he'd just found. "Now *that* sounds interesting."

"It's so *not* interesting." When Grey shot her a look, she continued. "Let's just say my dad isn't the world's warmest, most patient man."

"So you weren't the apple of his eye?" Slowly the puzzle pieces began fitting together—her wariness with men, her need for control. A beat of silence passed, except for the puffing of Shaman's breath as he chewed on the dog treats.

"My dad's always been proud of me. He loves me." Avery watched Shaman trot over to the boulders. "He's just . . . demanding."

"What about your mom?"

"She's been a doting mother and wife." Avery's tone indicated her remark had not been much of a compliment.

"Isn't a doting mom a good thing?"

"When you're a kid, sure. But sometimes, as much as I love and appreciate her, I feel like I don't really know her—the real her. Honestly, I wonder if she even knows herself. She's made my dad, Andy, and me the focal point of her life. Her friends were the mothers of Andy's and my friends, her outside activities involved school volunteering or the bridge club my dad wanted to join. From my perspective, she gave up her own identity for most of her adult life.

"Now she's in her late fifties without anything of her own. She's totally under my dad's thumb. I hate that, and then I feel guilty about my anger, because she's been so loving." Avery picked at some grass, her gaze hardening. "I doubt I could ever be like her—sacrificing everything that makes me who I am just to please everyone else. If that's what it takes to be loved or make love last, then I guess I'll be on my own." She looked at Grey, her expression solemn. "See why my former boyfriends weren't so stupid after all?"

"All relationships are different; some better than others. It's up to the people involved to figure out what works for them." He narrowed his gaze. "But just because *you* wouldn't make your mom's choices doesn't mean she's unhappy with them."

"I hope she's content. She doesn't have many options at this point." Avery twisted her mouth in a grim mood. "Enough about my family. Tell me about yours."

The thought of his mom always made him smile. "My mom is exactly how you'd picture a music teacher. Loves kids. Loves music. Creative and caring. Laughs easily—and bakes some wicked-good cakes and cookies. You can pretty much blame her for my sugar addiction." He paused and rolled onto his back, looking at the sky but seeing his childhood living room in his mind. "My dad is affectionate with her. They have a strong marriage. But he was tough on me. He had a hard time with my dyslexia, mostly because he worried about my future. Then, after Juliette died and I took off, well, he felt like I abandoned them."

Grey looked over at Avery before continuing.

"He's never really forgiven me for leaving. He couldn't understand why I didn't want to stay there surrounded by memories because, as he put it, a lot of them were good ones." Grey's chest constricted slightly, but he rubbed it away. "Then, when his dad died and left me his money, my using it to buy a business here instead of around Lake Tahoe was another nail in my coffin. Now he's convinced I'll lose everything. To him, my dyslexia means I can't run a business. But I've learned a ton about the industry from working with so many outfits at so many resorts. And Trip is a huge help with the paperwork."

He aimed for confidence, but really, Grey had no fallback position. Worst-case scenario—his lack of education, dyslexia, and inability to ski or climb would relegate him to a dreary future working minimum-wage jobs.

Grey'd bet his entire inheritance on making Backtrax work. He rubbed the space above his injured knee. "I know I can do this. I have to make it work, if for no other reason than to avoid the 'I told you so's.'"

Avery shivered as a strong breeze rustled the leaves of the nearby branches. Grey tugged her down alongside his body and wrapped one arm around her shoulders. Holding her close distracted him from his worries.

She set her chin on his chest. "You're disciplined, Grey. I have faith in you."

He smiled while playfully touching the tip of her nose. "Hopefully that faith extends to more than Backtrax. I want you to have faith in me as a man you can trust. One who isn't interested in changing you or holding you back."

He watched her face twitch. Personal discussions clearly made her jumpy. But she'd only promised him one date, so he had to make it count.

She stared at her fingers as they traced a circle on his chest. "Can I ask you a question about Juliette?"

His stomach tightened. "Sure."

"What was it about her, exactly, that made you fall so hard?" She glanced at him, then looked away as if she were afraid of the answer.

For someone who didn't like answering personal questions, Bambi sure could ask the big ones. But feeling the weight of her against his side, and suspecting she felt insecure, made it less painful for Grey to talk about Juliette today.

"It wasn't any one thing." He felt himself smile. "More like a million little things and experiences. And youth. Sometimes I've wondered, if she and I had met as adults, would we have been as good together? I can't really answer that question, but I think what made it work for us was mutual respect. I listened to her, and not just to what she said, but how she felt and what she hoped. I supported her dreams, and she did the same for me. We had absolute trust in each other. No secrets. She had my back and I had hers. She truly was my best friend."

"Sounds nice."

"It was." He tilted his head, and decided to unearth more about Avery. "You said something the other day that troubled me."

"I did?"

"Yeah. You said you'd never felt really loved by any guy."

Her cheeks turned pink, and not from the breeze. "Do you think I'm pathetic?"

"No. I just can't believe it."

"Look at how Matt betrayed me. Though honestly, even though I never hurt him, I didn't love him deeply. Not the way you loved Juliette, with your whole heart and soul. That's a connection I've never experienced. Maybe it's just not in the cards for me. I don't have the best attitude about love."

Her downcast expression made him want to punch Matt and every other guy who'd disappointed her. "Or maybe you just hadn't met the right guy until now."

Her lips quirked. "Until now?"

"Right now." Then he rolled her onto her back, holding himself above her. "I wouldn't want you to change a thing." Before she could respond, he bent his head and kissed her, gently lowering his body against hers. What he would give to make love to her, here and now.

Her hands found their way around his waist and back, and she kissed him back. Tightening and tingles shot through his body and straight to his groin. She felt so good, so right, so everything. He wanted to be the guy who would change her outlook on love. He *would* be that guy, even if he needed a sledgehammer to break through all her walls.

"Grey," she panted as his mouth found her collarbone and she tightened her hold on him.

Unfortunately, a loud bark and wet nose descended upon them, killing the moment. Grey pushed himself up on his elbows and grumbled, "I should've left Shaman at home."

"He's my bodyguard." Avery reached up to pet the dog under his chin. "Keeps you in line."

Grey kissed the tip of her nose. "Not for long. He'll be grounded this evening."

◆　◆　◆

Two hours later, Avery returned home to shower and change for dinner. She was humming to herself when she entered her house.

"Look who's home," Andy called from the kitchen.

Three things struck Avery at the same time: a bouquet of sunflowers and irises sat on the kitchen island, Andy's accusatory expression meant trouble, and Matt sat staring at her disapprovingly.

Avery dropped her keys on the desk, her gaze drifting from the flowers to Andy. "Hello to you, too."

"So, this was a bit of a surprise." Andy nodded at the bouquet before lifting the card from the holder. "'Avery, Can't wait for our first date. Grey.' Grey? You're going on a *date* with Grey Lowell tonight?"

Grey's lovely gesture had foiled her plans to keep things on the down-low. But instead of being upset by her brother's anger, the beautiful bouquet only fueled her desire to pursue the relationship.

"Yes." When she heard Matt sigh, she continued. "In fact, I just got back from spending the afternoon hiking with him and his dog."

"Really?" Andy returned the card to the holder then crossed his arms, his voice thick with sarcasm. "If he's hiking, maybe his knee isn't as bad as he wants everyone to believe."

"Don't start, Andy. Hiking on a flat path isn't anything like the kinds of stress and sideways movement backcountry skiing or climbing place on the joint."

"Great, so now you're defending the enemy?" Andy's eyes widened with betrayal.

Here we go. Avery resented having her great mood spoiled.

"Grey is not the enemy. He's the *victim.*" Avery placed her hands on her hips, challenging Andy to say more. "Besides, he's expecting a settlement from the OS, which should lessen the burden on you."

"You say that like it was *his* idea, instead of mine," Matt chimed in, swiveling toward her on the kitchen stool.

Why is Matt still in town?

"Please stay out of this." Having to defend herself to Matt in her own home scorched her pride. "It's honestly none of your business. Isn't it time you go back to LA and Sasha?"

Matt narrowed his eyes, but then appeared to swallow whatever angry retort he'd been considering.

"You know what, Ave, play the tough-sister act with me, but don't expect a lot of support when Dad finds out you're dating Grey."

"*You*—not me and not Grey—are the one responsible for this entire mess. I'm not planning on telling Dad anything at this early stage, so keep your opinions to yourself."

"Getting involved with Grey before everything is settled is stupid. And don't tell me you, with that big brain of yours, can't see what I'm talking about, Avery."

Avery's shoulders tensed as she clenched her hands and jaw while engaging in a silent showdown with Andy. Her brother glanced at Matt and then sighed in defeat. A wave of emotional exhaustion threatened to fell her, so she marched to the island, snatched the vase away from Andy, and strode to her room.

She set the flowers on the nightstand and collapsed onto her bed. Closing her eyes, she replayed her idyllic afternoon. Grey had obviously spent money he didn't have to spare on flowers and good food, but more importantly, he'd opened up to her. Even more surprising, he'd gotten her to open up a little, too. Something she rarely did, and never so quickly.

He hadn't even winced when she'd voiced her cynical thoughts about love. If anything, he addressed her concerns. Equality. Mutual respect. Absolute honesty. Unlike sweetness and deference, those were qualities she possessed. Promises she could keep.

Maybe Grey *was* the right guy for her. Maybe these cursed legal matters would resolve without hurting everyone she loved. Maybe she could take a chance on love after all.

Facing off with her father would not be pleasant, but she couldn't let go of Grey simply because the legal matter *might* affect her family. His effect on her—the way he relaxed her and made her hope—was too powerful to resist, no matter how illogical and fraught with risk.

◆ ◆ ◆

Avery was swallowing a piece of salmon-and-jalapeño sushi when Grey reached across the table and placed his hand over hers. "I brought you here because this is where I first saw you, so I assumed you liked it. But the way you're picking at your food tells me maybe I got it wrong."

"No, I love sushi." She smiled and took another bite.

"Okay, then." He squeezed her hand. "What's changed between three o'clock and now? Did I do or say something wrong?"

"No. God, no! You've done everything right." She smiled and squeezed his hand back, irked for allowing her brother's sense of foreboding to have interfered with their evening. *Absolute honesty.* "I'm sorry I've been edgy. Andy and I had a little tiff this afternoon."

Grey released her hand and sat back into his seat. "Ah, gotcha. He's not a fan of this," he said, waving his hand between them.

Shaking her head, she grimaced.

Grey inhaled slowly. "Neither of us can see the future. Not about my knee, or the lawsuits, or what's going to happen in your brother's criminal case, or if one of us will end up with another broken heart. I wish I had answers, but I don't. All I do know is how I feel about you right now."

He intertwined his fingers with hers. "I really like you, Avery. I like your fire, your quick mind, your smile, your loyalty to your friends and family, your honesty, the way you feel and smell. I like the whole package, enough to take a risk and see where things might lead. So I guess you have to decide whether or not you think I'm worth the risk, too."

Before she could respond, Kelsey arrived, with some forty-something guy, full of smiles and energy.

"Well, fancy bumping into you two here." Kelsey turned to her companion. "Wade, these are my friends, Avery and Grey. Guys, this is Wade Kessler. He's from Seattle, but is here in town for a commercial development project along Ute Creek."

"Welcome," Avery said, extending her hand.

Grey followed suit, shaking Wade's hand. "Pretty land over there. I lead clients on ski tours through the national forest near there."

"Grey, Wade's a big outdoorsman. Maybe you two could hook up at some point, whether through climbing or skiing."

Avery had to suppress a giggle at how quickly Kelsey had moved on to her latest plan to discover love and romance.

In any case, Grey appeared to appreciate Kelsey's plug for his business. "Happy to show you around the backcountry any time."

"I've been heli-skiing twice." Wade placed his hands on his hips. "Love that rush."

"I don't have a heli-ski permit, so we've got to hike or take a snowcat to our spots."

"Sounds like a good workout." Wade grinned.

The hostess cleared her throat and waved Kelsey and Wade to another table.

"Nice to meet you both." Wade nodded and followed behind Kelsey, who gave a little wave before sauntering off in the other direction.

Grey swallowed the last of his beer and chuckled. "Looks like she's found a new target already."

"We'll see." Avery had to give Kelsey credit. She never gave up. She put herself out there time and again, hoping to find that one guy who would love her.

Surely Avery could have at least as much courage as her friend. She pushed her empty plate away, thinking of the question Grey had posed before they'd been interrupted by Kelsey and Wade. "Are you ready to go?"

"It's only nine thirty. I hate to take you home so early."

Avery hesitated. "Is Trip home?"

Grey turned toward her, wearing a smirk. "It's Saturday night, Bambi. Have you *met* Trip?"

She wrinkled her nose. "I guess I'd thought his womanizing was largely an act."

"Nope." Grey shook his head. "I doubt he'll be home before sunrise."

"I can't believe he hasn't burned through the female population by now." Avery chuckled in wonderment. "I mean, it's a darn small town."

"Maybe he keeps some kind of rotating schedule." Grey shrugged. He reached for her hand, his eyes focused completely, and heatedly, on her. "I don't really want to discuss Trip right now, do you?"

"I suppose not." She couldn't take him to her house, a major source of conflict between them. Worse, Andy might be home. Most importantly, home was her sanctuary, and she wouldn't let him in there prematurely. Still, she noted the anticipation in his expression. "Can we go to your place for a while?"

Grey's eyes flashed with excitement and relief. "There's nothing I'd like more."

Chapter Sixteen

Avery fidgeted with the ties of her wrap dress while waiting for Grey to return from a quick trip outside with Shaman. Spending so much time near him today made her hot and restless, just like she'd felt the first time she'd seen him.

Now, despite the fact that she'd *never* slept with any guy on a first date, she was standing in Grey's living room considering it. More than considering, actually—fantasizing.

Then again, nothing about the day or evening had seemed like a first date. Working with Grey this spring had already established a rhythm of conversation and a level of trust. Today he'd listened without judgment and still wanted her.

Playing it safe had never kept her from getting hurt. Tonight Avery wanted to act on unbridled desire without fear of consequence.

Resolved, she marched into Grey's bedroom and sat on the edge of his bed—his very neatly made bed. She scooted back and tested its firmness before leaning down to seek his scent among his pillows. Sadly, his bedding smelled like fabric softener instead of his unique mix of testosterone and grape candy. She then noticed a new pillar candle sitting on top of his nightstand, and a book of matches at the ready.

Fresh sheets. Candlelight. Had he been planning a seduction? Rather than feeling indignant, she decided to push past her comfort zone and take the reins.

Her heart fluttered a bit as she lit the candle. Within a minute, she heard Grey and Shaman reenter the apartment. Ten seconds later, Grey called out, "Where are you hiding, Bambi?"

"Back here." She stood, gulping a breath.

What she would've given for a camera to capture Grey's shocked expression when he walked through the doorway, lollipop stick hanging from parted lips. "What are you doing?"

The wild abandon felt surprisingly good. And sexy. She toyed with the ties of her dress. "Breaking my rules."

Grey crossed the room in three quick strides, tossed the chewed-up stick on the nightstand, and crushed her against his body. She felt him shudder, his chest rumbling, when he kissed her. His words emerged in a husky tone. "Are you sure?"

"Let go and I'll prove it."

He cupped her face and delivered another passionate kiss before looking her directly in the eyes, his own blazing. "I've imagined this a thousand times. Each time, *I* undressed *you* while kissing every inch of your body." His silver eyes flashed with hunger and determination. "So *you* let go."

On his command, she released the ties of her dress and wrapped her arms around his neck. She needed to anchor herself to his strength before the promise of his words buckled her knees.

He backed her up to the edge of the bed, kissing her while cupping her butt and pressing his hips against her pelvis. Like a tease, he then eased away and slowly untied her dress, removing the garment as he rained kisses on her neck, shoulders, and down to her breasts. His gaze caressed her body from head to toe, leaving her exposed, nervous, and strung tight with anticipation.

She raked her fingers through his wavy locks and kissed him, then tried to tug him onto the bed, seeking his body's heat.

His firm grip stopped them from falling. "I'm not done." His fingers grazed her collarbone, making her shiver, before sliding underneath her bra strap.

"No fair." She grabbed his shirt. "You're still wearing *all* your clothes."

He grinned and raised his arms over his head, waiting for her to remove his top. Never one to take orders, she bypassed the shirt and went straight for the button of his jeans, surprising him. Before he could react, she'd unzipped his pants and pushed them partway down his hips. When her hand stroked the length of his impressive hard-on, he growled.

He shrugged out of his shirt, kicked off his pants, and unfastened her bra in a few fluid movements. His mouth began a hot assault on her neck and shoulders as he cast her bra aside. Then he turned her facing away from him, nudged her onto the mattress, and grabbed her panties. The minute his lips made contact with the small of her back, she groaned and lost all thought.

◆ ◆ ◆

Yes, yes, yes! Grey couldn't get enough of Avery. His hands roamed her back, waist, and legs. It was better than any of his daydreams. She'd shocked the shit out of him when he'd found her in his room, offering him everything he'd been dreaming of for months. His body had responded immediately with an insistent throbbing. The long, long wait was over. *Thank you, God.*

His tongue trailed down her spine, over her tight little ass, and down to the inside of her thigh. Her body bucked and arched in response until she twisted underneath him so he came face to face with . . . heaven.

But as much as she wanted him, he hadn't yet finished his exploration. Grey wasn't about to let her shortchange him any foreplay. He cradled her face in his hands and kissed her. Grey liked kissing a lot.

Always had. Kissing Avery felt so damned right. His tongue sank deep into her mouth, possessive and penetrating.

"Mmm," she purred.

He opened his eyes so she could see the crazy effect she had on him, then whispered against her neck, "I'm on fire."

"Me too."

He then kissed her lips, her eyelids, her cheeks, her jaw, the notch at the base of her neck. She twisted her body to meet his mouth, filling him with a crazy sense of victory.

The candlelight flickering in the room gave him a sexy view of the slopes and curves of her naked body. His fingertips traced the indent along the center of her stomach as he kissed her again.

Slowly and purposefully, his mouth began to work its way from hers, down her neck and to her perfect, *perfect* breasts. He cupped one, which filled his hand, and brushed his thumb across one tight, pale-pink nipple, which was begging for his mouth.

She arched her back in invitation just before he tongued her then sucked hard.

"Grey." Hearing his name on her lips made his heart pound.

Her hands roamed his back, reaching lower, but he wasn't in any hurry to leave paradise. He pushed her hands away, holding them by her side, while his mouth continued exploring her body, making them both ache with anticipation.

"Oh, yes," she whimpered, clutching fistfuls of his hair, sending another wave of shivers through him.

Her supple, smooth skin smelled like fresh flowers, but not too sweet. Exactly how he'd imagined. Better, actually, and he hadn't thought that possible. He grew painfully hard while his mouth began its descent along her waist.

"Avery." When he caressed the inside of her thighs, she rocked her hips forward and let her legs fall open. "I'm so hot for you." His voice scraped from some lust-tightened place in his chest. "You're so damned beautiful."

When her nails raked his back in unison with another of her sensual moans, he decided maybe she didn't mind swearing in bed, which was good because it was bound to happen again.

He parted her with his fingers before bringing his mouth between her legs and inserting two fingers inside her hot body. Her hips pitched and she cried out again, driving him half out of his mind.

Her scent, tangy taste, and wetness overloaded his senses. He circled her with his frenzied tongue and worked his fingers, sensing her rising tension as her fingers threaded through his hair.

"Oh! Oh, God!" Her breathing became ragged as her body spasmed until he tasted her orgasm. His heart soared until he could barely catch his breath.

As she settled, he kissed the insides of her thighs, her belly button, and beneath her breasts. When he tongued her nipple, her overly sensitive body twitched, making him smile.

Her muscles began to slacken, but his body remained taut and rigid, nearly in pain from needing release. He needed to sink deep into her body. To take her, the way he'd wanted for months. To claim her as his own for as long as she'd have him.

His hand caressed her cheek just before he kissed her mouth. A long, deliberate kiss to allow her another minute to recover before he aroused her once more. He grinned when her hand skirted over his chest and down his stomach to his monstrous erection. Apparently Bambi didn't need more time.

"I want you," she rasped, the gold in her blue eyes lighting with fire.

"You got me." His hoarse voice sounded as desperate as he felt.

He reached for a condom, which she helped him put on. His control started slipping when she took him in hand, but he'd waited too long for her to allow his overeager cock to ruin everything.

Without breaking their kiss, he moved on top of her, savoring the skin-to-skin contact. His body came alive as her hands and fingers traced the muscles of his shoulders, chest, back, and ass. He centered himself between her legs then pushed the tip of his penis inside her slick body, before backing out. He repeated the motion, each time thrusting slightly deeper. With each withdrawal, she groaned and gripped his hips, raising her legs to force him deeper. But he wanted to hear her beg before he satisfied that burning need they shared.

"More!" Finally, what he'd been waiting to hear.

"Look at me." He wanted to see her eyes, and to know that she saw him while he thrust fully inside her. "You feel so good."

He kept his gaze locked on hers as he continued to pump his hips. Another animalistic sound escaped his throat, but he didn't care, and apparently neither did she.

She kissed his chest as he started a rhythm. "Faster, Grey. Faster," she whispered before kissing his neck and raising her legs up and around his waist.

Hell, yes, faster. But in the midst of utter ecstasy, his knee began to ache. He flipped onto his back, keeping her with him. Like a freaking goddess, she reared upright on his lap. Those beautiful, full breasts pertly awaiting his attention.

He sat up, holding her waist, while his mouth latched onto one nipple. He kneaded her hips and nipped at her breasts as she slid herself up and down his throbbing, hot erection.

Nothing could get better than this, he thought, until she pushed at his chest, laying him flat against the mattress while she remained upright, then reached around behind her butt and cupped him. The shock of her maneuver almost made him jump off the bed, sending him into a sensual mania as she rode his body with confidence and lust, her breasts bobbing with each rise and fall.

His heart thundered at the sight.

He wanted to watch the erotic scene unfolding on his lap, but his eyelids grew heavy as his own back arched and he bucked to meet her pace.

Both of them were groaning and panting when they finally, and explosively, came together. A string of expletives shot out of his mouth before he could stop himself.

"Sorry for all the swearing," he whispered in her ear before he hugged her tightly to his chest.

"Forgiven." She remained collapsed on top of him, her head tucked up against his shoulder and neck. Her contented sigh filled him with satisfaction.

He stroked her hair and back while his heart rate settled. Candlelight danced on the walls of his room, the play of light and shadow enhancing the mystery of the intense sexual connection. The past fourteen hours had exceeded all expectations.

Snuggling closer, he noticed the dewy sweat on her skin, the scent of sex mingled with her flowery perfume, the little panting sounds of her breath, the way her fingers mindlessly traced his collarbone.

He kissed the top of her head and allowed happiness to wash over him. With any luck, she'd feel it, too, and it would carry away her doubts and worries. Reflexively, he squeezed her a little more tightly and felt her smile against his chest.

Moments later, he rose to remove the condom and deposit it in the bathroom just outside his door. When he returned to the bedroom, she was hunting for her clothing.

"What are you doing?" *What the hell was she doing?*

"Getting dressed." She blinked at him like he was crazy. "It's really late now. I should probably go."

"No." He shook his head and grabbed the bra out of her hand, tossing it to the ground. "Stay the night."

"I shouldn't."

"Why not?"

"Because of Trip."

"What's he got to do with us?"

"Well, he'll be here in the morning."

"So?"

"So, that'll be a little awkward."

"Trip will delight in teasing us as often as possible, so get used to it." When he noticed the crease in her forehead, he grew concerned. "Do you regret what happened?"

"No, but I guess I feel a little . . . I don't know, self-conscious. I told you, I've never done this so quickly. I don't want to presume anything."

She looked unusually vulnerable. He didn't think words would persuade her, so he kissed her. "I want you to stay, Avery. All night." He held her until he felt her resistance ebb.

"Okay." Her shy smile might have been one of the prettiest things he'd ever seen. Or maybe the wave of relief crashing over him simply heightened every little thing she did.

Grey pulled back the sheets and playfully pushed her back down onto the bed, crawling in beside her before snuggling his body up against hers. "Better?"

She nodded. His hands gently caressed her body as she relaxed against him and drifted off to sleep.

◆ ◆ ◆

Avery woke up sweaty in the middle of the night, momentarily confused by the unfamiliar surroundings. Lying on her side, she scanned the dark silhouettes of Grey's room. His arm and leg were draped over her body, his chest glued to her back. The languid rhythm of his breathing told her he was soundly sleeping.

He slept so peacefully—the opposite of how she felt. Her heart had recovered from Matt, but was it really strong enough to handle someone as overwhelming as Grey?

The bracelet Grey never removed drew her attention. Juliette. Just the name sowed seeds of doubt. Would he ever love anyone that much again, or does the heart lose the ability to give everything after it's been broken? And even if he could love so deeply again, could he love her, someone so different from Juliette? Insecurity acted like fertilizer, making those seeds grow like unruly ragweed.

She attempted to ease away from him in order to turn and look at him, but her movement roused him. A satisfied-sounding hum rattled in his chest as he nuzzled his nose into her hair and neck, sending little currents of anticipation zipping through her limbs. His hand slid up her waist and began to fondle her breast, immediately stirring her body.

At least I'm not the only one aroused, she thought as she felt him grow hard against her hip. His mouth—those beautiful lips—kissed her neck and shoulder as he deftly repositioned himself so he could minister to her breasts with one hand and all the other parts of her body with his other.

Grey knew how to handle a woman's body and deliver maximum pleasure. She turned slightly so she could kiss him while his hands did delicious things to her body.

In the midst of the mounting sensual frenzy, the rightness of being held by Grey in the dark silence hit. Her swift attachment to him was unexpected. For the first time, she understood why *they* called it falling for someone. Falling—into an abyss from which one might not wish to recover—described the feeling precisely. And despite the danger, her heart tumbled for this man.

Her thoughts scattered the instant he entered her body from behind. A heady blend of confidence and devotion laced every one of his movements. Somehow he'd already learned how to read her cues. He knew when to push, pull, kiss, touch, speed up, slow down. Dizzying, in the very best way.

Their bodies rocked together as he pushed her closer and closer to the edge. Small tremors convulsed as she tipped over that edge, then he abruptly pulled out, all the while repeating her name until his own body stopped shaking.

She turned over to nestle against his chest. The first hint of daylight had begun to creep through the edges of the blinds, enabling her to see all the contours of his shoulders, hairless chest, and stomach. Given her profession, she'd seen her fair share of fit bodies, but Grey's ranked up there at the top of her list.

He tucked one hand behind his head and watched her tracing the lines of his upper body. "Glad you stayed?"

She arched one brow at his rakish grin, but didn't deny him the answer he needed to hear. "Very."

"Me, too." He pulled her closer and snaked one arm underneath her shoulders. "Me, too."

She liked it there, in the crook of his arm, inhaling the smell of his skin and listening to the steady beat of his heart. Sated and tired, she allowed her mind to wander in and out of consciousness until the brightness of the room interfered with her ability to fall back asleep.

As much as she might like to stay longer, she was hungry, and she had to get home. Reluctantly, she pushed up onto one elbow, waking Grey.

"Mornin'." His sleepy eyes crinkled as he reached up and brushed her hair behind her shoulder.

"Good morning." She held the sheet up against her chest. "I know you're going to try to change my mind again, but I've got to go home, Grey."

He glanced at the clock. "It's only seven on a Sunday morning. What's the rush?"

"My parents are coming for *another* visit, and I've got a bunch of things to do to get ready."

"How long will they be in town?" He avoided her gaze, choosing instead to watch his own fingers as they slid along her bicep.

"I'm not sure. Why?"

"I'm assuming I won't see you while they're here." His voice dropped a few decibels.

Her stomach fell at the thought of her dad's reaction to news of her dating Grey. "I think that would be best, at least until we see what happens with the lawsuits, and with us."

"With us?" Grey's expression grew concerned. "Are you already expecting something to go wrong? 'Cause I gotta say, I think things right here are damn near perfect, Bambi."

She smiled at him and that ridiculous nickname she'd come to treasure. "Things are nice, but things always start off good, don't they?"

Grey sat up, appearing to be battling some unpleasant emotions. "No, they don't. And even when they do, that's not the same as this. This, by the way, isn't a normal start. You get that, don't you? We already know each other well. We've even had our first few arguments. This"—he motioned between them—"is already past the beginning. For me, anyway."

The vehemence of his tone surprised her. "You're right. We are somewhere beyond a beginning." She leaned over and kissed his shoulder to soothe his ruffled feathers. "Still, my family is under a lot of stress right now."

She felt Grey tense even as he glanced away. "Grey, I'm not like you. I don't rush into things, and even you must admit, now isn't the best time to introduce you to my family. Not when so much is unresolved for all of us."

Grey's scowl loosened a bit. "I'm not an idiot."

"Then stop pouting and let's eat before I take off." Avery saw her clothes in a pile on the floor. "Can you hand me my things so I can face Trip with some dignity?"

At least that remark caused Grey to grin. A welcome sight. He slid out of bed, giving her a great view of his very tight butt and broad shoulders.

He stood there completely comfortable in his nakedness, forcing her to concentrate on not dropping her jaw. If she looked that good naked, she'd probably be less modest, too, she thought. He dangled her bra from his finger.

"Sure you don't have time for round three before you go?"

He dropped her bra and lunged at the bed, apparently taking her two-second hesitation as a yes. Who was she to resist?

◆ ◆ ◆

An orgasm was a much better way to start the day than a cup of coffee, she decided while lying in Grey's embrace.

"You still hungry?" He peered down at her and kissed her forehead.

"Very." She propped up on one elbow. "Maybe a bowl of cereal or something before I go?"

Grey reluctantly got out of bed and put on athletic shorts and a T-shirt. "I think I can manage that for you." He walked to the edge of the mattress and kissed her quickly. "I've got to let Shaman out real quick. Be back in a jiffy."

After he left, she quickly dressed herself and pulled her hair into a ponytail. Before she left the safety of Grey's room, she braced for an onslaught of teasing from Trip.

Luckily, Trip wasn't in the living room or kitchen, and his bedroom door remained closed. Either he never came home, or he snuck in early and was catching up on sleep. Either way, she'd been spared the embarrassment of being caught in the clothes she'd worn last night—the dreaded "walk of shame."

Grey returned from letting Shaman out. He poured her a bowl of Fruity Pebbles and a glass of orange juice, then leaned his elbows on the counter and watched her eat, while the dog sniffed around her stool.

She stared at the fluorescent cereal and shot him a look. "Seriously?"

"I assumed you'd love such a colorful cereal." He grinned. "Don't judge until you try. They're awesome."

"I guess I should be grateful you didn't hand me candy." She chuckled before spooning crunchy sugared cereal into her mouth. She'd never admit it, but it did taste kind of good.

"So when can I see you again?" His fingers crawled toward her and stroked her forearm. "Is tonight too soon for another sleepover?"

"I can't sleep here tonight. I've got work tomorrow, and stuff to do, like I said."

"I'll come to you." He frowned. "Come on, before your parents arrive and I have to stay away."

Avery shook her head. "We just talked about this. I need a little time to warm Andy up to this idea, too."

"Fine." He stood up. "How about dinner tomorrow?"

"I can do that. This time I'll bring the picnic." She spooned the last of the cereal into her mouth.

Grey grabbed her hand and tugged her off the stool into a kiss—a steamy kiss that made her wish her parents weren't coming to visit. He sucked on her lip and then his tongue found hers, all while he held her firmly against his body.

If someone had asked if she would like all the touchy-feely stuff, she would've guessed not. She would've guessed wrong. She actually craved his demonstrative, romantic nature. A first for her, and a little bit scary.

Caution warned her to slow down, but her heart had galloped ahead of her brain and she couldn't find any reins.

She marveled at how bravely he exposed his feelings. Almost from the very first moment at Plum Tree, when he'd winked at her, he'd opened himself up to her rejection. Even when he'd been restraining himself as her patient, his interest had simmered just beneath the surface.

Juliette may still inhabit a special place in his heart, but clearly he wanted to make room for Avery. And so there, in his drab little living room, another chunk of the protective casing she'd wrapped around her heart for as long as she could remember melted.

Grey was a game changer.

When his hands rode up her back and into her hair, she pressed herself against him, kissing him as if she might die if they stopped.

The deadbolt clicked on the apartment door a second before Trip entered and caught them in the middle of their make-out session.

He stopped and grinned. "You didn't leave a 'do not disturb' sign for me. You think you'd know better. Next time I'll knock before entering." Trip removed his cowboy hat and smiled at Avery.

"Hi, Trip." She hid her discomfort by going on the offensive, and made a show of looking at her watch. In a joking tone, she said, "I'm surprised to see you getting home this late in the morning given your reputation for sneaking away before dawn."

"Is that right?" He scratched his head, wearing a wicked grin. "Let me think, now. According to *your* reputation, it seems we're both breaking all the rules this morning, hmm?"

The fact he said it with a big smile didn't make the hit less direct. Avery didn't wince, but her shoulders stiffened. She smiled and flipped her hair over her shoulder, hoping neither noticed her hot cheeks.

Trip sank into the sofa cushion and crossed his feet up on the coffee table. "What are you two doing today?"

"I'm on my way out, although I'm not sure it's safe to leave Grey here alone with you." She turned to Grey and teased. "Can you resist his bad influence?"

He kissed her just as Trip called out, "And here it was me being afraid of leaving him alone with you, sweet PT. You've got him all turned inside out."

Avery looked at Trip and tilted her head. "I can't wait to meet the woman who finally turns *you* inside out."

"Ha!" Trip laughed before his expression shifted to something more genuine than she'd ever seen from him. "I doubt she exists . . ." And then he immediately slipped back into character. "Who knows, maybe she'll be born this year. By the time she grows up, I'll be old enough to settle down."

Avery rolled her eyes while Grey mumbled something to his friend before walking her down to her car. He opened her door for her and then kissed her again before closing it. "I'll call you later."

"Okay." She waited until he backed up a step or two before she pulled away from the curb. In her rearview mirror she saw him, standing in the middle of the road, watching her drive away.

The past twenty-four hours had been blissful. Although she still felt somewhat off-balance by her decision to run headlong into the possibility of love, whenever she pictured Grey's smiling face, she couldn't imagine anything less than a happy ending.

Chapter Seventeen

A week later, Grey limped into the Backtrax office after his first bouldering session with a new client. He unclipped his chalk bag and tossed it on top of the banged-up green file cabinet. Traversing the boulder had strained his knee. Worse, his crash pad had done little to reduce the compression of his landing, which had further stressed the joint. Sent a razor-sharp pain through the damned thing, actually.

Fortunately, now the throbbing had dwindled to a steady ache, so he was ninety-nine percent sure he hadn't done real damage. The bigger worry involved the fact that he still couldn't rely on his knee for his work. For the first time, he started to consider the real possibility that he might never be able to do so.

After leaning his crash mat against a wall, he filled an ice bag with cold water and ice cubes, popped a couple of ibuprofens, collapsed onto his desk chair, and elevated his bad leg on a cardboard box.

"Tell me we aren't headed back to the hospital." Trip's voice cut through the air, his gaze riveted to the ice on Grey's knee.

"No. Just pushed it a little too hard today showing a client some heel and toe hooks." He hid his concerns behind a dismissive wave. "It'll be fine."

Normally Grey could count on Trip for banter and good times, so his friend's dead-serious expression pulled him up short. "Everyone warns you not to push. You can't just *will* that joint to heal right, Grey. Why in the hell would you risk screwing it up so soon? Don't you want to get back on the slopes one day?" Trip sank onto the chair opposite the desk and loosened the laces of his climbing shoes. "I'm doing everything I can to help you keep things afloat. Now do your part and let your knee recover, dammit."

Grey raised his hands. "Whoa, buddy. You knew I was taking a client bouldering this morning, so what's with the attitude?"

The new client—a novice twenty-something—had promised to bring some of her friends next time. Repeat business was still a primary concern.

Trip leaned forward, resting one arm on the desk, and quirked his brow. "I assumed you'd restrict yourself to spotting. Didn't realize you'd be so pigheaded as to teach by example." He shook his head and slouched back into his seat. "You can't afford to make stupid mistakes."

Grey glanced at his knee, careful to avoid eye contact. "I'm sick of sitting behind this desk, dealing with numbers and words. I didn't plan to climb today. But the sun was shining, the girl was struggling a bit, and you know the pull. I needed it, Trip. Needed to *do* something."

He grimaced at his moronic explanation. Still, it had been more than twelve weeks since his surgery. Countless hours in therapy. By most measures, his fit body could handle anything. So why the hell did a mere nine-foot drop make him feel like an arthritic seventy-year-old man?

"I'd worked on soft-landing jumps in therapy this past week, so I didn't think it would hurt. Other climbers have been able to do as much at about twelve to sixteen weeks." He held up his hand to keep Trip from interrupting. "I won't climb again until I get the green light from Donner. Promise."

Trip's facial muscles relaxed into a grin as he reached across the desk and wiggled his pinky finger. "Pinky promise?"

"Asshole." Grey batted Trip's hand. "How'd it go with your group?"

"Jon and I led a group of four from Durango—three guys and a chick. They paid cash." He plunked down a wad of bills on the desk. "Along the route, we crack climbed a chimney. Good day. I think we'll see them, or at least her and some of her other friends, again."

"Did they rebook?" Grey gathered the money, counted it, and stuffed it in the cash box.

"No, but she was a flirt. I made sure she got her money's worth." Trip scratched at his forearm, the self-satisfied gleam in his eyes causing Grey to chuckle. "Trust me, she'll be back."

"If Backtrax is doing double-duty as a personal escort service, make sure I get a cut of whatever you're raking in," Grey joked. He tossed the pencil aside and clasped his hands behind his head. "Maybe we should add a 'Local Lady-killer' tab on the website and post a big picture of your face. What's your fee?"

"*Triple* the going rate of other guys. Of course, you'd have to switch up your tagline. 'High Altitude Adventures . . . and . . . nooky? Stud services?' Ah, how about 'High Altitude Happy Endings'?" Trip playfully rubbed his chin. "Whatever. It all sounds good to me! Too bad Avery won't let you participate in that side of the business."

"Don't feel sorry for me. I'm plenty happy with my situation, thanks." Grey reached into the drawer for a sucker and tossed one to Trip. "Let's get back to *real* business."

With a heavy sigh, Grey scratched the back of his neck, resigned to the fact the pain in his knee would quickly be replaced by a headache. He turned on the computer and printed a draft of an article he planned to submit to some online adventure magazines.

"I wrote an article I need you to proofread. Hopefully someone will pick it up and print it in October." He picked up the draft article, trying to read through it one more time. As usual, letters jumped around the page like they were playing hopscotch. Grey passed the papers to Trip. As an afterthought, he tossed a red pen at him, too. "You'll need this."

Trip folded the pages and stuffed them in his front pocket. "Have you heard from the OS?"

"Not yet, but I'm counting on a big insurance settlement." Grey repositioned the ice bag. "I just want all this to be over."

Trip leaned forward again, this time resting his elbows on his knees. He stared at the ground for a moment before meeting Grey's gaze. "Listen, that ice bag should be a big red flag, Grey. Don't settle your claims for the bare minimum. There are no guarantees about your recovery. More importantly, there's no guarantee that laying off Andy Randall will result in a fairy-tale ending with his sister."

Grey crunched up the last bits of his lollipop before throwing the stick in the trash. Trip wasn't wrong, but if Grey pressed hard against Andy, that *would* guarantee the end of everything with Avery. "I hear you. I won't roll over, but I am going to do whatever I can to avoid hurting her."

Trip rolled his eyes. Of course, Trip didn't know squat about love relationships, so Grey shouldn't expect a different reaction.

"Well, I can see I'm talking to a brick wall, so I may as well put my mouth to better use. Too bad we haven't booked my stud services yet," Trip kidded before he cracked his knuckles and stretched out in his chair. "Think you can manage to hobble to Grizzly's for some brews and a round of pool?" When Grey glanced at his phone, Trip clucked. "Henpecked already? Honestly, Grey, it's way too soon for you to need permission to go out with me, or anyone else, for that matter."

"I don't need permission. It's just that I'm expecting her to drop by on her way home. With her parents in town, we haven't seen each other."

"That's a good thing. You've jumped into this thing with Avery no-holds-barred. A few days apart will give you time to locate your brain and stop daydreaming."

Grey flung a thick pink eraser at Trip's head, which Trip caught. "I don't daydream."

"Oh yeah, you do. You've been sporting a goofy, lovesick face since last Saturday. Hell, you barely paid attention to the Rockies' game last night." Trip shook his head, chuckling. "It's sad, man. Just sad."

"What's sad?" Avery arrived on cue, smiling.

Although the back office lacked windows, the space brightened up like a cloudless summer afternoon. Her visit made Grey's heart skip and prompted a huge smile, which seemed to further goad Trip.

"See what I mean. Just plain sappy." He turned toward Avery, grinning. "You're a menace."

"Jealous I stole *your* title?" She joked, until her gaze landed on the ice bag covering Grey's knee. Her expression shifted to concern. "What did you do?"

Before Grey could answer, Trip volunteered, "Took a client bouldering and showed off his own skills instead of spotting her."

Grey knew Trip hadn't meant to provoke Avery's insecurities, but he watched Avery take a step backward at the inference he'd been flirting. "Oh, really? So you ignored all my advice and put that kind of strain on your knee already?"

Why couldn't anyone understand his urge to conquer the rock? "I just got a little excited out there today. Lesson learned. Can we move on, please?" He lifted the bag from his knee and tossed it to the floor. Glancing at Trip, he jerked his head toward the door in a silent plea for a little privacy. "How about you and I discuss that article later?"

Trip crossed his legs at the ankles, apparently enjoying making Grey squirm. "How 'bout you give me an answer about pool tonight?" When Grey tried and failed to look at Avery without getting busted, Trip slapped his thigh. "I knew it."

He stood up and, walking in a tight circle, tucked his hands under his armpits and flapped his arms like a chicken. *Bwok, bwok, bwok.*

Then he laughed out loud as he exited the office.

Avery stared after him—arms crossed, head tilted to the left—then shook her head and redirected her attention to Grey. "What was that about?"

"Nothing." He reached both hands toward her, and she quickly complied with his silent request. He pulled her onto his good leg and kissed her. "You miss me?"

She squirmed a bit, but didn't deny it. "I want to talk."

"You mean you're not here to sexually assault me?" He nuzzled against her neck, but she pushed him away.

"That's next, so stop distracting me."

"I wasn't even trying hard. Let me bring my A-game." He pushed up her shirt, but she shoved it back down.

She smacked his shoulder. "Seriously, I want to talk about how I might help you drum up more business."

Grey drew back a bit, wondering what she could possibly do to help. "I don't want you worrying about my business."

"Come on. It'll help prepare me for when I finally start my own clinic." She smiled. "I'm happy to help you, Grey."

"Last I checked, you weren't a certified climber or ski guide." He stroked her back, unable to restrain the urge to keep touching her.

"No, but I'm a decent writer, so I could help with your website redesign or marketing brochures or blogging. And you should give Kelsey and Emma a bunch of brochures. Kelsey's always meeting rich people like Wade, so she can help promote your business. Emma's inn is also an easy place to reach potential clients. And I know everyone in this town, so I can introduce you to whomever you haven't yet met."

Her eyes shimmered with energy and intelligence and enthusiasm.

"I like it when you get all fired up." Grey wrapped his hand behind her neck and pulled her in for another kiss.

She bit his lower lip and pressed away from his chest. "So you'll let me help?"

"I'll think about it. Like I said, I can handle my own affairs." He threaded his fingers through a hank of her hair, unwilling to accept being seen as a dyslexic illiterate. Like a man who couldn't take care of himself. "You've got enough on your plate now with your own job and your family."

She whacked his hand, her brows pinched together so tight it drew a deep line in her forehead. "Don't just treat me like some pet, Grey. If sex is all you want, then go hang out with Trip and I'm sure you'll find plenty of willing partners." She tried to wiggle off his lap, but he clamped his forearm around her waist.

"Settle down, Bambi. You know what I feel isn't just sexual," he said, then grinned and nipped at her shoulder, "although that's a nice side effect."

"Then prove it. Don't hide a weakness from me, or play macho. I was a great student. I'm a strong reader and writer. You've got dyslexia. Let me help you in that area, just like I'll let you help me with my weaknesses."

"You've got a weakness?" Grey tickled her. "Where? I don't see any."

"Quit it. I'm serious." But he caught her grinning before she scowled again. "Are we on the same page, or not?"

He held up his hands in surrender for the second time that afternoon. "Okay. Yes, I hear you. Help away!"

She slid a sideways glance at him. Grey's fingers toyed with the buttons of her Alpine-PT pullover. "Seeing you in this getup makes me all kinds of nostalgic. Donner doesn't look half this good at therapy."

"I have a hard time believing you find this outfit sexy." She placed her hand on his chest.

"Honest to God, you have no idea how hard it was to hide my woodies at your clinic." His hand stroked her arm and rested under her hip. "Frankly, I don't miss that part of working with you."

She reached between his legs. "I guess I can't argue with this evidence. Who knew the track-suit look was so hot?"

"I want you so bad right now." Grey reached up and drew her in for another kiss. "I'm guessing you wouldn't be comfortable going upstairs, with Trip in the next room."

"Not particularly, no." Avery shivered when his tongue stroked her neck.

"Your house is out?" He nipped at her earlobe, his own stomach now clenching with desire.

"Yes." Avery looked across the room. "Does that door lock?"

Grey's mouth nibbled on her neck as he pressed her tighter to his chest. "Uh-huh."

"Hang on." She jumped up, locked the door, then returned and sank to her knees. Her quick maneuver dumbfounded him for a second. Long enough for her to free his erection. "Avery!" He couldn't complete his thought as her pretty pink lips locked around him. "Oh, baby, that feels so good."

His eyes closed briefly, but he forced them open so he could watch her take him in and out of that sassy, pouty mouth of hers. His legs twitched and tightened, so he straightened them and sank a little lower in the chair. "Yeah, like that."

In a distant recess of his mind, he thought to stop her—to give pleasure rather than take it—but it wouldn't happen just yet. Thinking he could give up this bliss so soon was about as fruitless as trying to kick his sugar addiction.

She tongued him and used her hands along his shaft and elsewhere, making everything from his chest to his toes tighten in an agonizing form of ecstasy. He dug his hands into her hair, unable to resist applying a little pressure to her head as he watched her with lustful fascination.

◆ ◆ ◆

Avery felt herself being lifted off the floor at the same time a growl ripped from Grey's throat. He sat her on the edge of the desk and ran his hands through her hair, down her back, and under her hips, yanking her up against his chest.

"Woman, what you do to me." He planted heated, wet kisses behind the ear and down to her collarbone. His touch and groans made her entire body tingle. He grabbed the hem of her shirt and shoved it up over her head. "Off."

He tucked her bra to the sides and under her breasts, which pushed them together and upward. His roughness heightened her anticipation—her desire. He kissed her, thumbing her nipples until she whimpered and arched into him. His mouth sucked on her breast, while his hands caressed her waist and kneaded her hips. Grey grunted and shivered, which sent delicious tremors fanning throughout her body.

"You like that," Grey muttered in her ear just before yanking her sweatpants down and pushing her onto her elbows as he dipped his head down between her legs. *Oh yes, I like that.* His hot tongue explored and probed her, as did his fingers. Her hips bucked off the desk, but she didn't want to come without him. She sat up, trying to pull his hips to hers.

"My knee," he winced.

She hopped off the desk, pushing him into the chair.

"Condom," he uttered.

"On the pill now and clean. You?"

"As a whistle." His eyes flickered, like light hitting liquid silver, as he reached for her breasts.

She straddled him, needy and ready. "God, you feel good," she moaned as she sank down the full length of his throbbing, hot erection. He filled her completely.

His hands didn't seem to know where they wanted to be, stroking her arms, running through her hair, caressing her breasts, kneading her ass. Everywhere he touched her skin left a trail of goose bumps. Wherever he kissed her, the stubble on his jaw burned her skin in the best way. Every nerve in her body vibrated.

His ragged breath heated her neck, urging her to rock faster and harder against him. "Avery, wait!"

He pumped his hips up against her bottom, making her insides clench and tighten, seeking release. "Don't stop," she ordered, as she swiveled her hips against him. "Deeper."

"Come on, baby!" Grey cried out as his control slipped. His frantic grinding tipped her over the edge, causing her body to convulse and collapse against his chest. He clung to her, kissing her temple, his hand stroking her hair, his uneven breath gushing from his lungs. "Look at you, having sex on my desk in the middle of the afternoon. You're naughty." His fingers stroked under her chin and tipped her head up for a kiss. "I love it."

Avery grinned, refusing to think too much about the fact she'd never been nearly so unrepressed in the past. Grey brought out some kick-ass sexy side of her she never knew existed. As she lifted off his lap, he used the bottom of his shirt to wipe them both clean.

Suddenly she felt shy, standing there practically naked in the middle of his office. Grabbing her clothes, she quickly dressed while he merely had to scoot his pants up.

"Don't do that." Grey came up behind her and wrapped his arms around her waist, resting his chin on her shoulder.

"I can't stand here naked."

"Debatable." He squeezed her and then his voice dropped a decibel or two. "But I'm talking about how you start running away every time we're together."

Her body stiffened. "I do not."

"Yeah, you do. Every time. You retreat, like you're uncomfortable looking at me."

She twisted around to face him. Her breath caught looking at his flushed face and gorgeous eyes. Eyes that focused on her, reflecting a dozen emotions she wanted to believe and yet feared.

She couldn't let her heart roam free so fast. Couldn't forget the risks. Couldn't get hurt again because loving then losing Grey could be devastating. "I do not, Grey."

"Fine." He sighed and dropped his hands to her hips. "Wanna grab some dinner?"

"I can't. I've got to pick up Andy in fifteen minutes, and then get home for dinner."

"When will I see you next?" Grey nonchalantly played with the ends of her hair.

"They leave in a couple of days." She brushed his bangs out of his eyes.

"Two more days?" He scowled.

"Maybe I can sneak away and meet you for lunch." She eased from his arms. "But right now I've got to run."

"Guess I'm stuck going out with Trip tonight."

Avery frowned. "Maybe you two will bump into the woman you took climbing today."

She closed her eyes, wishing she could retract her childish, jealous remark. Her cheeks heated, and only grew warmer when she opened her eyes and saw Grey's smirk.

"You're wondering if she was pretty, aren't you?" He tilted his head and smiled the warmest, most sincere smile she'd seen. "Truthfully, she was cute. But no one's as cute as you, Bambi. I'm not Matt. You can trust me, okay?"

"I trust you. I just don't trust her, or other women—or that gigolo of a best friend you've got dragging you around town."

"Don't rag on my buddy. He's not forcing anyone to do anything they don't want to do. As far as I can tell, so far everyone's been plenty happy with the arrangement."

"Hmph." Avery grimaced, imagining Trip and Grey together, surrounded by women eager to seduce either man. "Maybe it's a little early to discuss this," she said, gesturing between them while hating the catch in her voice, "but I'm assuming we're exclusive. I mean, we're together now, right?"

"Damn straight we are." Grey glared at her, apparently aggravated by the mere thought of her running around with anyone else. He hugged her tight against his body. "You're mine."

Avery didn't enjoy being thought of as a possession. However Grey's Neanderthal declaration curled her toes in a good way.

"Don't worry about tonight." Grey kissed the tip of her nose. "It's just beer and pool."

"Famous last words."

Chapter Eighteen

Later that evening, Grey followed Trip into Grizzly's, then shuffled up to the bar, antique wood floors creaking beneath his every step. Hammered copper trims and smoky mirrors gave the old bar a rosy glow. Too bad it stank like stale beer. Thankfully the place was fairly empty, which meant Trip might not want to stick around too long.

"Two Red Rockets." Trip slid a twenty on the bar and took a seat next to Grey. "Hey, buddy, if you're gonna make it as my wingman, you need to smile a little."

"I'm here for a beer and round of pool. Period." The last thing Grey needed was to be stuck in the middle of Trip and a group of rabid women.

When the bartender arrived with their drinks, Grey might not have noticed him had the guy not gawked while handing him a bottle. The tall blond looked familiar, but it took another minute for Grey to work out where he'd seen him. More importantly, why he remembered that face at all. *Matt.*

Apparently Avery's ex really had decided to move back to town. Possessiveness coiled around Grey's chest like a python. He sized Matt up when the guy turned his back. Matt looked to be an inch or two taller than him, well built, and probably considered good-looking by women. An unwelcome image of Avery wrapped in that man's arms drifted through his mind, kicking open a nest of fire ants in his gut.

That jerk knew how Avery looked when she got fired up. Knew how she sounded when she laughed real low. Knew how she looked naked. Worst of all, Matt knew how she felt cradled against his skin. *Push it aside.*

Trip, who clearly didn't recognize Matt, raised his bottle in a toast. "To living single and drinking double."

"Original?" Grey clanked his bottle and took a swig, hoping the cold beer would dilute the acid in his stomach. Yet Matt's presence loomed behind them, causing the hairs on Grey's body to prickle.

"Nah." Trip sipped his beer, eyeing the young guys playing pool in the corner. "David Lee Roth."

"That's random as hell." Grey focused on his friend rather than obsess about Avery and Matt's past. It was, after all, her past—and a painful one, at that.

Trip shrugged and adjusted his cowboy hat, his wolflike gaze inspecting the few women in the joint. Grey knew a few things about his friend. One: Trip wasn't interested in a relationship that lasted more than a few hours, so a great personality wasn't a draw. Two: the guy had a definite preference for blondes, preferably ones with big boobs and long legs. And three: all the women in the bar were garden-variety brunettes who, while possibly being great women, wouldn't capture Trip's interest tonight.

Given his knowledge, Grey wasn't surprised when Trip turned to Matt and asked, "Where the hell are all the women?"

"Probably hiding from you." Matt delivered the line in a playful tone, but Grey caught a whiff of malice.

Hypocrisy must be another of that lousy cheater's traits.

"Oh joy. A frustrated stand-up comic working as a bartender." Trip smiled, and pulled another long draw from his bottle. Few men seemed as comfortable in their own skin as Trip. He might be a bit of a cad with women, but he was honest with them and fun to be around, so Grey knew Trip didn't give a shit about Matt's opinion. Or anyone else's.

"I'm going to investigate the situation at the pool table. See if we can barge in on the game." Trip glanced at Grey's knee. "Wanna come, or stay put until it's time to play?"

"Stay put." Either way would be uncomfortable, but curiosity kept Grey parked in front of Matt. Avery had believed she'd loved this guy at some point, and Grey wanted to figure out why. Especially if Matt actually intended to try to woo her back. If Grey had to fight for Avery, he needed to know his enemy.

The minute Trip sauntered away, Matt crossed to the sink closest to where Grey sat.

"Looks like you're babying that knee. Do something to hurt it recently?" Matt cleaned a glass, keeping his eyes on his work.

Grey had never had much interest in playing games with people. Now he knew Matt had a sneaky side. No great shock, considering his history, and how he played the whole Outpost thing with Avery and her brother. Grey despised sneaky. Did Avery *like* sneaky? "I know who you are, so you can drop the phony banter. If you've got something to say, say it plain."

Matt held up his hands. "Relax, Lowell. I'm just making small talk."

Grey glanced over his shoulder at Trip before finishing his beer. His grandfather once taught him the best way to win a battle of wits was to stay quiet long enough to let the other guy hang himself. He'd followed that good advice for most of his life. No reason to stop now.

"I'm surprised you're here trolling for action with your partner instead of spending time with Avery." Matt rested his butt on the back bar and crossed his arms.

Grey's stony silence provoked Matt, just as his grandfather had promised.

"Then again, her folks are here, right?" Matt lifted off the back bar and leaned closer to Grey. "Guess you're not high on the list of people they want to see."

"Maybe not, but I'm probably not as low on their list as you." Grey shoved the empty bottle toward Matt.

"Don't count on it. Unlike you, I'm trying to help that family avoid financial disaster. We'll see where things stand once all the dust settles." Matt's smirk hinted at some kind of inside information he was dying to share, but Grey wasn't about to let the guy best him. At least he'd learned what he needed to know: Matt was, in fact, going after Avery and planning to use Grey's potential lawsuit as a wedge to split them apart.

"You know, the minute I heard about how you cheated on Avery, I suspected you must be the world's biggest dumbass. Damn if you didn't just go and prove me right." Grey stood up. "I wouldn't spend much more time trying to win her back. You may have shaken her faith in men, but now she's moved on."

"A temporary setback, Mister Rebound. I've got time. She's got her rules, after all. And she's even slower to give her heart." Matt turned his back to tend to another customer, leaving Grey fuming and his fist itching to punch Matt in the face.

Although some smug part of Grey wanted to see Matt react to the news that she'd broken her rules about sex for him, he'd never betray her trust. He wanted to dismiss Matt's dig, but like a splinter beneath his skin, the harder he tried to get it out, the deeper it burrowed.

"Grey!" Trip called out, waving him to the corner of the room. "We're up!"

◆ ◆ ◆

The next morning, Grey squinted in the sunlight as he biked toward Donner's office. A few months ago, he'd been traveling the same road on a different bike. Now planters spilling over with flowers replaced the mounds of snow on the sidewalks. Gravel—not ice—littered the edges of the road. The air, devoid of the crispness of winter, carried a woodsy scent laced with wild herbs.

Grey arrived at Donner's, stopping two doors down to lock his bike to the public rack on that block. As he strolled toward the clinic, his phone vibrated against his thigh. Adler.

"This is Grey."

"Grey, it's Warren. Do you have a minute? I've gotten a response from the Outback's insurance company."

Grey stopped. This could be it. The answer that would eliminate a significant roadblock between him and a future with Avery. He sat on the bench in front of the bakery next door to the clinic. "I hope you've got good news."

"They've offered you ninety thousand dollars to settle your claim against the bar." Warren fell silent while Grey's stomach dropped.

"I thought you said something about one fifty." Grey scrubbed his free hand through his hair, as if he could rub away the oncoming headache.

"One fifty's the *maximum* anyone can collect on this claim in Colorado. But I also told you Dram shop cases are tough to win. This is a good offer."

Grey's lawyer would take a third of the payout, leaving him with sixty grand. Sixty instead of the one hundred he'd planned to clear. Sixty, which made it harder—plain stupid, according to Trip—to settle for Andy's insurance offer of only twenty-five thousand.

He glared at his knee, which ached from yesterday's climb and this morning's cycling. Dammit. "So I guess I should take the money."

"We're not going to get a better offer, and I can't guarantee we'd get more if we filed a lawsuit. In all likelihood, we'd wait forever for a costly trial and you'd end up with less."

He heaved a sigh. *A bird in the hand.* "Take it, then."

"Good decision. Don't forget, you still have a claim against the driver. Once your doctor signs off on your MMI, we'll be able to determine the full extent to which this injury has an impact on your future. After we estimate your damages, we'll file your suit. In the meantime, this settlement with the Outpost will give you some cash in your pocket and help you offset the medical expenses."

"Listen, I'm late for my therapy appointment. Do you need me to come in and sign anything?"

"Yes, you'll need to sign a release. I'll call you once I've had time to review it."

"Thanks, Warren."

Grey shoved his phone back inside his pocket, rested his elbows on his thighs, and hung his head in his hands. When would he catch a damned break?

He sat up, twisting his neck side to side, recalling Matt's sneering face. Inhaling slowly, he gave himself a mental kick in the ass. There'd be no ifs when it came to his skiing again . . . only a when. No way would he let his knee and stupid money stuff be what kept him and Avery apart.

He marched into Donner's clinic, more determined than ever to overcome his injury.

◆ ◆ ◆

Avery snatched the take-out bag of chicken enchiladas from her passenger seat, and strolled through Backtrax's front door. "Grey? You back there?"

When she got to the back office, she found it locked. Spinning on her heel, she called out again. "Grey?"

She wandered up the interior stairwell and knocked on the back door of his apartment. Shaman's muffled bark greeted her, and then she heard Grey's voice through the door. "Get back, boy."

The lock clicked and the door swung wide open. "Hey." He smiled and held up a finger while speaking to someone on the phone. "Ma, I'll call you back. Avery's here now." After a brief silence, he said, "You will when you come visit." He grinned and nodded. "Okay, love you, too. Bye."

Setting the bag down, she clasped her hands in front of her body. Knowing him, his easy declaration of love for his mom didn't shock her. "Is your mom coming to visit?"

"No immediate plans." He grabbed her around the waist and kissed her.

"How often do you two talk?"

"Almost daily."

"Really?"

"I'm her only child. She misses me. It makes her happy when I call and tell her about my life, my work, you." He nuzzled her neck. "Why are we talking about my mom?"

"I can't believe she already knows about me."

"I told her about you a while ago, before things got personal." Grey eased away and tilted his head. "I take it from your expression you still haven't told your family a thing about us."

"Not yet." She avoided his gaze and removed lunch from the bag. "Chicken enchiladas, Christmas-style," she said, waving her hand over the tin loaded with green and red sauce.

"Smells good." He glanced at the tins, then narrowed his gaze on her. "Can I ask why you're still hiding our relationship?"

"Andy knows. But there's nothing to gain from adding to my parents' tension right now."

"Is that the truth, or do you still have doubts about me—about us?" Grey sighed. "I need to know if we're in this together before *I* get in any deeper."

Could she trust him?

"A hearing date has been set in Andy's criminal case. Early July." As usual, thinking about her brother going to jail triggered some sort of speaking disorder—one that fired sentences out in rapid succession without any breath in between. "We can't believe his lawyers haven't been able to negotiate a plea. No reduction in the charges, no elimination of jail time. Honestly, Grey, aren't there worse criminals out there that the prosecutors should be putting in jail? And the bills from the law firm are putting a strain on all of us." Grey wiped a tear from her cheek with his thumb, effectively stopping her rant. "Sorry. I know you've got your own set of problems related to this situation."

"Don't apologize for being worried about your family. Besides, your problems *are* my problems." He hugged her again, his firm embrace somehow steadying her erratic emotions. "I'm sorry I can't do anything to help."

When she stiffened a bit, he asked, "What? *Is* there something I can do?"

The memory of his disappointment when she'd last inserted herself in his legal matters flashed like a road construction warning light. "Never mind. Where are the plates? Let's reheat this food. I have to get back in thirty-five minutes."

"Avery, stop." He gently squeezed her arms. "Tell me what you want me to do."

"It's more like what I don't want you to do, or to have already done." She glanced at the floor, shifting her weight to one leg.

Grey reached out to tip up her chin. "I promise you can trust me."

His gray eyes focused on her face, scanning every millimeter as if he were searching for the key to unlock her thoughts, making it impossible for her to hide.

"Andy thinks maybe you're one of the reasons his lawyers are having trouble with the prosecutor. I told him you wouldn't do that. I know he's not your favorite person, but you didn't go to the prosecutor and insist they play hardball, did you?"

"No." Grey stepped back, his expression disheartened. "I told you from the beginning, I'm not out to hurt anyone. Especially not someone so important to you. The only things that matter to me are you and my business. Seeing your brother rot in jail isn't going to do squat for my bottom line, and it sure wouldn't make me someone you'd want to spend time with, would it?"

Even though she'd known in her heart Grey wouldn't seek vengeance, hearing him confirm it lifted her spirits. She hugged him tight. "Thank you."

His arms locked around her waist. "Listen carefully, Bambi. I'll *never* intentionally hurt you or the people you love. No matter what." He kissed her head and then nuzzled against her neck. "Feel better?"

She nodded, inhaling the scent of his skin. Funny how his scent settled her so quickly. If her stomach hadn't growled, she could've stayed locked in his embrace all day. "Let's eat. I'm starving."

"Okay." He used a spatula to plate the food to reheat in the microwave. Although he'd just been cuddling her and making promises, his furrowed brow indicated discomfort.

"You seemed preoccupied."

He waved it off. "Nothing, just thinking about stuff."

"Stuff? Did something happen this morning, or last night with Trip?"

"Both, actually." He grabbed silverware from a messy drawer and set it on the counter. Rubbing one hand over his face, he sighed. "I heard from my lawyer this morning about a settlement offer from the OS. It's not as much as I'd been counting on."

"Oh." She waited, afraid of saying the wrong thing. Of course, Grey's anxious expression proved they both realized this news could affect her entire family down the road.

"If I knew for sure I'd be skiing again—this year or, at the very least, next—I'd take your brother's insurance money and call it a day. But I might not be able to lead out-of-bounds teams again, ever. If that's the case, I need a lot more compensation because then this injury truly screws with my life—personally and professionally. Between my dyslexia and lack of college education, I've got no plan B. So, I can't settle until I know about this knee—or win the lottery." He accompanied the deadpan delivery with a quirk of one side of his mouth. "I asked Donner for a prognosis, but he won't make any guarantees, just like you never would."

The microwave beeped, so Grey retrieved their lunch and took a seat. His posture, slumped over the plate, warned her to tread lightly. Avery sat beside him, absorbing his last remarks in silence.

Her brother had screwed up Grey's life. Deep down she knew there was a possibility his knee might never handle skiing his way. Setting aside Grey's professional concerns, how bitter might he become if he couldn't pursue his passions? How much might he come to resent Andy, her family, and possibly her?

Her stomach now churned with a fresh wave of doubts, so she barely picked at the lunch she'd been craving minutes earlier. She glanced at Grey, who was shoveling giant bites into his mouth.

"This is great." He squeezed her thigh with one hand. "Thanks."

"You're welcome." She placed her hand on his forearm. "Grey, I know you're frustrated. But as I told you in March, you should expect nine to twelve months of recovery and therapy before you'll be able to truly test your knee. You've got to be patient and keep working. I believe in my gut that you will ski again—even in the backcountry—although I've got to tell you, I'm not keen on you putting yourself in the middle of avalanche danger on a regular basis."

He grinned, cupped the back of her neck, and pulled her into a kiss made spicy by the lunch he'd devoured. "Thanks, Bambi."

"Sure. So now tell me what happened last night? Did a posse of angry women chase you and Trip out of all the bars?"

"Nope." Grey chuckled. "Beer and pool, just like I promised."

"So what was the problem?"

He set his fork down and sighed. "Your ex was bartending. Seems he's planning on sticking around for a while."

"Oh, brother." Avery waved her hand in the air. "He's clueless."

"He's pretty convinced everything's not dead between you two. I need you to tell me straight up if there's any part of you that still cares about him." Grey reflexively twisted his bracelet around his wrist, subconsciously turning to Juliette whenever he felt discomfort.

"I'd understand. I know you can't always get over loving someone just because you want to. And I'm willing to fight for you, but I need to know exactly what I'm up against. Don't sucker punch me later with the fact that he still means something to you."

She met Grey's even gaze, her breath catching in the face of a man so straightforward. So open. So sincere.

Being jealous of Grey's enduring affection for Juliette's ghost wouldn't help Avery move forward. She had to choose to see it as a positive sign of his capacity for love rather than fearing it as something she could never match. To earn his love, she needed to be honest.

"I'm grateful he's been a friend to Andy now, when so many others have shied away, and I remember some good times. However, what I once thought we had was never what it should have been. It was comfortable, but it wasn't true."

"Okay." Grey pushed his plate aside, tugged her close, and wrapped his legs around her hips. "I feel better."

"Me too." She wound her arms behind his neck and kissed him.

"Can we take this to my bedroom?" he asked.

She glanced at her watch. "T-minus twenty minutes."

"I can work with that."

Chapter Nineteen

"You've had that slaphappy look on your face for the past few weeks now. If I didn't know you better, I'd swear you were stoned." Trip shook his head and tossed his hat aside. "Let me guess, you were just talking to Avery."

Grey shook his head and reached into the bottom desk drawer for a grape Tootsie Pop.

Trip glanced at his watch. "It's only ten o'clock. Can't you wait until after lunch before chain-eating those things?"

"I'm celebrating." Grey smiled and grabbed another lollipop to hand to Trip, eager to share his good news. "Care to join me?"

"For later." Trip tucked the Tootsie Pop in his front pocket before sitting down. "What are we celebrating?"

"I just hung up with the president of Denver's Daring Denizens." He leaned forward and drummed his hands on the desktop for emphasis, only to be met by Trip's puzzled expression.

"Who or what is the triple D?" Trip shifted in his seat, raising crossed fingers while joking, "Please say it's a group of strippers."

Grey shook his head. "You think my candy habit's a problem, but your sex-capades will cause a lot more trouble—for your health and your sanity." Grey stretched his hands over his head, cracking his knuckles. "'Triple D' is a group of adrenaline addicts living around Denver. They organize all kinds of adventures for their membership of twenty-five hundred *and growing*. Backtrax is now on their list of certified program providers. They've just booked three large groups for September climbing trips with a promise to plan several winter ski trips, too. If I keep tapping into these kinds of groups, I can build a solid following by word of mouth. Repeat customers, that's the key."

"Well, this *does* deserve a celebration." Trip rested one big cowboy boot across his opposite knee. "Maybe we should bring some bubbly to the jazz festival tonight."

"Avery is finally introducing me to her brother, so I'm not going to make him uncomfortable by drinking." Grey started sifting through one pile of mail on his desk. "You coming with us, or just meeting us there? Kelsey and their friend Emma will be staking out a good spot and marking it with a bunch of red balloons so we can find them."

"Eh. No booze on top of the fact that jazz isn't really my thing makes it a less-than-exciting proposition."

"Not enough twang and tears for you, I suppose. But apparently the whole town comes out." Grey then joked, "Seems like having all the women corralled in one place would be right up your alley."

"Good point. Guess I'll slip in toward the latter half and see where the night leads."

Grey chuckled, then his gaze fixed on an envelope from Pyramid Insurance. He tore it open and withdrew the check he'd been expecting. Normally a healthy five-figure check would have him doing somersaults. Not this check.

"What's that?" Trip leaned forward as if sensing money.

"OS settlement check." Grey tossed it on the desk and watched Trip check out the amount.

"Seems a little light considering how badly that bartender screwed up." He sat back and laced his hands behind his head. "Sorry, Grey. I know you've been hoping to avoid filing a suit against Avery's brother."

Grey crossed his arms, uninterested in another lecture about money. Trip just didn't appreciate Avery's importance in Grey's life. There'd been other women since Juliette, but none that made him think about the future. None that made him feel everything more intensely. None that made all other women invisible.

"Not too long ago I'd assumed we'd be in the red by this point." Grey clicked off the screen and picked up the check. "I'll use this insurance money to settle some of the debts I've racked up because of my knee. But thanks in large part to your efforts, it's not impossible to think we can keep Backtrax afloat until I'm fully back in the game, even *if* I choose to settle for Randall's twenty-five grand."

Trip scrubbed his hands over his face; his irked tone grated through the room. "You've guaranteed a big loan, Grey. And you still don't know whether you'll get full use of your knee back. Wouldn't it be better to have a bigger buffer?" He tapped his pointer finger against the desk several times. "Quit putting Avery's needs ahead of your own. If she cares as much about you as you care for her—she'll want you to be treated fairly. She'll want you to have some breathing room and not risk everything just so she can keep her house. It's just a house, for God's sake."

"It's her *childhood* home." Grey sat back, crossing his arms again, fully aware she'd yet to invite him there. She'd kept him away, as if she were protecting it—and her heart—from him. So unlike Juliette. He didn't know how to handle his disappointment about that distance, or how to make inroads beneath her defenses. "If her family loses it because of me, it'll be over between us."

"If that happens, it's because of Andy, not you." Trip planted both feet on the ground and placed his elbows on the desk. "I'm serious, Grey. Don't you make any decisions until your doctor gives you the final call on your knee."

Grey raised one hand. "Stop. I haven't made a decision yet, and I don't want to go ten rounds with you about it now. Let's change the subject and talk about how we're going to handle these new bookings." When Trip nodded, albeit reluctantly, Grey continued. "I'm still limited physically, but Donner's giving me a green light to do some light climbing in another two weeks."

"Now *there's* something to celebrate." Trip high-fived Grey and then they started to brainstorm ways to devise climbing trips to accommodate various levels of expertise.

◆ ◆ ◆

Later that evening, Avery sat between Grey's legs, leaning against his chest while listening to the second band in the lineup. Last year, she'd begrudgingly attended the festival, still smarting from Matt's rejection. She winced at the memory, recalling the various looks of pity and curiosity she'd endured.

Now the sexiest, most caring man she'd ever met was cuddling her on a blanket in the middle of the crowd. Although he appeared to be enjoying the guitar riffs gently weaving through the crowd, he seemed preoccupied.

"What's wrong?" she asked.

"Nothin'." When he looked at her, his eyes twinkled with warmth and sweetness, which washed pleasure through her like a sip of hot cocoa.

"You look distracted," she said, touching the spot behind her ear where his murmur had tickled.

"Just disappointed your brother decided not to show up. I'd hoped to officially meet him so we could get past the rough start."

"I bet he doesn't want to be on display in front of the whole town. With his hearing at the end of next week, meeting you now isn't the best timing, anyway. I shouldn't have suggested it."

"You're probably right." Grey's smile looked unconvinced.

"Hey, *I'm* here with you. Doesn't that count for something?"

Sliding his arms around her waist, he purred, "Yes. You make me happy."

Avery turned to kiss him, stroking his jaw with her hand. The deep growl in the back of his throat set off a spark of heat, which sizzled as he tightened his grip on her waist.

"Hey, you two. Save it for later," Kelsey taunted. "There are kids here, you know."

Grey chuckled and loosened his grip. "Sorry, ladies."

Kelsey and Emma were seated in folding chairs next to an open cooler containing assorted drinks and snacks. Shaman lay on the corner of the blanket, gnawing on his braided bully stick.

"Where's Trip, Grey?" Kelsey asked as she looked up at the cluster of red balloons floating above them. "Is he colorblind or something?"

"He said he'd probably come late. Should I tell him you missed him?"

"Hardly!" Kelsey snorted, brushing off a mosquito. "But Emma here has never met the infamous ladies' man."

"That's okay." Emma blushed. "He doesn't sound like my type."

"What's your type?" Grey asked, leaning back on his elbows.

"Sincere, not showy." Emma's blush deepened to dark red, like her hair. "Sorry, I know he's your friend."

"No offense taken." Grey winked at Emma.

Avery breathed a contented sigh, pleased with how Grey had been making an effort to get to know her friends this evening. She hadn't realized how nervous she'd been about whether Kelsey could handle being with them. Fortunately, her concerns had been unfounded. With the exception of Grey's disappointment about not meeting Andy, the evening had been perfect so far.

"In fact," Grey continued, "You sound a lot smarter than the women who think they can get him to settle down."

"See, Em, that's why dating older men makes sense. They're settled, not still bent on proving themselves a stud." Kelsey crossed her legs and chugged her beer.

"Did someone just call my name?" Trip's jovial baritone voice snuck up behind them.

Beer shot from Kelsey's nose while Shaman barked hello. Avery and Grey laughed; Emma's cheeks turned dark purple.

Kelsey wiped her face, then quipped, "Only *you* would act like that nickname was some kind of compliment."

Trip knelt to purr in Kelsey's ear. "Nicknames are so interesting, aren't they? Bambi here seems to have made peace with hers. How about you, Kelsey? Any nicknames you're living down? I feel like there is . . . in fact, it's on the tip of my tongue."

Although Kelsey waved Trip away, Avery held her breath and pinched Grey, who then subtly cleared his throat. With a satisfied grin, Trip turned his attention to Emma.

His smile widened, presumably over discovering newfound prey. "This beauty must be the elusive Emma, whose breakfast food I often smell on my way out of the Weenuche."

"Dial it back a notch or two, if that's possible," Avery replied. "You're not her type."

"Always with that forked tongue." Trip tipped his cowboy hat, first at Emma, then Avery. "I think Cobra is better suited to you than Bambi."

"Hey, now. Bambi works." Grey sat forward, the heat of his chest warming Avery's back.

"How about you, Emma?" Trip ignored everyone else. "Any nicknames?"

Emma shook her head and swallowed a large gulp of beer, clearly tongue-tied by Trip's velvety voice and perfect bone structure. Her shy withdrawal seemed to capture Trip's interest because he started to move toward her.

"I'm trying to enjoy the music!" Kelsey nudged Trip with her foot. "Not listen to your yammering attempts at seduction."

"Don't be jealous, sweetheart." Trip snatched a soda from the cooler and sat next to Grey and Avery. "There's more than enough of me to go around."

After the group's collective "grow up" groan, Trip had the good grace to laugh at himself. "All right, I'm done."

As everyone settled in, Avery believed the evening would continue to play out as smoothly as the notes flowing from the saxophones. She should've known better.

"Oh," Emma uttered as she sat up straight and waved to catch the attention of someone in the crowd. Avery followed Emma's gaze and saw her brother and Matt only a few yards away, cutting through the horde. Apparently her brother had changed his mind.

Grey's muscles clenched around her even as he smiled.

"Hey, Emma." Andy nodded, grinning, then he turned toward the others. "Sis, Kels."

"Hi," Avery replied.

Just as an awkward pause settled over the blanket, Grey stood and extended his hand toward Andy. "Glad to finally meet you, Andy. I'm Grey. This is my friend, Trip."

"Hi." Andy reluctantly shook Grey's hand and nodded at Trip, his cheeks suddenly rivaling Emma's in hue. He glanced at Grey's knee and then briefly met Avery's gaze. Without looking directly at Grey, he mumbled, "I'm sorry about the accident."

Andy's obvious shame pulled at Avery's heart.

"I know you are." Grey's relaxed expression eased the knot around Avery's chest. "For your sister's sake, let's set it aside."

When Andy's slumped shoulders straightened a bit, she appreciated Grey's kindness all the more. Grey then slid a less friendly glance toward Matt. "Matt."

"Now I remember," Trip blurted out. "The bartender from Grizzly's! Frustrated comic."

"Just Matt, thanks." Matt folded his arms, sighing. His heavy gaze fell on Avery. "Evening, Avery."

"Hello," she said coolly, pulling her knees to her chest.

Matt's presence complicated everything. Perhaps her brother could've become more acquainted with Grey tonight if Matt weren't with him. Now, what already was an awkward introduction had turned tense. She aimed for brightness, but her voice sounded flatter than she'd hoped. "Andy, I'm glad you changed your mind about coming."

"I realized this might be my last festival for a while." He sipped his seltzer without saying more.

Just like that, the threat of his sentence hung over all of them like a dense storm cloud, causing a chilling silence.

"You don't know what will happen." Emma's gentle voice drifted into the void.

Grey briefly looked away and then sat down, leaning back on his hands, strategically placing one of them behind Avery in a maneuver she suspected was, at least in part, an effort to mark his territory in front of Matt.

Another pronounced pause hung over the group. Avery felt grateful Trip hadn't used the moment to provoke anyone with a snarky remark. Apparently he had some sense of timing after all.

Kelsey jumped in to break up the discomfort with a change of topic. "Hey, did you all hear about Wade Kessler's big project? Huge commission." She cast her arms wide. "Huge!"

"Look at you, Little Miss Moneybags." Trip raised his drink. "What's his big project?"

"Don't you read the paper? He's building a first-class boutique hotel and condominium complex, with a spa and other amenities." Kelsey's eyes sparkled as she spoke. Apparently Wade had made quite an impression. Avery prayed her friend wasn't clinging to unfounded romantic fantasies about the guy. "The subdivision plans were just approved for the fifty acres behind the slopes, along Ute Creek. The closing is on Monday."

"Where, exactly, is this acreage?" Trip's uncharacteristically serious tone caught Avery's attention. Was he jealous or something?

"Off Big Fir Trail." Kelsey ignored Trip's concerned expression and smiled at Avery. "Girls' weekend soon, my treat. I'm thinking Santa Fe."

"Sounds fun." Avery grinned before noticing her brother staring out over the crowd, wearing a melancholy expression. For a moment, she'd forgotten about him and his bleak future. Now the girls' weekend, and pretty much everything else about the night, seemed a bit frivolous.

"Will Wade's hotel hurt your business, Emma?" The concern in Andy's voice surprised Avery.

"I hope not," she replied. "Our customers like our historic building and décor, which I doubt they'd find at a fancy new place."

"And don't forget about your cooking." Andy smiled.

"Aren't you going to sit down and hang out a while?" Emma asked.

He shook his head, casting another quick glance at Grey. "Not tonight, thanks. This is just a flyby."

"Don't leave on my account," Grey quickly said.

"We're meeting up with some old friends." Matt looked directly at Avery. "Maybe another night." After a few good-byes, Andy and Matt meandered into the throng.

Avery watched her brother disappear. His bowed head weighed on her.

The reminders of his situation made Avery want to escape the music and Kelsey's celebratory mood. She rested her head on Grey's shoulder. "I'm sorry, but Andy's mood tanked mine. Would you mind leaving early?"

"Not as long as I'm with you."

She smiled to herself, thankful for his supportive nature. "Are my friends safe with Trip?"

"They've got his number." Grey kissed her head.

"Okay, then. Let's go."

Within fifteen minutes, they'd walked to Backtrax, Shaman trotting alongside them in relative silence. The late evening sky, tinged with faint pinks and lilacs, provided a gorgeous backdrop for the jagged peaks of the San Juans. The music, climate, and picturesque evening would've been the ultimate romantic night under other conditions.

Avery stopped on the sidewalk near her car. "I'm sorry I cut short your first-ever Sterling Canyon Jazz Festival, especially on such a gorgeous night."

"Night's not over yet." Grey fished around his pocket for the keys to his apartment.

For weeks she'd been coming to his place, meeting him in town, and generally doing everything she could to keep him separate from her brother, their home, and her family. Suddenly all her efforts seemed selfish and silly. She wanted to move forward and cement the relationship. To forget about competing with Juliette, and bring him further inside her world.

"Hey, let's go to my house tonight."

Grey's brows shot upward. "You sure?"

Avery nodded. Grey's grin made her chastise herself for waiting so long to take this step.

"Let me get Shaman settled," he said. "I'll be right back."

When he returned, he slid into the passenger seat. "Now that I've finally met your brother, maybe next time it won't feel quite as uncomfortable."

Avery pulled away from the curb, her eyes on the road, her thoughts elsewhere. "I can't imagine that happening for a long time, although I do appreciate how you're not holding a grudge. Most people in your position wouldn't be as forgiving. In fact, I doubt I would."

Grey shrugged one shoulder. "Let's not go overboard. If it weren't for you, I doubt I'd be so easygoing about everything. But I've got my priorities."

"You do?"

"I do." He reached across the gearshift and rested his hand on her thigh.

Avery's stomach tensed as she approached her cul-de-sac, wondering what Grey would think of her home. As she pulled into the driveway, she watched his eyes scan the yard and exterior of the house, the corners of his mouth tilting upward.

"Home sweet home." She led Grey in through the front door so he could get the best first impression. From the entry, the immense picture windows lining the rear of the house typically offered a spectacular view of the mountain range. Of course, at night it looked like a wall of mirrors, reflecting the explosion of color inside.

Grey's grin widened as his eyes were drawn from the living room to the dining area and then the kitchen.

"You must've thought you died and went to hell when you first set foot inside my apartment." Grey looked at her and then pulled a face. "Sorry for swearing."

She shrugged, unwilling to lie, but equally unwilling to insult him. "Well, your place does have one advantage over this house." When he shot her a puzzled expression, she continued. "You're there."

"Good to know that counts for something." Grey winked and then walked around the living room, inspecting it more carefully. He frowned briefly when he came to the doorway marred with hash marks denoting Avery and Andy's heights at various dates throughout their childhood. He gently traced the indents with his fingertips. "I can imagine this being a great place to grow up."

"It was. There were other kids on the cul-de-sac, although most of them have moved away." She watched Grey study the family photos on the mantel. "So many people always looking for someplace more exciting, like the location will make their lives more fulfilling. I don't get it. How could any place be better than this one?"

"Well, having moved around a lot, I can vouch for the fact that some places are better than others." He walked over and wrapped his arms around her. "This town is great, but what matters is the people in your life, not the place where you live."

She couldn't help but detect a double meaning in his words, but she brushed it aside when he continued the conversation.

"When I first met Bill Batton, I thought fate brought me here to buy his business." His drew his thumb along her jaw. "Now I think it meant for me to find you."

"So the accident was destiny forcing us together?"

"No, not the accident. I saw you before that happened. If I'd have made it home safely that night, I'd have found some way to get to know you better." He kissed her forehead. "Now you're the first thing I think about in the morning and the last thing I picture at night. You occupy a lot of my daydreams, too."

"I don't know what I did to earn such devotion, but I won't complain."

"Speaking of devotion," he said, molding her against his body, "how about you let me show you instead of just talking about it?"

"Good idea." Her arms wound around his neck. She loved the solid feeling of him. His sexy smile. The grabby hands that always sought her out.

"Can't wait to see where you sleep most nights." He flashed a wicked smile. "I've been trying to picture it for months."

"I suppose we'll see how good an imagination you have, then." She led him to her room. He squeezed her from behind, resting his head on her shoulder as he took in her white wrought-iron bed and floral-print bedding.

"Very feminine. I guessed pretty well, though honestly I expected brighter colors instead of these soft pinks and yellows." She felt him grin against her cheek as his hands began to caress her abdomen. His voice dropped to a low, sexy tone. "Wrought iron gives me some ideas."

Although he left the details of his naughty thoughts unspoken, her body tingled in anticipation.

Suddenly, he turned her to face him. "Thank you for bringing me here tonight. I know how hard it is for you to trust in us, but I swear you won't regret it."

Letting go of her just long enough to close her door, he then returned and cradled her face, kissing her in a way that made her feel precious. He stroked her neck, shoulders, and ran down along her waist. Easing away, he held her arms out to the sides, letting his gaze roam her entire body.

"I love looking at you," he said as he gently slid her top up over her head. "These pretty sky-blue eyes, flecked with sunlight." His lips landed on her jaw and worked their way down her neck. "The little freckle behind this ear," he whispered. "The notch at the base of your neck," he said before kissing it. "The swell of your chest." A soft groan vibrated in the back of his throat as he unclasped her bra. His response elicited a tremble from her.

He continued kissing her while unzipping her jeans.

"Grey." She yanked his shirt off him and ordered him to take off his cargo shorts. He sharply inhaled as her fingertips traced the sculpted muscles of his torso and chest.

Her breath came a little quicker each time they were so close, so exposed, so vulnerable.

Both of them were still in their underwear when she tugged him onto the mattress. She could easily put into action the emotions she struggled to put into words.

The moonlight cast shadows around them, shrouding them in a private cocoon. She watched Grey's muscles flex, his wavy hair falling across his face, the intensity in his gaze. "You make me so hot." His roughened voice rasped across her neck.

Grey kissed her stomach and stroked her thighs, hips, waist, scorching her skin with his touch. His hands then cupped her breasts until he drew one into his mouth, the tender ministrations stoking a need deep within her. Making her want more.

He slid his body along hers and held her face in his hands. Then he closed his eyes and kissed her like it was the most important thing he could do. Like she was the most important thing in his life.

She felt hot and dizzy with lust before he'd even moved his hands along her inner thigh. Her eyes closed and her back arched as he used his mouth and fingers to stoke the excitement building inside. Her hips gyrated, seeking him out, needing more.

She ran her hands down his back, reaching for his hips, urging him to enter her body. "I want you now."

He opened his eyes, which reflected everything she felt. "I want you always." His deep voice rumbled over her skin, causing her to shiver just before he drove inside her. "God, I love being with you."

He slowly withdrew and thrust several times. The power of his body, his voice, his stare overwhelmed her, crushing through every barrier she had built around her heart.

Tonight he seemed intent on a mission to force her to slow down and open up, to let go of all her fear, to meet him on his emotional plane.

Panic collided with pleasure and desire. Grey was everything she'd ever wanted in a man. Could she let go with him without losing herself?

His mouth crushed against her neck as he quickened his pace, driving into her possessively yet tenderly. As he moved inside her, she felt the coil of tension, the wave rising within her body, the craving for release. His breath, hot and wet against her skin, set off ripples of goose bumps.

"Faster," she pleaded, and he complied. Within seconds his muscles tightened beneath her hands and, just as her own orgasm seized her, he shouted, spending himself inside her, his ragged breath falling against her hair.

"I love you," he whispered once their bodies quieted.

Her breath caught. When she didn't immediately respond, he rolled onto his side and stared at her. A lopsided grin graced his face. Sweat plastered his bangs against his forehead, so she brushed them away.

"I think I just freaked you out a little," he said, not looking the least bit anxious or uncomfortable. How she envied him and his ability to embrace his emotions.

"No. I . . . no." The three words he wanted to hear sat on the tip of her tongue. He deserved them, but she couldn't spit them out.

"I don't want to scare you or force you to say anything, but I want you to know how I feel, Avery. I'm in love with you. Everything about you makes me smile. The neon wardrobe, the way your left eyelid droops whenever you're mad, these deep dimples," he said, gently placing his finger against her cheek. "Your smarts, your wisecracks. The way you push back when cornered even though you're actually a little afraid. I'll take all of it. So whatever does or doesn't happen in the future, always remember that much."

Her nose tingled. "I—"

"Don't." He pressed three fingers against her lips. "Don't say it just because I did. If you love me, you'll tell me in your own way and your own time. It'll mean more to me that way, too. Okay?"

Once she nodded, he removed his hand and kissed her again. Her heart soared. Grey understood her. Her flaws—her resistance to vulnerability—didn't intimidate him or put him off. He didn't want to control or manipulate her, and that freed her in a way she couldn't explain.

She wrapped her body around his, snuggling into his arms. Perhaps the words wouldn't come today, but in every other way, she would show him how she felt until she could admit aloud what was in her heart. For the first time in her life, she drifted off to sleep believing she'd finally found true love.

Chapter Twenty

Grey slid into the booth at Drafts Pub to meet Trip for lunch. He'd arrived a few minutes ahead of schedule, so he used the free moment to call Avery. Her parents were due to arrive today in advance of Friday's hearing, so he wanted to make sure she wasn't being driven over the edge by all the pressure.

When she didn't answer, he hung up. Just as well, because Trip showed up on time.

Before they could even say hello, the waitress arrived tableside with water and menus. Trip cast Grey a quick look. "Pizza?"

Grey nodded. His stomach chimed in, too.

Trip tipped his hat to the waitress, whose rapt attention almost made Grey chuckle aloud. "Extra large sausage, onion, and green pepper. Well done, please. And two drafts."

"What kind?" she asked.

"Surprise us." Trip smiled at her and Grey could practically hear her hormones raging in response. Once she turned away, Trip's smile vanished. "Listen, Grey, I think you've got big trouble."

Grey edged forward on the bench seat, not sure how much more trouble he could handle. "How so?"

"Did you realize Kessler's big project includes a tract of public land we've been using to access portions of the national forest covered by your permit? Without that entry point, we can't reach some of the most challenging terrain. If we can't find safe alternatives, it'll become a lot harder to attract repeat skiers."

"That can't be right." Grey scratched his neck. "My permit must grant some kind of right-of-way over that land. Otherwise private developers could come in and basically void permits."

"Maybe that lawyer of yours can do a little investigating?" Trip acknowledged the waitress with a grin when she delivered their drinks.

"I'll ask Warren, but I don't think he's that kind of lawyer." Grey chugged half his beer, his mood darkening. "Am I crazy, or does it seem like the universe has it out for me? What the hell have I done to deserve so much bad luck?"

"I'm just glad you didn't settle with Randall yet. If that development cuts us off, you'll need to regroup and submit for a new permit for other land, or, well, I don't even know what else. But I know this— you'll need time and money."

"Dammit. I don't want to sue Andy. And it's the last thing I want to tell Avery this week, when she's so concerned about her brother's hearing." Grey pinched the bridge of his nose. "I don't know how much more her family can handle. Are you positive we can't access that land anymore, or find another access point nearby?"

"There's no other road access within a couple of miles of that ridgeline, and the forested parts aren't passable in the snowcat. I'm pretty sure I'm right, but I'll double-check. Maybe Kelsey can confirm it." Trip's brows drew together as he drummed his fingers on the table.

"Maybe my dad was right. Being an expert skier doesn't make me an expert in the business of skiing. I should've just invested that money for retirement and kept working as a guide." Grey stopped talking while the waitress delivered the pizza and two plates. "What the hell will I do if I lose everything?"

"Okay, enough of the pity party. We're two smart, tough guys. We can figure this out. Maybe you can get a permit for 'copters. I promise, you won't lose everything." Trip lifted a steaming hot slice of pizza onto his plate. "But we need more info, more time, *and* more money."

Trip's eyes looked distant when he made that final remark, causing Grey to wonder about that sugar mama they'd joked about recently. Had Trip tried that avenue and been refused? Grey wouldn't impose on his friend. He'd accept Trip's help if offered again, but he wouldn't pressure him. Besides, a heli-ski permit was still a pipe dream at this stage.

Grey took a bite of the pizza, though his appetite had dulled thanks to the topic du jour. He glanced at his watch, but realized he couldn't interrupt Avery at work. He forced himself to eat another slice and finish his beer. After they paid the bill, they left the pub and stepped into the bright sunlight.

"Let's not panic. I'll go pump Kelsey for info. You call your lawyer and find out what you can. We'll regroup tonight and plan your next steps."

"I really don't know what to say to Avery. It sucks that I might not be able to keep my promise."

Trip tilted his head and studied Grey. "Like I said before, if she's as invested in you as you seem to be in her, she'll support you." Trip batted a fist against Grey's bicep. "Buck up. I'm going to hunt down Kelsey. See you at home later." He turned on his heel and began walking toward Kelsey's office.

Grey pulled out his phone and called Adler. "Hey, Warren. It's Grey. What do you know about U.S. Forest Service permits and real estate?"

Ten minutes later, no closer to an answer, he hung up feeling pessimistic. He went back to his office to further research the legal terms Adler had mentioned: easements, rights-of-way, adverse possession. He also studied the fine print of his permit documentation, hoping to find some kind of grant of access. Of course, his damned dyslexia made the task doubly challenging. He unwrapped his fourth sucker, but no amount of candy could lift his mood today.

◆ ◆ ◆

At four thirty, he dashed across town to catch Avery at the clinic before she went home. Looking back on the first time he'd blown through these doors bracing for a confrontation, it seemed less fraught with trepidation than the confrontation about to occur. When her last patient strolled out the door, she approached him.

"I didn't expect to see you here today." She gave him a quick kiss, but her fidgety body language indicated her distraction. "My parents are here already, so I can't join you for dinner or anything. My dad's barking at me to get home."

"I need five minutes." He clasped her hand. "I wish I didn't, but I do."

"I don't like the sound of your voice." She narrowed her eyes. "If this is going to upset me, can it wait until next week? I really can't handle anything else until after Andy's trial."

"No, it can't wait. Believe me, I wish I didn't have to deal with this either, but things are happening that are making it impossible for me to settle for Andy's insurance proceeds."

"What things?" She glanced at his knee. "Did your doctor give you bad news?" The concern in her voice tugged at his heart and burned though his stomach. *Fuck.*

"No. This is about business. In a nutshell, Wade Kessler's new project cuts off our access to a substantial portion of land covered by our special-use permit, and that will wreck my business. I'm going to need time and money to come up with some alternatives."

"How is that related to the accident and Andy?" She withdrew, her expression confused.

He drew a breath, hoping she'd understand his perspective. "I've been willing to consider taking less than I need—less than I deserve—because of my feelings for you. But now making that sacrifice would very likely cost me everything. That doesn't seem fair, especially when this injury isn't my fault."

"I know it's not fair. Nothing about our situation is fair." Avery's troubled expression dug beneath his skin. "I'm not sure what you expect me to say. Are you asking for my blessing?"

"No. I'm telling you so you don't hear it from someone else first." He reached out for her hands. "I came to you as soon as I realized what was happening. You know I want to keep my promise not to hurt you or drag your family through some ugly stuff. I'm hoping maybe you, your brother, and I can sit down and find a solution together so we all get what we need."

"Well, with Andy facing jail time and life as a felon, I doubt he cares much about his financial trouble, let alone yours." Avery eased free of Grey's grip and ran her hands through her ponytail, her eyes darting around the clinic, her teeth worrying her lower lip. He'd rarely seen her look so flustered. "Sorry, but I warned you I'm not at my best today. I've got to go home. My dad's already called me twice today. He's got something important to discuss. I guess we'll talk about this tomorrow, or next week, after Andy's hearing."

"Call me later." When he pulled her close, her stiff body set off alarms. He tipped her chin up and stared into her eyes. "Avery, I'm still looking into alternatives. If there's any option that lets you keep your house and me keep my business, I'll take it. And I promise I won't do anything without telling you first, okay? We're in this together."

"Thanks." Her weak smile offered little comfort. "Listen, I probably won't call you tonight. You know how my dad wears me down. I don't want to end up arguing with you because I'm keyed up about what's going on with my family. We'll talk about this legal mess later, all right?"

"I wish I could comfort you, Bambi. If you're upset, I want to be there for you."

"There's nothing you can do or say to make it better, especially given what you just told me." She wiped her hand over her face. "I'm not blaming you. This is just a difficult time for all of us."

He didn't say another word as he walked her to her car. Her quick kiss good-bye left him anxious and unhappy.

Naturally, because God had it in for him, he crossed paths with Matt on his way home.

"You don't look nearly as cocksure as you did at the jazz festival." Matt stopped on the sidewalk in front of Grizzly's, tucking his hands under his armpits.

"Mind your own business."

"Contrary to your opinion, the Randalls are my business." Matt sighed. "You don't have to like it, or me, but you should get used to seeing me around town, and around Avery."

Grey's hands balled into fists, but he counted to ten in his head. "You seem to enjoy trying to get a rise out of me, but as I said before, I don't think all the Randalls are as eager for your company as Andy."

"I made one big mistake, but I'm not a terrible guy, and I do have history with them and this town. Maybe I'll earn a second chance with them—maybe sooner than you think." Matt shot Grey a two-finger salute before stepping inside the bar.

Grey stared at the door, debating whether or not to take the bait. His grandfather's voice echoed in his head, telling him to keep his eye on the prize and not get distracted by other people's bullshit. With much effort, he backed away and walked home, desperately hoping for a magical solution to his dilemma.

◆ ◆ ◆

"Smells good." Avery closed the oven door after taking a quick peek at the lasagna Andy had prepared for dinner with their parents. She glanced at the ceiling, hoping he couldn't read the extra distress in her face. "I need a glass of wine before Mom and Dad come down."

"Lucky you." Andy placed the final napkin and set of silverware at the table. "I have to face Dad sober these days."

"Sorry, but I really need this right now." She gulped down a big swallow of Cabernet Sauvignon. "We're all dealing with a lot these days."

"Some of us more than others." Andy pulled at his collar and stared at his feet, avoiding her direct gaze.

"I know you're worried about the trial, but I told you, Grey hasn't even talked to the prosecutor. If they ask for a statement before sentencing, he won't make things worse. You've done everything your lawyer suggested. I have to believe it will all make a difference to a judge. I think things will not turn out as badly as you imagine, at least not in the criminal trial."

"The way you just said that makes it sound like Grey is changing his mind about not suing me."

"Things are forcing his hand, but he's still looking for alternatives, Andy." She recalled the distraught tone of Grey's voice as he relayed his circumstances. "He's making every effort to avoid turning our lives upside down."

"Well, it won't matter if he sues us anyhow." Andy then seemed to check himself. His cheeks turned pink as he turned his head away.

"Why do you look so guilt-stricken?" She tipped her head, awaiting his response. "Andy?"

"I hear Dad coming down the steps." He swiped his palms across his shorts twice before rubbing the back of his neck. Their dad had made Andy nervous for most of his life. Since the accident, it had been even worse.

"Oh, joy." Avery downed the last drops of wine in her glass and set it on the counter. "On second thought, maybe you should've sneaked one, too."

Andy grimaced. "Probably."

Closing her eyes, she drew in a deep breath and then forced a smile, mostly for her mother's sake.

"Welcome home, Mom." Avery hugged her mother until she heard Andy clear his throat as their father stormed into the room.

She never knew what to expect from her dad. While she didn't think he intended to blow through their lives like a hurricane, it often played out that way. "Dad."

Their dad had never been particularly talkative.

"Avery," he said in response to her tremulous smile.

"How was the drive?" she asked as he gave her a stiff hug and peck on the head. A hint of cigar smoke tainted his skin. Thank God her mother had always managed to keep him from smoking inside the house. But he'd never fully given up the bad habit.

"Uneventful." It was then Avery noticed the folder in his hand.

Avery's mom immediately began busying herself, fluffing the sofa pillows and refolding the throw blankets. Her reddening cheeks sent Avery a warning. *Uh oh.*

Avery craned her neck to peek at the file. "Whatcha got there, Dad?"

He opened the manila folder and pulled out two documents. "These little beauties will protect us all from that Grey Lowell."

She rolled her shoulders and sighed. "*That Grey Lowell* is not an enemy combatant."

"Avery, he's playing Mickey-Mouse games with our finances and now he's probably stringing you along, too." He waved his big hand in the air. "Don't start denying it. I've heard you've been dating the man."

Avery glared at Andy. He bowed his head, and her stomach fell to the floor.

She'd been hoping for an opportunity to feel her parents out before dropping the bombshell about her relationship with Grey at their feet. Thanks to Andy, her dad was now staring at her as if he'd been told she'd quit the clinic to become a porn star.

Avery slid another disappointed look at Andy before returning her attention to the papers in her father's hand. Deciding she didn't owe her parents an explanation about her love life, she refocused on the documents. "What exactly are those papers?"

"A promissory note and mortgage." He shook them in the air. "First thing tomorrow, we're going to the town clerk's office so you and your brother can sign these documents in front of a notary and then we can file them there with the deed. After that, we'll all breathe a little easier at night."

"What?" Avery stepped closer.

"We're going to formalize our loan arrangement so, if Lowell gets a judgment against Andy and you two are forced to sell this house, your mom and I will get paid back first."

Avery took the papers from her dad and looked at Andy, who merely shrugged. "I don't understand." She quickly scanned the first page of the note. "Did you contact a lawyer to draw these up?"

"No." For once, her dad looked a little uncomfortable—almost apologetic. He cleared his throat. "Matt's sister sent them over."

Surely she'd heard wrong.

It took Avery thirty seconds or so to remember Matt's sister, who lived in Denver, was a paralegal. He must've called her for advice. Why the hell was he still inserting himself in her business?

"Avery, I haven't forgotten how Matt broke all our trust last year, but I can't let that stand in the way of protecting my family. He's come back and has been a real friend to your brother. He's been watching out for our family's interests, unlike your new boyfriend." Her dad must've noted Avery's dismayed expression. "This protects both of you, too, missy. It makes it much less attractive for Lowell to force a sale, because the money left on the table will be a lot less than what he expects."

Avery's mind—typically sharp—slogged through swampy emotions, unable to fit the pieces of this puzzle together. "I'm sorry. Not following. Can you explain how these will keep Grey from suing Andy?"

"It doesn't stop him from suing, just makes it fruitless. Without them, if he gets a hundred-thousand-dollar judgment against Andy, he could file that lien against the house and then collect his money after forcing a sale. But if this mortgage is filed first, it will have priority over his judgment lien. So after the house is sold, there won't even be a hundred grand left on Andy's side of the table. In fact, Andy will probably be able to declare bankruptcy, which also means he'll get to keep some equity under another law. Basically these papers mean Lowell will be no better off going after this house than he will if he settles for Andy's insurance offer." Her dad nodded proudly.

"This all seems unfair or fraudulent or something," she sputtered. "I mean, Grey has a legitimate claim, Dad."

"It's not my fault he hasn't filed a lawsuit."

"He hasn't filed because his doctor hasn't made a final determination of his long-term condition, so they can't estimate his damages. Besides, he's been pursuing solutions that won't affect us, like the thing with the OS. He's also been diligently attending therapy to minimize his losses." Avery slammed the papers on the kitchen island, her voice rising. "He stands to lose everything if he can't ski and climb again . . . all because of Andy! This move feels like we're taking advantage of his good will and delay."

Her dad's face turned as red as a Santa suit. He spoke in a lethally controlled voice. "I'm not taking advantage of anything. I'm simply formalizing the loan that *already* exists. I'm doing what I should've done from the start—protecting my family. *You* should be worrying about all of us instead of him, young lady."

Avery glanced around the room, hiding the tears clouding her vision. She loved her home. All her memories—old and new—lived there with her. Her dreams for her future had always been played out in these rooms. Being forced to sell the house to strangers so Andy could pay Grey would hurt, but she didn't want to see Grey lose his business either.

Her mother continued to avoid eye contact, while Andy suddenly looked relieved for the first time in a long while. A sense of betrayal twisted through her lungs, but she'd deal with him later. First she had to get her head together.

Was her father right? If he'd paid a lawyer when they'd made the transfer, loan documents would have been signed and recorded long ago. The debt was real, not phony or newly trumped up. Following her father's orders enabled her to keep all her equity after a sale without feeling guilty about her parents being shortchanged, which set her up better for finding a new place. In fact, as a debtor, she probably couldn't ignore her father's demands anyway.

Bottom line, she owed him his money.

Would this feel so wrong if Grey were a stranger? Did that matter? Morals were supposed to be static, not something tied to personal feelings. Yet she couldn't untangle the doubts clouding her reasoning.

How could she, when she'd just left Grey knowing how hard he was working to find a solution that wouldn't hurt her? When, every time she thought of him, she envisioned his smiling face beholding her like she was some kind of superwoman. When he'd been honest, unselfish, and full of good will since the day they met. *We're in this together.*

"Fine. I can't argue with you, and I do owe you the money, but I want to talk to Grey first, as a courtesy."

"No, Avery. We're doing this tomorrow, and I don't want to risk him finding some kind of eleventh-hour loophole that will trump my move."

"What could he possibly do between now and tomorrow morning?"

"What if his lawyer can file something to stop us? I don't know, and I don't want to know. It's not worth the risk."

"Maybe not to you, but what about me? Dad, I want to be the one to tell him . . . *before* it happens. Otherwise, I look like I'm sneaking around stabbing him in the back." She cast a pleading look at her mom. "He deserves better from me."

"What about what *I* deserve from you?" her dad asked, his hurt tone burying her in guilt. "Didn't I sell you this house at a discount when I could've easily gotten more money—and been paid in full—on the open market? Weren't you the one who wanted to hold on to this house for sentimental reasons? Don't you owe me, *your father*, more consideration than you owe Grey Lowell? Don't your mom and I deserve to retire in peace, without financial worry?" He shook his head, sighing. "Please don't argue with me. Not now, when we still have so much going on with your brother's trial. What I want—what I expect—from you tonight is your loyalty to your family, not to Grey Lowell. He's not your husband. He's not even your fiancé. For all you know, he'll be out of your life a year from now. Don't put our whole family's future in jeopardy because of your infatuation."

Trapped! If she forewarned Grey and he did find a loophole, her family would never forgive her. If she didn't, Grey might never forgive her, either. A lose-lose situation.

"How will I face Grey with this latest maneuver?" she mused aloud.

"Head held high, like I've always taught you," came her dad's quick reply.

Chapter Twenty-One

The next morning Grey licked the remains of two chocolate-glazed donuts with sprinkles off his fingers before opening the door to the town hall. He squinted at the directory in the lobby, searching for the location of the town clerk's office. Adler had told him he could search the public land records to find maps of the property in question. If any easements or rights-of-way existed, they'd be noted in surveys or land descriptions. Of course, Grey's disability meant reading those maps could very well turn into mission: impossible.

Grey strode down the musty hall thinking about what he had at stake. Matt's smug face and remarks had run through his head all night and morning. He'd tried to ignore the idiot, but his gut warned him to prepare for bad news. When he'd called Avery last night, the call went straight to voice mail and she hadn't returned the call—a first since they'd starting dating a month ago.

He shook his head, needing to focus on the task at hand. A middle-aged woman behind the counter smiled as he approached.

"Good morning," he began, reaching into his pocket to retrieve the paper with the property information Trip had finagled from Kelsey. "I'm hoping to take a look at any surveys and subdivision plans filed in connection with this property. Can you pull them for me, or show me how to find them?"

The kindly-looking woman took the paper from him and studied it. "Give me a minute." She disappeared behind a few rows of books. Moments later, she returned carrying a large book with Grey's notepaper stuffed in its pages like a bookmark. "You can sit over there and take a look." She pointed to a metal table pushed up against the wall.

"Thanks, ma'am." Grey plunked the book down and opened it to the page the woman had marked for him. It took him a few minutes to orient himself with the creek and road they parked along last winter. Then he used the legend to try to map out the general outline of Wade's proposed purchase, which did look like it would include the access point they'd been using. Unfortunately, Grey didn't see any kind of easement or other right-of-way denoted on the survey.

After ten minutes of chasing his tail, he closed the book, sat back, and scrubbed his hands through his hair. Another dead end. Wade's development would cost them a third of the best runs they'd found. Just as he pulled out his phone to call his partner, it rang. Grey didn't recognize the number.

"Grey Lowell."

"Mr. Lowell, this is Brad Michaels, the prosecutor in the State's case against Andy Randall."

Oh shit. "Good morning." Grey straightened up in his chair. "What can I do for you?"

"I'd like to talk to you before the hearing. I don't need you to testify because we've got solid evidence without you, but I'd like to get a victim impact statement. It can be helpful with sentencing. Do you have some time this morning?"

Grey glanced at his watch. A favorable statement would help put Avery's family at ease. At least he could do one positive, productive thing today. "I can stop by now."

"Great. We're located on the third floor of the courthouse. Just come to the DA's offices and ask for me. See you soon."

Grey sighed before standing and returning the book to the clerk. "Thanks."

"No problem," she said.

He turned to go, dialing Avery to let her know about the latest development in his morning, when she and her entire family walked into the clerk's office.

"Hey, I was just calling you." He put his phone away and nodded at Andy. "Andy."

Then he waited to be introduced to her parents. Only then did he notice Avery's pasty complexion and panicked expression.

"Grey, what are you doing here?" she asked.

"Looking for a solution to our problem." He tilted his head, peering at her. "What are you all doing here?"

She tugged at her ponytail and cleared her throat. "Mom, Dad, this is Grey Lowell."

Grey reached out his hand toward Mr. Randall, who shook it without making direct eye contact. "Sir," he said, then smiled at Avery's mother, who remained standing behind her husband. "Ma'am, it's nice to meet you."

"Hello." Mr. Randall gave Avery a quick look before saying, "We're here to file papers to formalize some old business."

"Well, then, don't let me hold you up." Grey smiled, but it didn't ease their obvious tension. "Avery, can I talk to you for a second privately?"

"We need her to sign some papers first, then she can step into the hall with you." Her father's unreadable expression raised the hairs on Grey's neck.

"Okay, I'll sit right outside while you take care of your business."

She nodded at him and, two minutes later, came into the hallway.

"Well, that was awkward, but at least it's out of the way." Grey leaned in for a kiss hello, his lips brushing her cheek when she glanced at her feet.

Avery forced a lame-ass grin. "Yep."

Grey tipped her chin up to look in her eyes. "What's the matter, Bambi? You're acting way too distant for my taste right now."

"I'm sorry. I should've called you last night." She squeezed his arm, but her hunched posture made him uneasy. "I wanted to speak with you in person."

"I'm listening now." Everything about her demeanor made his chest tighten. "Is your family pissed at me for something new?"

She splayed her palm on her forehead and squeezed her eyes shut. When she opened her eyes to speak, her voice raised in pitch and tone, her eyes were pleading. "Just so you know, I'm very upset about this entire situation. I can't figure out what's right and wrong. I can't find solutions that benefit everyone. And now . . . now I've done something that makes it harder for you to recover money from Andy."

Grey's spine stiffened as he withdrew his chin and scowled. "You what?"

"Andy and I executed loan documents formalizing the arrangement my dad and mom made with us when we bought the house. My dad's recording the mortgage now, which will give him priority over any other creditors who come next, including you, assuming you get a judgment lien in a lawsuit against Andy."

Grey couldn't understand all her legal mumbo jumbo, but he could read guilt and dread all over her face. "Slow down. What are you trying to tell me?"

"Basically, whatever remains of Andy's equity in the house probably won't be much more than the insurance settlement you were offered."

Despite her palpable anguish, his muscles went rigid from his forehead to his feet, and two words escaped his throat in a whisper. "Fuck me."

"Grey!"

He stared at her with defiance. "Don't ask me to apologize for swearing right now, Bambi. I've had my fill of bad news for a lifetime this week."

"It hasn't been a cakewalk for me either, you know."

"And yet you and your family have managed to come out on top, haven't you?"

"I'm sorry, Grey." Her eyes filled with tears. "I didn't have a choice. I owe my parents the money. I had to sign the documents."

"All this time I've been running down rabbit holes looking for options that wouldn't hurt you, then you go and take away the only option that saves me from disaster." He rubbed his temples. "Why didn't you tell me first? Too busy conspiring? I was sick about hurting you yesterday. Barely slept last night. You could've spared me all kinds of upset if you'd have simply told me your precious house would be protected."

"I didn't know about it until I got home. Apparently Matt gave Andy the idea."

"Well now I know why he was so cocky yesterday." Grey spat out, planting his hands on his hips. "I can't believe you didn't call me, Avery. I would never have done something like this without warning you."

"I'm sorry." She began retreating into herself, putting on a stiff upper lip and relying on that backbone he'd previously admired. "My dad demanded my loyalty."

"Did I get *any* consideration? For God's sake, I've turned myself inside out these past months to keep this nightmare from touching you. I've changed therapists; I lived broke until last week. I refrained from going full force after your brother because of you. This is how you repay me? *This* is how little my feelings matter to you?"

"Grey." She reached for his arm, but he shrugged away from her. Her family spilled into the hallway in time to see and hear his anger.

"What's going on here?" Mr. Randall's brusque voice cut through the air.

"Nothing. Nothing at all, it seems." Grey's voice was thick with disdain, disappointment, and anger.

"According to my daughter, you weren't planning to sue Andy and take the house, so nothing done here today should make a difference, unless you were lying to her." His gall only fueled Grey's disgust.

A joyless laugh escaped Grey's throat as he looked at Avery. "I just love how this keeps getting turned around on me when I'm the victim." He turned toward her dad, practically bellowing, "I'm the damned victim!"

He watched Avery's mom's eyes widen, but he wouldn't apologize. His head hurt, seething with betrayal and disillusionment. He raked his gaze over her family, letting it rest on Andy. "Speaking of which, I'm late for an appointment with the prosecutor."

A little zing of vengeful thrill rippled through him as he watched Mr. Randall's superior expression fade and his face go pale.

"You promised you weren't going to do that, Grey." Avery's dismayed voice drifted through the hallway.

He whirled around to face her. "I was calling you to tell you I'd just been asked to give a victim impact statement, but you weren't answering my calls. Seeing how you didn't feel the need to give me a heads up on this little plan," he said, "you're in no position to judge." He still couldn't believe she'd undercut him that way—working against him instead of with him—knowing he had no fallback position. Closing his eyes briefly, he tried to figure out how to scrape his heart off the floor. "At least you won't have to worry about avoiding my calls in the future."

When he turned to walk away, she cried out. "Grey!"

He stopped, hoping she'd apologize or ask him to forgive her for how she'd basically spit on everything he'd been trying to build between them.

She came around to face him. Her splotchy cheeks and perspiration started to soften his attitude, until she spoke. "What are you going to tell the prosecutor?"

His breath caught as an avalanche of bruised pride, heartache, and humiliation crashed over him and carried him away. She didn't care about him or their relationship. She only cared about her family and her house. Well, he hoped she'd be happy without him, because he'd had enough of being her fool.

"Good-bye, Avery."

"Good-bye?" Her face crumpled as she clutched his forearm. "Wait! Don't go. I'm sorry!"

He shook free and strode away. A pained sob erupted behind him, but then her father's sharp voice silenced her with a single command. "Avery!"

Grey barreled down the hall and out the front door of the town hall without glancing back.

◆ ◆ ◆

Avery hugged her body, only vaguely aware of her parents and Andy standing behind her. She watched Grey storm down the hallway and out of her life. The memory of his repulsed expression replayed in her mind, making her dizzy. She closed her eyes and squeezed her waist tighter, bending over slightly to avoid fainting.

When a hand touched her shoulder, she sprung away and turned to face her family. Her mother's stunned expression stopped her from yelling. Avery looked at her dad and Andy, and shook her head. "Are you happy now? Do you feel good?"

Andy looked as white as the plaster walls. If Avery weren't so devastated by Grey's obvious hatred, she might feel sorry for her brother. "This is your fault, Dad! If you would've let me talk to Grey last night, he wouldn't be making a beeline to the prosecutor's office to throw Andy under the bus. He wouldn't hate me, either. You've just ruined Andy's last hope regarding a light sentence, and you've blown up my relationship. I should've listened to my heart."

"If Grey Lowell were the man you thought he was, then he would've understood what we did here. He wouldn't be blaming you or expecting you to side with him over your family."

Avery straightened up. "He's not furious because I signed those papers. He's upset that I didn't warn him. That I didn't discuss it with him first. That we didn't all sit down together to look for a fair solution, like he'd asked. Instead of working with him, we've stolen all the cards without so much as a hint." Avery strained to control her breath, remembering how Grey had described his perfect relationship with Juliette: one of absolute honesty and trust, of having each other's backs. No secrets.

In one fell swoop, Avery had just proven to herself and Grey that she wasn't worthy of the love he'd shared with Juliette.

She grabbed her waist and bent over, breathing in through her nose and out through her mouth.

"I'm sorry, Avery." Andy's quiet voice echoed in the hallway. "I should've talked to you before going to Dad. I've just been feeling so guilty about putting the house and everything at risk, I charged ahead without thinking about how it would affect you and Grey. I didn't realize he meant so much to you. You never said anything."

Avery didn't look up. She couldn't argue that point. For weeks she'd been minimizing her relationship with Grey. Segregating her life to make it easier. To avoid getting hurt.

Ha! How stupid she'd been. Given that Grey's brush-off just tossed her heart in a meat grinder, she hadn't avoided being hurt at all.

Once her breathing settled, she stood and looked at Andy. "Now we're all going to pay a high price for our pride and stupidity, aren't we?" She glanced over Andy's shoulder at her dad. "Even you, because it will be a long time before I have a kind word to say to you, Dad." She only winced at her mother's pained expression, but even that didn't stop her from turning on her heel and walking away from them.

Throughout the rest of the day, she tried calling Grey, but he wouldn't answer. Her attentiveness to her patients hit an all-time low. She'd been so preoccupied with her thoughts, she'd zoned out at least six times. One patient thought Avery might be having a stroke.

Her lunch sat, uneaten, on the corner of her desk.

Her red-rimmed eyes hurt.

Avery had never experienced a sense of loss and pain this profound. Every time she realized Grey had cut her out of his life, her chest tightened. Only days ago, he'd professed his love. He'd given her a glimpse at a life so full of love she could barely believe it. Her lifelong doubts—her fear—had kept her from loving him as he deserved to be loved.

She could blame her brother, her dad, and even Matt . . . but she couldn't hide from the ugly truth. The person most responsible for the fact that Grey was finished with her was looking back at her in the mirror.

Chapter Twenty-Two

Grey strode out of the courthouse feeling marginally better than he had an hour earlier. Bonus—in the midst of giving his statement, he'd gotten an idea about Wade's project. Now he needed Trip and Kelsey's help.

He dialed Kelsey first. "Kelsey, it's Grey. I need Wade Kessler's number."

"Why?" Kelsey's tone sounded cautious. Protective, even.

"I have a proposition for him." Grey stopped on the sidewalk, placing one hand on his hip.

"What kind of proposition?"

"A business one." He tamped down his impatience, forcing himself to stop tapping his foot against the pavement. "Can you give me his number, please?"

"Sure. He's actually in town this week. Staying at the Sterling Canyon Resort."

Grey's brows rose. "You don't send him to Emma's place?"

"Wade likes modern resort amenities."

Figures. Grey nearly dismissed the thought, but then realized Kelsey probably knew a lot about Wade. Details that could help him negotiate. "Seems like you're getting to know him pretty well."

"We've spent a lot of time together looking at properties. He's very interesting."

"Guess he's easy to work with, too?"

"Better than most of my other clients. No bullshit, no games. Decisive."

"Good to hear. Hope he's treating you right."

"He's very professional and courteous. But so far there's nothing more going on . . . at least, not yet." When Grey heard Kelsey's feminine giggle, he knew Boomerang had locked in on a new target.

He couldn't help but grin, knowing Wade had no idea what he was in for in the upcoming weeks or months. But unlike Grey, maybe Wade would be interested in Kelsey. "Good luck with that, but watch your heart."

"Easy for you to say now that you're happily involved."

All the words got stuck in Grey's throat for a minute. Until an hour ago, he'd thought he'd been given a second chance at love with an incredible woman. But he'd been too blind to see it had been one-sided. Avery's betrayal made her dead to him—a heartache different from, but equally painful to, losing Juliette.

Somehow he managed to say good-bye to Kelsey. He looked around at the storefronts, wishing for something to hit or kick. Nothing. Certainly not here in the middle of this gossip-riddled town.

Shaking his head, he refocused on the task at hand and called Trip. He might've lost out on love a second time, but he wasn't going to lose his future, too. "Buddy, I'm coming back to the office. Don't go anywhere. I have a plan we need to discuss."

◆ ◆ ◆

Wade Kessler greeted them in the lobby of the resort. The man was probably forty two, but still fit. Clean cut. He flashed a friendly smile at Grey. "Good to see you again, Grey," he said as he reached out to shake hands.

"I'm Trip." Trip also shook Wade's hand. "I work for Grey."

"Shall we sit?" Wade gestured toward an intimate seating area in the corner of the lobby.

"Thanks for agreeing to see me on such short notice. I wanted to talk to you about your development's impact on my operations," Grey began. After explaining the basic conflict, he said, "Based on the circumstances, I'd like to float a proposal by you."

"I'm listening." Wade sat forward, attentively.

"I'd like you to grant us an easement over the sliver of property we use to park our vans and take clients up the backside of the mountain." Grey leaned forward, anxious and uncomfortable. "In exchange, I'll give you free ski and rock-climbing tours twice per season for as long as we own the business."

Wade's surprised expression turned thoughtful. "Where, exactly, do you cross the property?"

Trip jumped in. "The short dirt road that turns off Big Fir after the small bridge, right where the guardrail breaks."

Wade scratched his cheek just below his eye. "How often do you use it, and how many people are with you?"

"During ski season, one of us is there at least five days per week. The total number of people could be anywhere from six to fifteen, give or take." Grey's stomach sank a bit as he watched Wade's brows rise. "We park the vans and leave them there for the better part of the day while we hike up those ridges."

"You're asking me to take on a lot. Not only would I be putting an encumbrance on my land in perpetuity by recording an easement, but I'd also be taking on additional liability for your guests and property—like your vans—while they're on my land." Wade sat back, crossing his arms. "What if I flip the property in ten years? Buyers might not want that on the title, and that could affect the salability of the property."

"I have to think there are ways to deal with those issues, whether with money or whatnot." Grey rubbed his jaw, his mind racing but unable to offer solutions.

"There are liability and insurance issues, too," Wade said. "Not to mention that I can't have a bunch of old ski vans parked in the middle of my five-star resort."

"The area we're talking about is on the fringe of your property, not in the center," Trip interrupted.

Wade nodded with a shrug. "I'd need to take a hard look at our development plans to see if we can find a spot that wouldn't interfere with the hotel access or parking, or be a blight to the condo owners."

"I understand that, and I'd be willing to work with you to find a parking location that is out of your line of sight." Grey glanced at Trip. "I'll sign whatever releases and waivers you'd need. Pay for the additional insurance rider, if need be. I'm not asking for a gift; I'm just asking for help so you don't end up putting me out of business."

"What if other outfits come and ask for the same rights?" Wade sat forward again.

"They won't. I have an exclusive forest service permit, so no one else can lead anyone into that part of the mountains. Some town kids will hike back in there on their own now and then, but that's about it."

"You're the *only* business who can take teams back in there?" Wade narrowed his eyes.

Grey nodded, wondering what else Wade was thinking.

"I appreciate the offer to give me free treks, but that's not really enough value for me to justify giving up so much." Wade crossed one foot over his knee. "But maybe if you give my hotel guests and condo owners a fifteen-percent discount on any tours they booked, then we'd have something to talk about. That could give me something to add as part of my marketing package."

Grey shot Trip a questioning glance, relying on Trip to help him decide whether or not Wade's counteroffer was affordable. Of course, if he refused, he'd be out of business. Decision made, Grey said, "We don't have huge margins, and we're a seasonal business, so fifteen percent is a bit steep. Would you settle for ten percent plus a one-time fee for the easement?"

Wade's gaze drifted for a few seconds before he responded. "Let me track down my lawyer and ask him a few questions before I give you an answer."

When Wade stepped away, Trip kicked Grey's foot. "That was pretty smooth, my friend. Pretty smooth. You've got some big balls trying to negotiate when you don't really have any power here."

"He seems like a fair guy," Grey replied. "Worst he could do was stick to the fifteen percent at this point. It sounds like a lot will depend on his lawyer's advice."

Ten very long minutes later, Wade returned. "Fellows, I can't give you a quick answer. My lawyer's going to look at the subdivision plans and all the other obligations and contracts we've got going on with this project to make sure there aren't any conflicts. But as long as there isn't any non-negotiable conflict, I think we can probably work something out, assuming we can come to terms on a right-of-way and indemnity. I'll accept the ten-percent discount, too, but will get back to you about other costs that may be associated with this deal."

"Thank you." Grey stuck out his hand. "Can we buy you a drink?"

After two rounds of beer and conversation about the town, Wade excused himself, and Trip and Grey walked back to the office.

"Well, it's not quite a done deal, but it's looking good, right?" Grey glanced at Trip.

"Looks real good, Grey. I think the only thing holding it up is the lawyer shit."

Grey's phone rang. He looked at the screen and saw Avery's name for the fourth time in the past hour, but he didn't answer.

"I'm going to butt in here, because in addition to your being edgy and hyped up, I'm noticing you aren't taking Avery's calls." Trip kept his eyes on the pavement as they continued walking. "What's happened?"

After Grey described the confrontation at the town hall, Trip frowned. "I'm sorry she burned you, Grey."

"You warned me not to jump in so fast, but I really thought . . . well, it doesn't matter. I thought wrong." Grey unlocked the office door. "I've got to keep my eyes on this business and do whatever I can to avoid disaster. I hated to give away that discount, but I couldn't think of any other way. You think we ought to talk to Kelsey and get her help with Wade? They seem tight."

"Not yet. Let's see what happens. I've got a good feeling." Trip sat in his usual chair, across the desk from Grey. "I actually have an offer of my own I'd like to discuss. One that will also help alleviate the financial strain of the business debt."

"Bring it on." Grey sat forward.

"I want to buy a stake in Backtrax and be your partner. I know I'd only promised to come for a year or two and help you get things going, but this place has grown on me. Funny how your injury forced me to get more involved . . . and I *liked* it. Anyway, I know what you put into the business, and what is still owed. If I come up with a hundred-fifty grand and cosign the loan guarantee, would you make me an equal partner?"

Grey whistled. "Where are you coming up with that kind of cash?"

Trip shifted in his seat, averting his gaze. "I've got money."

"You mentioned that before, but never said how." Grey didn't mean to be rude, but he couldn't help it. He'd known Trip for four years. Never during that time had Trip won the lottery or lived like a guy who had access to six figures at the drop of a hat.

Trip slid deeper into his chair and pushed the brim of his cowboy hat back. "Family money, but I'd rather not get into details, if you don't mind."

Grey held up his hands. "Sorry, and hell yeah, I'll take your money and make you my partner. Honestly, Backtrax wouldn't still exist if you hadn't taken over when I got hurt."

Trip flashed his gigantic grin at Grey and stuck out his hand. "Thanks, buddy. You won't be sorry."

Grey shook his hand, but then sat back, brow furrowed. "I have to ask you something. Why didn't you make this offer sooner, especially when you saw me struggling with Avery? Might've made things with her a lot easier for me."

"For one, I wasn't sure I was ready to commit myself completely to life here in Sterling Canyon. Also, getting my hands on that money will open some doors I'd rather keep closed, but I don't want to get into all that with you. As for Avery, well, that just wasn't my responsibility, was it?" He frowned, his gaze distant. "Sounds bad, I guess. Sorry if I let you down."

"Don't apologize." Grey flicked a paper clip. "Looks like you were right to have your doubts about her commitment, too."

"Doesn't make me happy." Trip's earnest tone made Grey glad for his loyal friendship.

◆ ◆ ◆

Avery dreaded going home that evening. She'd avoided Andy and her dad's calls this afternoon, but she couldn't put off the inevitable any longer. Her blood pressure practically exploded when she saw Matt's car in her driveway.

After snatching her purse from the front seat, she slammed her car door closed. She stood in the driveway and rolled her shoulders twice, trying to alleviate the tension in her muscles.

When she finally came through the front door, her mother greeted her with a nervous smile, much like she used to greet her husband when he'd come home after work. "Oh, honey, you're finally home." She patted Avery's arm and quietly said, "I know it's been an upsetting day, but we have some relatively good news to share."

"Good news, Mom. Really?" Her mom winced at Avery's sharp tone as Avery glanced around the room. Her father was suspiciously absent, but Matt's gaze homed in on her. Had he heard about her and

Grey's falling out? "Not that anyone cares much about my feelings lately, but I'd rather not discuss family matters in front of Matt."

"Avery." Matt approached her. His sheepish expression only made her want to toss her purse at his head. "I heard about what happened at town hall. I swear, I was only trying to help your family."

"If that were true, then you might've come to me before going to my dad. Your sneaking around makes it pretty clear you were just exploiting the situation to try to get between Grey and me."

"No. I didn't come to you because I thought you'd accuse me of using the situation for my own benefit. But that's not the case. I told you before, I've always cared about you, and your family. I just wanted to help make sure you didn't all suffer because of Andy's accident."

Avery looked away, unable to decipher the truth anymore. She'd been worn down, turned inside out, and depleted. "Well, whatever your motives, you've seriously interfered in my personal life. This is the second and last time you'll ever hurt me. I won't order you out of this house when everyone else seems happy for your company, but if you care about me at all, you'll leave now."

Matt sighed, cast a quick look at Andy, and then conceded. "We'll talk later."

"*We* won't be talking later. If you want to stay in town, I can't change that. If you and Andy have picked up where you left off before California called your name, so be it. I'll even thank you for giving my parents and Andy some peace during this difficult time. But I do not want to hang out with you, confide in you, or do anything else with you. So please, quit provoking Grey with your comments about me, and stay out of my way, okay?"

"I'm sorry." He set his glass down and turned to Andy. "I'll call you tomorrow."

The minute Matt strolled out the door, Avery whirled around and asked her mom, "Where's Dad?"

"Upstairs, packing." Her mother was tugging at the cuff of her shirt, glancing between her two children.

"Packing?" Avery crossed her arms. "He's buttoned up the finances, so now you're leaving before Andy's hearing?"

"Avery, don't talk about your father that way. He's a good man. He's worked hard his whole life to take care of all of us. I know you've got issues with him, and with me, but enough is enough. I didn't raise you to be so disrespectful to your parents." She squared her shoulders in a brief show of strength, but her eyes darted to Andy. "As for Andy, there isn't going to be a hearing. His lawyers finally negotiated a last-minute plea agreement with the prosecutor."

"Really?" Avery's head hurt from trying to keep up with the events of the day. "How did that happen?"

Andy stepped forward. "Apparently Grey spoke on my behalf. Told the prosecutor about how I'd been going to AA, talking to teens about drinking and driving, even mentioned the icy roads and stuff. His statement, combined with the pressure the DA has in terms of its schedule, and the fact that it's my first offense, convinced the prosecutor to structure a felony plea that will be reduced to a misdemeanor after one year of parole, assuming I don't screw up during that year. The judge will have to approve the recommended sentence and add fines and community service, but since they usually go with the prosecutor's recommendation, I probably won't go to jail."

"Grey helped you even after I hurt him?" Her thin voice hung in the air.

"He did." Andy grabbed her hand. "I called to thank him, but he didn't answer, so I left a message. I guess you haven't spoken with him?"

Avery shook her head, tears pooling in her eyes. "He won't take my calls." Her throat ached.

Andy hugged her tight. "I'm sorry, sis. Really, I am. I've done nothing but bring trouble your way for the past few months while worrying about myself."

Her mother's sniffle caught her attention. "Don't cry, Mom." Avery drew a deep breath. Who the hell had she been to judge her parents' marriage, or her mom's choices and happiness? Thirty-three years of marriage was a better record than Avery had when it came to love. "Listen, I'm sorry I snapped at you. I didn't mean to be disrespectful. And I'm glad for Andy's news. I know eventually things will look brighter for me, too, but right now I'm wiped out. My head is pounding. I just need to be alone for a while."

Her mother hugged her. "Go rest. I'll call you when dinner is ready."

Avery kissed her mom and then went directly to her room. The sun had lowered, casting amber light around the space. She lay across the bed, remembering being there with Grey only days ago. Wrapping her body around a pillow, she let the warm tears spill down her cheeks.

An hour later, she'd made a decision—one that required her brother's consent.

She sat up, brushed the hair off her face, and steeled herself for another family meeting. This time she would do the right thing no matter what they had to say.

♦ ♦ ♦

Four days later, Avery left Kelsey's office. Tonight she had one last chance to make up with Grey.

When she parked her car, she could hear a somber classical piano tune drifting through his open window into the evening air. Clutching her bag and folder of papers, she kept her face lifted toward the window as she walked around the side of the building.

She nearly ran into Trip when he came through the side door with Shaman. He leveled her with a malevolent glare. "Haven't you done enough damage yet?"

His anger pulled her up short, but she tipped up her chin. "I'm here to see Grey, not trade barbs with you."

Shaman sniffed her legs and whimpered. She was grateful for the distraction, because she was too wiped out to argue with anyone. After scratching Shaman behind the ears, she stood and tried to sidestep Trip.

"I think you need an attitude adjustment." Trip moved sideways to block her attempt to scoot by him. "Grey is a good guy with a big heart—one you tore to pieces. If you think I'm going to stand by and let you take a second stab at him, you've badly misjudged me."

Avery's shoulders slumped. "I'm here to fix things, Trip. I promise, I'm not going to hurt him again."

"Fix things?" Trip's voice kicked up a few decibels. "You think you can fix things now? It's too late. Turn around and go home, back to your family and your white knight, Matt What's-His-Face."

"You can't keep me from talking to Grey." Avery placed her hands on her hips, now ticked off. "This is a silly standoff, especially out here on the sidewalk. It's not up to you to decide whether or not Grey talks to me."

Grey popped his head out the window. Apparently their argument had made its way inside. "Trip, I don't need a mother hen." He glanced at Avery, and her heart sank at the hollow look in his eyes. "Let her in."

Her. No Bambi. No Avery. No smile. Let *her* in, spoken in an abject tone. Avery drew a deep breath and met Trip's stony gaze. "Excuse me."

Trip shook his head and muttered, "You'd better be worth it." Then he whistled at Shaman and walked toward the park.

Avery started up the steps when Grey opened the door at the top. He stared at her but said nothing. The muscles in his jaw and chin were drawn and clenched. The ice in his eyes practically froze her in place. Everything about him stood at odds with the casual stance he'd adopted by leaning against the open door.

When she got to the top of the stairwell, he stepped aside and waved her inside. After closing the door, he leaned his back against it and folded his arms, waiting.

"Can we sit?" She fumbled to push the words through her closed throat.

He gestured toward a chair, but didn't follow her. She would've been completely without hope had she not noticed the slight glistening in his eyes. He remained glued to the door, gnawing at the inside of his cheek.

She cleared her throat. "First, I came to thank you for what you did to help my brother. It was unexpected, under the circumstances."

"Unexpected?" he barked. "Even though I told you on several occasions that I wasn't out to hurt anyone."

"You did." Avery glanced at her hands, which were tightly clasped in her lap. "But after what happened, I assumed you'd change your mind."

Grey raised a hand in the air and let it slap against his thigh. "Proving how little you've ever understood about me. I don't go for revenge. I just let go."

Her hand clutched the spot on her stomach where his cutting remark had landed a solid punch. "I'm sorry I doubted you. I'm sorry about all of it, Grey. Truly, I never wanted to hurt you."

"Betray me, you mean?" His narrowed gaze, so unlike most of the looks he'd ever cast her way, appeared to be closing the door on any hope of reconciliation.

"That's fair, I guess. I had to sign those papers because I owe my parents the money, but I should've called you first. My dad bullied me, and I was torn between loyalty to him and you. Either choice would hurt someone, so I chose my dad. But not because I didn't care about you, Grey." She looked at him, pleadingly. He, however, remained rigid and removed.

"That's why I'm here—so you know how much I care. To prove it, I've made a decision." Avery pulled the papers from her purse and set them on the table, her voice quaking slightly. "Andy and I are going to sell the house. Kelsey thinks we can list it at close to six hundred thousand, although it won't sell at that price. Still, even once we pay back my parents, there should be roughly two hundred thousand dollars left. I don't know if that will end up covering all your losses, but it's the best I can offer."

Grey's cool demeanor shifted as he studied her. Neither of them spoke for a minute or two. He held her gaze as he pushed off the door. When he came within three feet of her, he stopped and rested his hands on his hips. "And where will you live, then? If you give me your money, you won't have anything left to buy a new place."

She shrugged. "I've got a little money saved."

"Weren't you saving that money to invest in your own business?"

"So I'll put off those plans for a while longer. I'm not unhappy at the clinic. For now, I'll have enough money for a first and last month's deposit on a rental at least. It doesn't matter. Like you said the other week, where I live isn't as important as who is in my life."

"But you love your house." His eyes softened. "You've told me so more than once. I've seen it with my own eyes."

She stood up, shaky from nervousness. *Now or never,* squeaked a little voice in her head. "But I love you more, Grey." She noticed the muscles in his cheek twitch, but he didn't move. She stepped closer. "I know I hurt you, and I hate that. Maybe you can't forgive me or trust me, but I still don't want you to lose everything, especially not because of my family. And I needed you to know that, even though I didn't show it sooner, you meant—you mean so much to me."

If she'd expected him to melt at her feet upon hearing her declaration, she'd be disappointed. The silence in the room suffocated her, but she couldn't move or speak. Did her words really have no impact on his feelings?

"What are those papers?" He gestured toward the listing agreement she'd set on the table.

"The listing agreement." Her mind had to work extra hard to process their conversation simultaneously with her own jumbled thoughts. "I just left Kelsey's office. She's probably adding the house to the MLS as we speak."

She'd never admit it to him, but her heart sank a little at the thought.

"Call her now and pull the listing." His brows lowered.

"No." Avery stood firm, shaking her head. "I've made up my mind. This is the right thing to do. I wish I'd done it sooner. Maybe if I had, things would've turned out differently for us."

"Is that what you want?" The hard edge faded from his voice. "For things to be different?"

She forced herself to risk rejection, to look him directly in the eye. "I want things to go back to how they were last week, before all this happened."

"Call Kelsey and pull the listing, Avery." He stepped closer, but didn't touch her. Still, the heat of his body pulled at her like a magnet attracts nickel. "I don't need the money."

She tilted her head. "What?"

"I worked out a deal with Wade, and Trip's buying a stake in the company, so I don't need the money. Even if I did, I wouldn't take it from you."

Her head was swimming through unspoken questions as she tried to catch up, but all she really heard was that he didn't want anything from her, not even her help.

"Oh." She turned away to hide the tears collecting in her eyes. After retrieving the listing agreement from the table, she stuffed it back in her bag. "I'm glad everything has worked out for you, I guess," she paused, "I guess I'll go."

His hands rested on her shoulders while her back was still to him. Her heart sped up as he ran his hands down her arms. He leaned close and whispered, "Thank you for being willing to give up your house for me. Tell me again why you did that."

She turned to face him, her hands clutching his shirt. "Because I love you."

His gray eyes flickered, the outer edges crinkling as he grinned. "I'm sorry, but I think all that piano playing has made me a little deaf. Can you speak up?"

"I love you, Grey." She wound her arms around his neck, determined to never let go. "Forgive me."

"No more secrets?" His intense gaze had turned serious as he pulled her against his body.

"Never again. I swear it."

"Forgiven." He reached his hand behind her neck and pulled her into a desperate kiss.

Avery clung to him, weak from the stress of the past few days. "I missed you. I hated myself, probably more than you and Trip hated me."

"I never hated you." He kissed her again, slow and hot, melting her insides. "But you have to believe in this, in us, Avery. We have to put each other first, or it will never work."

"I know." She burrowed her face into the crook of his neck. "I swear, Grey. You never have to doubt my loyalty again."

He squeezed her hard, both their hearts pounding. When he eased away for a second, he smiled. "Trip won't be back for at least thirty minutes. How do you feel about make-up sex?"

"Pretty enthusiastic." She nuzzled his neck again.

"That's my girl." He tugged her into the bedroom, kicked the door closed, and stripped out of his clothes.

Any reservations Avery had been harboring after making herself so vulnerable faded the minute he captured her in his arms. In that moment she knew, no matter where she lived in the future, he would always be her home.

Acknowledgments

I would like to thank my husband, children, parents, brother, and friends for their continued love, encouragement, and support.

I am grateful to my agent, Jill Marsal, as well as my editor, Irene Billings, and the entire Montlake family for believing in me, and for working so hard on this story.

A special thanks to my friend, Herb Cohen, who patiently answered my questions about personal injury law, and to Bill Scrima for answering questions about arrests, arraignments, and other police matters. For the sake of fiction, I took liberties with the information they provided, but their time and input were invaluable.

I also owe much to The Revisionaries (Monique, Annette, and Rob), and my Beta Babes (Christie, Siri, Katherine, Suzanne, Tami, and Shelley), for their input on various drafts of this manuscript. And many thanks to the Alta 8 (Dusty, Jordan, Dan, Carol, Charlie, Pete, Stacey, and Brad) for helping me retitle this book.

As always, the wonderful members of my CTRWA chapter provided endless hours of support, feedback, and guidance, and I love and thank them for it as well.

Finally, thank you, readers, for making my work worthwhile. With so many available options, I'm honored by your choice to spend your time with me.

About the Author

Jamie Beck is a former attorney with a passion for inventing stories about love and redemption. In addition to writing novels, she also enjoys dancing around the kitchen while cooking, and hitting the slopes in Vermont and Utah. Above all, she is a grateful wife and mother to a very patient, supportive family.

Facebook page: facebook.com/JamieBeckBooks

Newsletter: oi.vresp.com/?fid=e24107dc99